THE ISLE

THE ISLE

JORDANA FRANKEL

KATHERINE TEGEN BOOKS
An Imprint of HarperCollins Publishers

Katherine Tegen Books is an imprint of HarperCollins Publishers.

The Isle
Copyright © 2016 by Jordana Frankel
All rights reserved. Printed in the United States of America.
No part of this book may be used or reproduced in any manner
whatsoever without written permission except in the case of
brief quotations embodied in critical articles and reviews.
For information address HarperCollins Children's Books,
a division of HarperCollins Publishers, 195 Broadway,
New York, NY 10007.
www.epicreads.com

Library of Congress Control Number: 2015939178
ISBN 978-0-06-209537-4

Typography by Erin Fitzsimmons
15 16 17 18 19   PC/RRDH   10 9 8 7 6 5 4 3 2 1
❖
First Edition

For my cousin Lauren, who is secretly a disco ball made out of fossilized bat teeth, and who speaks a language I'm lucky enough to be even somewhat conversant in.

THE ISLE

PROLOGUE

REN
9:00 P.M., THURSDAY

Those pennies keep piling up.

Day four, and hundreds of lucky copper thank-yous are still outside Benny's garage door. We've been bringing 'em in, but people don't stop dropping 'em off. The Blight's nearly done with, but everyone knows it wasn't Governor Voss's doing.

We got them the cure—me and the other racers.

They know. They know, and they're thanking us with luck.

If only I believed in luck.

I squeeze one of two penny charms hanging from my necklace—the one Aven gave me. Callum's is on the same chain, but I know which is which. They just feel different. I kiss the copper, remembering the night she asked to be

1

friends. She told me "Good skill" instead of "Good luck." Didn't believe in luck then, either. It's too unreliable.

Aven understood.

And I let her get taken.

Some friend I am.

Dropping the necklace, I see my nails for the first time in days. They look like they got caught in the props of a running mobile, cuticles mangled from where I can't stop picking. I don't care.

He's going to hurt her. *He's going to hurt her.*

He's going to—

Derek sees me stewing. He draws my fingernails away from my teeth. "We're getting her back, Ren—tonight. We're just working out the details. It takes time."

I grunt. Governor Voss said he'd do it, it wasn't an idle threat. Called it "clinical research"—a sanitized version of the truth.

He wants to experiment on her.

According to Callum's intel, Voss took her to the FATE Research Center—a multipurpose government lab. I know about it from my DI days. Quarantine is a regular house of horrors. It's where Chief Dunn, my ex-boss, imprisoned everyone convicted of spreading the Blight.

That's not its only function, of course; it's much bigger. Voss's scientists worked there trying to find a cure for the virus. And I'd wager money it's where Voss has been trying to re-create the water.

FATE: Fight Against Terminal Epidemics.

To Voss, death *is* a terminal epidemic. He'll kill Aven if it meant killing death.

"She could be dead in the time it takes to work out the 'details,'" I mutter, and continue making mincemeat of my hands. Don't much care that I'm leaving bits of skin and nail on the floor of Benny's garage.

"Enough, Renata!" Benny howls. My patron saint of racing and all things mechanical stands up. He wags a pointed finger in my face. "Worrying does nothing. Only action does something. And we are in the process of acting."

I drop my hands. My face burns as I glance from Derek to Ter, avoiding Benny's steel-cut glare. I just got schooled. It's the worst.

"I did not decide to work with you so many years ago because you were a worrier," he goes on, "but because you are a warrior! So please. Enough."

I roll my eyes—hero speeches make me gag. Play me some vintage heavy metal and it'll work better. Still, I know he's right. I'm not doing Aven any good by worrying. As her best chance at escape, I need to be in full form. Not a distracted, cuticle-less mess.

Ter tips his chair forward, balancing on its front legs. "You sure there's nothing you need me to do?" he asks. "I'd rather not wait here while y'all are risking your necks."

"You'll be more help if you're not there," I say too quickly. It sounds like an insult I don't mean, and I watch him recoil.

Ter leans back in his chair. Both legs drop, slamming the floor. "Thanks for the overwhelming vote of confidence."

3

Now, on top of the sick, alone feeling I've had in my gut since Voss took my sister, I'm also a brack friend. I don't want to fight with Ter. *I just want to leave.*

"Terrence . . . Renata is not doing a sublime job expressing herself," Benny says, leaning against the bumper of his Cloud9. "Which, considering the state of things, is forgivable. . . ."

Benny—the same Benny who just threw me out of my own pity party—has my back a moment later. I add this to the billion other things I want to thank him for someday.

"I believe she meant to imply that you and I are needed as a last line of defense, so to speak. If she and Derek are caught—"

I lock eyes on him. He amends his mistake.

"—*which they won't be.* But if they were, in this highly unlikely and hypothetical situation, we would be the ones to come in and get Aven."

I meet Ter's eyes. If I had a tail, it'd be curled between my legs right now. "That is what I meant, really," I say quietly.

Ter looks back at me, his Astroturf eyes warmer. "I believe you."

"There's more than one opportunity for this plan to backfire," Derek adds. "I can lead Ren to the lab, but Kitaneh and the others will be watching it, I have no doubt. If things start to look grim, we'll need you both ready."

Kitaneh. Derek's wife—by arranged marriage—but still. She'd love to shove a blade in my back and call it a day. Everyone in Derek's family, the Tètai, thinks I'm a liability . . . 'cause they're a bunch of lunatics. Misguided "protectors of

4

planet Earth." They believe that the miracle must be kept secret, because someone might abuse it.

Someone like Voss.

When I found the spring, I used it to help people—my sister, and anyone else with the Blight. Unfortunately, the Tètai have a strict policy on this subject: you find the spring, you die.

Ter nods. "All right. I get it. You need me here. But I need to know what's going on—comm me at the first sign of trouble. Or if you make it through easy. It don't matter. No news is *not* good news."

"You got it. Ren, have you heard from Callum again?" Derek asks.

"Nope," I say. Aside from some back and forth about the *details*, and one random comm wanting the miracle spring's dimensions, Callum and I have hardly spoken. I flip through my comms and reread his last message. "Nothing since he agreed to be our getaway ride."

"And you're sure he said she's in Basement A?"

I swallow the latest rock in my throat. "It's the prisoner surgery level, right next to Quarantine. Callum operated there a few times."

"All right," Derek says as he stands. "We leave in four hours to arrive in time for the graveyard-shift change. And I've got a distraction planned while Ren finds Basement A."

Benny wiggles his fingers together. "Quite a plan," he says, nodding. When Benny approves, we've got something. I may actually allow myself to start hoping.

"Four hours," I say softly.

The room goes quiet. Since I'm no longer allowed to pick at my fingers, I've switched to obsessively chipping red paint from the seat of the chair. Pieces fly off into the air. I don't watch where they land.

"Get some sleep?" Derek says, gently squeezing my shoulder. I look up at him. His palm lingers, so familiar, with so much care.

I can't help it: I go stiff under his touch, waiting for some flicker of feeling. Anything. . . . How badly I wanted him to touch me like that before. But all I can feel in my stomach are the ghosts of some dead butterflies killed off the moment I got caught up with Governor Voss.

The moment I found the spring. The miracle. The curse.

How can I sleep?

Nothing will work right until I get Aven back. Not my head or my body or my heart.

"Sure," I lie. "You too."

1

AVEN
WEDNESDAY

A voice whipcracks in my ear. "She's waking."

Am I?

It feels more like I've been dead, and now I'm bringing myself back to life. My nose is the first thing that works. I'm not at Ward Hope anymore, I know that right away. The room smells different. Emptier. The other room smelled like life, and plants, and the color yellow. It smelled like puppy love—that was Derek's crush on Ren stinking up the place.

He was there when I woke up. *He woke me up.* He gave me the special water. The same stuff Renny found, but way more of it, he'd said. So much that I wouldn't get sick again. It made me feel better, a hundred times better. Stronger too— like I could carry the world on my shoulders and not strain a muscle. And when I fell asleep, it smelled like Renny.

It doesn't smell like her now.

So where am I?

I risk a glance toward the voice, blinking a dozen times. This room is so bright, you'd think someone had plucked the sun from the sky and pushed it into a lightbulb. Except there's no warmth. The walls, the floor, the ceiling—everything's dull and gray. It's a prison. Worse: a hospital prison.

A bubble of panic pops in my throat. I try to talk—*Why am I here?*—but my tongue feels all rubbery. They gave me something. My voice comes out as a gurgle and that's the next thing to scare me.

Standing over me is a lady in a white dress and a white cap. She looks at me like I'm not human. That's not new. When you're sick—even if you're not contagious—people don't see you as "normal" anymore.

Except . . . *I'm not sick.*

I can just tell. My head is full of Hudson fog, still slow from what they gave me, but it also feels empty. Like there's no tumor inside weighing it down. I don't hurt, not even the smallest bit. I want to believe what Derek said, that I'd only need one dose. But pain has a way of coming back.

The woman stares down at me over her beaky nose. Her black hair won't move. It's like she's wearing a soldier's helmet, and she's going into war. "Good morning, Aventine," she says, her words clipped and angry as though I've done something wrong. She uses my whole name too, just like my mama did when she really was mad at me.

Then, looking down at a clipboard, she says, "How do you feel?"

"Athena made it out alive," I mumble, still coming back to life.

"Come again?" The lady looks up from her clipboard. Her eyebrows are two scrunched, confused caterpillars.

If Ren were here, she'd understand.

I close my eyes. The drugs are pulling me under again. "Never mind," I murmur.

I'm back in the abandoned school where I found the book. It told me about Zeus, the lightning god from Greece. He gave birth to a girl out of his head, Athena, and she grew up to be a goddess. She was good at wisdom and war. When I first felt the thing in my head, I had hoped I was Zeus and it was Athena inside, not a tumor. I kept pretending even after we found out the truth. It helped, imagining I was hurting so something good and strong could be born into the world.

"Child," the lady snaps. "When I ask you a question, you're to answer it directly. Do you understand?" She shakes my jaw side to side until I open my eyes for her. *She shakes me.* I can't believe it. . . .

Even back at Nale's—in a crummy orphanage—we were never touched, or shaken, or anything like that. I touch the skin at my neck, confused. Then a shiver tunnels down my back and it burrows far into my chest.

I've been taken.

Derek giving me the water, Ren being on the run from the Blues . . . that's why I'm here. Wherever "here" is.

My throat gets tight and I swallow. And swallow. And swallow again, until my spit is as dry as those crumbly yick protein bars Ren makes me eat.

I push aside the paper neck of my hospital gown and, out of habit, I reach for my penny necklace. Ren has one too. I made it for her. I wonder if she's touching hers. I wonder if she'll look for me. *Of course she's looking for you. She wouldn't let anything happen to you.*

"One more time: How do you feel?"

That question. I hate it.

What doctors really want to know when they ask this question is, how does the sickness feel? Not *me*—*I'm* afraid. I don't know why I'm here, and I don't trust her.

But she doesn't care about that. She cares about the tumor. The sickness.

Defeated, I answer her. "My head feels fine. No pain."

"Wonderful," the lady responds. She doesn't say it like it's wonderful. She says it like she knew, and she isn't surprised.

"What's this?" I ask, scratching the inside of my arm and finding a tube stuck there. It's an IV. I had one of these in Ward Hope. I hate seeing tubes poking around in my body. It makes me feel like a machine, or like that monster with snakes for hair. "Do I need it?" I raise my arm slightly.

"What caused your recovery, Aventine?" the woman asks, ignoring me.

I bite my lip. *Is the water a secret? Ren never said. I only know she found it for the Blues before we realized what it could do. It made me better, but then it made me worse. I ended up comatose in the hospital because I didn't drink enough for it to fix me for good. And I stayed that way right up until Derek came and woke me.*

10

"You were given a very special liquid. Almost like water. Am I correct?"

The woman says all this without looking at me. She's at the foot of my cot with her back turned, arranging sharp tools on a tray. I'm scared. I've never been this cold in my life. Not even when I was running from sickhouse to sickhouse after the Blues nabbed Renny. Fear makes everything colder. I push myself back into the cot as far as I can go. She's going to do something to me. Something sharp.

I shake my head. "I don't know."

"I don't believe you're telling the truth." Sweetly, the lady smiles and tilts her head, but it doesn't look real. "We have video footage from your stay at Ward Hope. A young man brought you something."

"Flowers," I tell her. I'm not trying to lie; I just want to remember the flowers and nothing else right now. . . . They had a yellow, trumpeting smell I liked.

"That's not all," she singsongs, like I'm an infant.

"I woke up, and he was there—I swear."

The woman sighs.

"I didn't see him give me anything, really."

"It was through your IV, then. Obviously," she says, shaking her head. "Did he say anything about it? Did he tell you what it was? How strong it was? And what about your friend, Renata Dane? Didn't she tell you anything about it?" The questions come like cannonballs.

"Ren isn't my friend. She's my sister," I interrupt, but the woman just snorts. It looks ugly on her. "Parents can adopt

11

children, can't they? Then I'm allowed to adopt a sister. And no, my *sister* didn't tell me anything. Neither did her friend." I'm raising my voice now, though I'm smart enough to know that's not a good idea. Not with the tools over there.

"Nothing? Really?" The woman raises one brow as she stands. "So you know nothing about what happened that night?"

I meet her eyes. Ren said she was going to do something impossible, but that's all she told me. "What happened?" I ask quietly.

"Governor Voss is a hero!" She gawks at me in disbelief. "That night will go down in history as the night he eradicated the Blight."

"He what?" I croak, staring back, wide-eyed. "How?"

"I only heard the radio transmissions, like everyone else. But you can ask him about it yourself, if you wish. The governor will be here tomorrow to oversee the procedure."

My heart retreats far into my chest, like it's going into hiding. "Procedure? W-what procedure?" I glance around the room, eyes darting from floor to ceiling for some way out. There's the door they must have dragged me in through, but I can't use that. A bathroom tucked in the far corner is no help either. I'm thinking, thinking . . . but nothing turns up.

Narrowing her crow eyes at me, she says, "Governor Voss believes that while you were in Ward Hope, you were given something very powerful by that young man. It cured you of the Blight, but the governor feels it's capable of more."

What do they think it can do? Looking down at my skin-covered body, I try to see through to the bones and the blood and the muscle underneath. No, I do not understand.

I understand those sharp tools, though. They sit there, waiting.

"Some Dilameth, to keep you calm." The lady fills up a syringe with clear liquid.

I tighten my forearms against the sheets.

"Now don't be difficult." She rips my arm away, stretching it across her lap like I have doll bones inside me. "Make a fist."

Ren—she'd make a fist, but it wouldn't be the kind this lady's expecting. Ren wouldn't let anyone stick her with a needle. She would fight. And then she'd escape, all on her own.

Am I smart like that?

I don't know, I realize. I make the fist she asked for.

2

"How much longer?" I ask Derek for the hundredth time. My voice carries too loud through the miles of unused track that'll lead us to the lab. A rat squeaks in the darkness.

We lost our flashlights for good reason—any one of Derek's centuries-old, assassination-happy family members could be following us. The delightful Kitaneh could be hanging back in the black right now, waiting to make her move.

"Soon." He stops. The rope leash around my wrist slackens—that's how I can tell. "Sooner than the last time you asked, at least."

"*Brack*—" I curse, bumbling backward under the weight of my waterproof pack. I've just flat-tired Derek, walked

14

straight into him, nearly pulling his boot clean off. "Why'd you—"

He grabs my elbow, first to steady me. Then, like it's some sort of road map, his hand travels down to find mine. The hairs on my arm prickle, standing tall as he brings my fingers to his lips. Between my knuckles, he whispers a soft *"Shh."*

I shut my trap and freeze all my bones, listening.

We stand in the pitch-black for what seems like hours, our hands welded together. Another rat squeaks, and Derek exhales. Releases me from his grip. I feel him step away and the rope that's tied between us grows taut again. *He's moving.*

We fall into a quicker pace this time.

"You sure the Blues don't know about this route?" I ask in a low voice, worried that maybe Derek was wrong about that bit. We don't need unforeseen trouble; the Tètai are trouble enough.

He stops short and a puddle splashes under his sole. "The DI knows the PATH exists. They're just under the impression that it's still flooded."

The PATH. He hadn't called it that before, but now that he's using the tunnel's old, pre–Wash Out name, my DI training kicks in—his information is good. As a former Blues mole charged with scouting the UMI for freshwater, I had to study maps galore: underwater, above water, geology, topography, history, too. This route travels under the Hudson River, now a strait. It connected Manhattan with New

Jersey, now the Ward and the West Isle.

Then the asteroid hit. Screwed everything up. *Big-time.*

Sea levels rose. Ground water aquifers turned too salty to drink. Couldn't even desalinate with an underwater power plant upriver. Upstate was left with the only good, clean water on the East Coast, streaming down from the mountains. And those brackheads bolted once they saw they could make a quick buck. Didn't want to be the sole supplier of fresh on the eastern seaboard no more. So they seceded.

Left New York City high and dry, literally. Leftover landmasses banded together—including a few Jersey towns. They renamed themselves the West Isle. Together, we became the United Metro Islets.

Since we had no army, the police force became the Division Interial. Or the Blues, if you ain't the fancy type. And without funding, routes like the PATH stayed out of commission. People from the West Isle weren't exactly clamoring for a way in once the Blight took over in the Ward either.

"So you and your family—the six of you—you just went ahead and drained an entire underwater railroad system? Like fixing a clogged pipe?" I whistle, ducking around the puddle that he'd missed. "Impressive."

Derek chuckles. "Lower your voice," he says softly. "And no. It was just Kitaneh and me, her sister, Sipu, and Lucas—they're also married. My other brother Pietr and his wife weren't there."

"And where were they while you four were off doing all the heavy lifting?"

He doesn't answer, not right away. Maybe I'm imagining it,

but the thick dark of the tunnel starts to feel oppressive, like I've asked something that doesn't have a good answer.

"They died that day."

Dammit, Ren, why you gotta go and ask so many questions? I kick myself, about to say how sorry I am, but he goes on—

"It was supposed to be a simple recon mission: learn how much water Voss had in his personal supply. That was all. We knew he'd found one of the spring's locations back before the Wash Out. What we didn't know was just how much he'd made off with, and he'd been evading us for years. All our attempts at assassination failed. Somehow . . . Voss knew we were following him. He was ready for Pietr and Takhi when they came."

"But . . . I thought you guys couldn't die?" I ask, unable to stop myself. I've been wondering that since I found his photo album. *From the 1800s.*

"There are ways," he tells me. "Humans have basic needs: Fresh water. Air. The spring's unique properties don't change that."

"I'm sorry, Derek. About . . . everything," I say, but the words sound so limp once they're out of my mouth. As we continue in silence, I wonder if he's hurting now, still, after so many years. I'd hurt every day for the rest of my life if I lost Aven.

"Something else has me confused . . . ," I start, needing to break the uncomfortable quiet.

"Go on."

"You guys have a zero-tolerance policy, so when Voss finds the water, you try to off him. Don't matter what he'd use the water for—you've also tried offing people who'd do good with the spring, like Callum. And me."

Derek's discomfort at the reminder runs like a line of electricity through the rope 'round both our wrists. It's taut with guilt. "So here's my question: Why not just bomb the hell out of the spring? Destroy it. Why go through all this trouble to keep it hidden in the first place?"

Derek answers on an inhale. "We've tried. We can't."

Behind us, something crumbles. Derek raises his hand as the dull racket of a rockslide echoes down the tracks.

"Structural damage, right? Your people would never be so clumsy."

Derek don't answer immediately. Waits for the tunnel to fall quiet again.

He grabs my hand, harder this time. Our soles hit the ground. Rubber squeaks against the metal rails, and we're running, giving every step away.

3

AVEN
WEDNESDAY

I need more time. My brain doesn't work like Renny's does. She thinks things over so fast.

I yank my hand back from the lady in white and cross my arms. "I have to use the bathroom!" I shout. "It's an emergency. I'm serious." And I am. I really do have to pee.

She doesn't believe me. Her helmet hair actually stiffens around her head.

"Do you want me to go in the bed while I'm under?"

The lady exhales through her nose, flat-lipped like a dead fish.

"A bed full of pee is no fun for anyone. . . ."

She nods toward a door in the far corner. "There's the bathroom. I'll be waiting for you."

I'm sure you will. If Ren were here now, she'd know how

19

to escape in the amount of time it took to pee. I don't know if I'm that smart. Steadying myself, I place both feet on the floor and take all the time in the world. Then I stay like that for a bunch more seconds.

"Sorry," I say, breathing heavily. "I'm so dizzy. And my stomach hurts." I clutch it, the same as when I'd skip class at Nale's to go penny-hunting.

The lady doesn't respond.

Once I'm finally inside the bathroom, I look around. It's a normal bathroom with normal bathroom things: sink, toilet, toilet paper.

How will any of this help me? I can't flush myself down the drain. Above the toilet there's a metal air vent. If I followed it long enough, could I eventually find a way out? It looks like I could unscrew it, too. *But what if I get caught?*

My fear embarrasses me. Ren wouldn't think like that.

Still mulling over the vent, I lift the hospital gown above my waist and pee, since I was telling the truth about that part. I'd need to get the lady out of the room—at least for a few minutes—if I were going to try for the vent. At Nale's, other girls used to spend hours and hours in the bathroom. They'd rather be in a smelly bathroom than in class. They'd say they had their period. I've never had mine. Survival trumps baby-making, Ren told me once.

I could get it, though. . . . I clap my hands together. Today's as good a day as any.

I decide to scream.

"Oh my god, oh my god! There's blood!" I start fake crying.

"What is it, child?" I hear the lady say from outside the

door. She's banging on the metal, announcing to me that she's coming in. Since the door doesn't have a lock, she's able to walk in on me like this, squatting on the seat, knees locked together.

"What are you doing?" I howl, blushing furiously, clutching my penny necklace. "Go away!"

Quickly, she shuts the door and says from the other side, "Don't you know what a period is? Jesus, child. That's nothing to scream about."

"Please, I hate blood. I need . . . something," I answer through the tears.

"All right, all right," the lady mutters. "You stay where you are. And stop your crying." I hear her walking away, and then a door closes.

It worked.

I . . . I don't believe it. I stifle a giggle. I'm not sure I've ever felt smarter than I do in this very moment. This was just the first hurdle—there are more to go—but I can't help it. If Ren were here, she'd—well . . .

First she'd tell me to get over myself. Then she'd tell me to keep moving. Last, when I was definitely out of danger, she'd tell me she's not surprised in the least.

With that thought keeping me afloat, I hop onto the toilet seat and examine the vent. My fingernails are too short to twist the screws free. I try anyway and end up with a bloody thumb.

What can I do? I'm not even sure how much time has passed. . . .

In bed, time never seemed to pass. Since I drank the water,

time moves so much quicker. I rub the copper penny between my fingers, staring at the screws, chewing on my lip, and getting the squirmy feeling in my stomach.

The penny! I tug off my necklace and fit the copper piece into the end of one screw. *Work, work,* I think, and I turn it like a key, twisting as hard as my fingers can manage.

The screw budges. I spin it round and round until it drops onto the floor. I have to work fast on the next three. *Twist, twist, twist, pull, repeat.*

I don't notice the door as it swings open. The lady is staring at me with her black hair-helmet, a square package in her hand. Quickly, I hide my hands behind my back. The last screw drops out on its own. The vent falls. It clatters against the linoleum.

We stare into each other's eyes.

The contest lasts less than three seconds.

She grabs my wrist. I'm dragged off the toilet seat and out of the bathroom. "N-no," I groan, digging my bare heels into the floor. It does nothing. A cool sweat has covered every inch of my skin. "I need some assistance in Lab A1," the lady says into a tiny mic at her neck.

I'm breathing through a pinhole. "You can't keep me. You can't do this!"

The lab door opens. A young man in white runs in, rushing to my other side—but . . . he's not here to help me. He's helping the lady instead.

Together, they grip my wrists. I've got so much fear in me, so much adrenaline swimming around, that I jerk and jolt, swinging as far as my arms will let me.

They're too strong, or I'm too weak. I'm dragged along like a toy, soles squeaking against the linoleum, until they throw me stomach-down onto the bed. With both arms crossed behind me, it's useless. I choke on the dead smell of bleached linens and my own sour tears.

A needle pierces my vein. I flinch, and from the corner of my vision, I watch the syringe pump itself empty inside me. *Don't close your eyes*, I tell myself, repeating, repeating, but the words lose their meaning. They become a lullaby.

Soon every one of my eyelashes is a building, heavy and lumbering against my eyelids. I have no choice. I have to close my eyes—the room rabbit-holes away from me. From the cobwebby corner of a memory there's a smell like the color yellow. It kisses the tip of my nose, nodding good-bye, and again I'm made of doll bones.

4

Derek and I run, palms jostling, but we stay tight together. "Are we close?" I huff.

He slows to a stop. He's not listening to me, but he is listening to *something*. If he were a dog, I imagine his ears would be perking up right now. "Do you hear that?"

A few moments of silence pass, then—

"Brack." Someone is definitely behind us. Each second, their footsteps pound closer. I wait for Derek to make the next move. Ain't used to doing that sort of thing, but he knows his way through the PATH and I don't, plain and simple.

"Derek," I hear Derek's own voice say.

And yet, of course, I know it's not Derek. Same timbre, same cadence. How can two totally different people be so similar? Their features, their bodies, the sounds that come out of their mouths . . . it confuses me to my very core.

"She's not worth it," Derek's brother Lucas says.

I'm flattered he thinks this is about me, but he's wrong. It ain't—not entirely, at least. Derek's been part of a family that refused to help when hundreds took sick. Can't Lucas imagine that maybe—just maybe—Derek's feeling guilty after sitting back and doing nothing for so long?

Lucas's flashlight flickers on, and I search the tunnel's graffiti-worn brick for a place to hide. Behind us I find a small alcove, shielded in shadow, with a recessed metal door tucked neatly out of sight. *Jackpot.*

Derek nudges me into the nook. I feel him slip the leash from his wrist; we're no longer connected. He pushes his bag into my arms and the contents clink softly, sounding fragile. He wastes no time. Stepping into the center of the tunnel, Lucas's flashlight finds him immediately, as he meant it to.

"Brother," Derek says, like he don't care that his own blood is out for his blood. Even his smile seems sincere. He draws the beam a few more feet away, and I stay hidden.

"She's with you. I heard her." Lucas sounds frantic. The warped circle of light darts up and down the tunnel, searching. But the alcove is deep. If I keep myself pressed against its side, I'm safe. "Do you think she'll like it when you're a corpse, Derek?"

A corpse? Shrinking back, the realization cuts straight to my marrow.

Derek's going to die soon.

How didn't I think of it? If he doesn't keep drinking the water, his age will catch up with him. And the moment

Derek got booted from the Tètai for helping Aven, he left his own supply too. I go so stiff, so cold, I may as well have turned into the corpse first.

"It's not too late for you to come home," Lucas says, and Derek stops breathing. "She'd accept you as family, if not her partner. With some help, Kitaneh's gotten over you fairly easily; you'd be surprised." At this, Lucas snickers to himself, exactly like an older brother. "We don't need to speak about what you've done, but this must stop, here and now. Your girl is a risk, Derek. Say Governor Voss catches her. If it'd get her friend back, would she tell him the spring's in our basement?"

Derek's silence frightens me.

"You have to let her go."

Would he do it? Would he go back to them? Though I'm fully out of sight, both legs ache from the sudden rush of adrenaline. Not from fear of being found, but from fear of being left.

Please don't, Derek, I find myself praying. Under the flashlight's yellow, his hair burns. He's the brightest thing in the tunnel. I watch him like a wildfire. Waiting for his answer, I've forgotten to breathe.

Somewhere back the way we came, shoes crunch gravel—I whip my head. I find nothing. *I'm imagining things.*

"She is not the risk," Derek says after an eternity. He moves closer to Lucas, his footsteps tightwire steady. Ten feet off, I hear scuffling. *Someone else is here.*

Lucas flicks his flashlight in its direction. Finding no one, he says, "Your girl's a coward, Derek," and turns the beam back on his brother.

"Governor Voss is the risk. Or have you forgotten? This is larger than the four of us can handle. We've made too many mistakes."

Derek's words are slow. Too slow. He's stalling. *He wants me to make a move. A distraction until he steps in—*

The light follows him, keeping me well out of sight. I lower both packs and ease over, ignoring the size of Lucas's muscled arms. They're Derek-sized, which says enough. I hesitate before moving in; a surprise attack by a five-foot-tall teenage girl might not end in my favor, but I'm the best we've got.

"Voss never should have survived this long," Derek goes on, his words smooth and deliberate. "We should have caught on earlier that he'd kept so much water. Over and over we failed. Now the rules must change. *We* must change. There are not enough of us to continue as we have."

Under my feet, tiny bits of asphalt shift around. *I'm being too loud*, I think, stopping, but Lucas doesn't notice. Derek's speech is doing the trick. I can't walk straight toward Lucas—that'd put me in the way of his flashlight. Instead, I inch along the wall and cross the tracks behind him. About five feet off—when I'm so close I can hear him breathing— someone's foot finds a puddle. It makes a soft, slurping noise.

Brack. I freeze.

Lucas spins around with his flashlight. "Where are you?" he asks, but I wasn't the one who stepped in that puddle.

Who the hell else is here? His light zigzags from one side of the tunnel to the other.

He doesn't know I'm right behind him. I guess there's one advantage to creeping around in an echo chamber—the sounds could be coming from anywhere.

Derek rushes his brother fast, flashlight dropping to the ground with a thud. The two of them lock together, grappling on the tracks. They're throwing punches and playing scrappy, each going for the other's throat.

Each other's *throats.*

This is how they die, I realize. *Suffocation.* Humans have basic needs, like air, Derek just said, and the spring doesn't change that.

I could actually lose him. Right now, I could lose Derek.

I have to do something. I strain my neck, but I can't tell who's who. All I can make out are big muscles and red hair, which help me a sum total of zero.

I make a dash for the flashlight—it's a few feet away, doing no one any good. The rope leash still tied to my wrist drags as I scoop up the light. I turn its beam on the two brothers. At the same time, they stop to look at me.

I scan both freckled faces for the jaw so square you could learn geometry off it. I thought Derek had one of those until Lucas. Hoping I'm not wrong, I pick out the jaw that best fits the bill and decide Lucas is on top. Derek's lost the advantage.

The rope still dangles from my wrist. I hate the idea it's giving me, but it may be my only option. I've got my trusty knife strapped to my thigh, as always, but if Lucas has been drinking the water every day, who's to say he'll even feel it?

The rope, however . . .

But what if I do kill Derek's brother?

I can actually hear the air hissing from Derek's lungs like a nearly flat tire, deflating fast. His forehead is red with blood, his veins blue and bulging—

I drop the flashlight to the ground. It shudders, then strobes. The brothers' bodies flicker in and out of sight. Pulling the rope tight between both hands, I move closer. The bristled cord shakes in my palms. Each fraying millimeter is rough to the touch. I don't want to kill. I don't want to do it.

Turns out, I don't have to. . . .

A shape, small and thick, tosses me aside. *Kitaneh?* I think, but almost immediately, I'm proven wrong. Jostled backward, I hear a dull thump. Lucas's head rocks and sways; he's been hit in the skull. In the strobing light, I watch as his eyes roll backward and his body rolls forward. He collapses over Derek, utterly still.

Derek gasps. Gripping his neck for air, he pushes his brother off. "Ren?" he chokes out.

"Not Ren. Me," a girl says softly, holding Lucas's head in her lap. She caresses his forehead, like she didn't just smack the living daylights out of him. Her dyed blond bob hangs unevenly against the dark skin of her jaw.

"Sipu," Derek wheezes, sitting up and taking deep drags of air. "What the hell are you doing here?"

I step around the girl, Sipu, and pick up the flashlight, only to hit it against the wall a few times. Sure enough, it quits its dance-party antics and gives us some solid light.

Trying not to blind anyone, I aim it onto the ceiling.

Sipu reaches into her backpack, her eyes two sunken shadows, and pulls out a spool of twine. "Lucas was lying," she says. She lifts his limp body and winds the spool round his hands, binding them together first. "Kitaneh would kill you if you returned. He thought . . . maybe if he could get you home—if we could just go back to the original plan—" Here she looks at me and shrugs. *Killing me. That was the plan.* "Then perhaps he could get Kitaneh to reconsider." She pauses and swallows hard. "They've become . . . close," she says finally.

Lucas hinted at the same thing, but I'd written it off as classic brotherly competition. From Sipu's face, though, I see he wasn't lying about that.

Derek crawls toward her. "And you came to warn me? Why?" Together, they pass the spool back and forth around Lucas's body.

Sipu avoids his gaze. "It takes only one falling domino to set the rest in action," she answers, her body stiff. "The same can be said for guilt. You don't know the half of it, Derek. Kitaneh's made decisions for all of us. I don't believe in hell, but if I did . . ." Her voice wavers.

Derek looks at her briefly but doesn't ask what she means. They tie off a bound and gagged Lucas, laying him down on the tracks. Taking Sipu's hand, Derek asks, "Come with us?"

"I can't," she says, unable to take her eyes off Lucas's face. "Our cause was worthwhile, our means were not—he must see this. I'm just not ready to give up on him yet. You two keep going. He'll wake soon."

30

"And if he saw you knock him out?"

"I couldn't see my husband kill his one remaining brother, only to live an eternity with that kind of guilt. It's true enough."

Derek and I throw our packs over our shoulders. "I never wanted to be at war with my family, Sipu," he says, his face haggard under the flashlight's beam. She nods. We turn and walk, following the tracks in silence. I'm sure we're both thinking the same thing.

He's been at war since the moment he saved Aven.

5

Mama always said I should love my hair.

"I've got it too," she'd croon. I'm no more than six, long and sprawled along her lap, and we're mushed together in a big rocking chair, watching the strait float by. "So blond it's silver, like an old person's but with more butter mixed in. When I touch your hair, I'm touching my mama's hair too. And her mama's hair, on and on, backward into infinity. We've all had it. Hair that's old before our time."

Her voice tickles my ear, and then it's gone.

Whatever they gave me, it's wearing off. My skull aches. I'm waking up faster than I want, but it's unstoppable. *Why do I hurt so much?* I feel like I'm holding the sun in both my hands.

Pain forces my eyes open, but I don't want to see where it's coming from. "What's going on . . . ?" I murmur, my voice toady and croaking. "I hurt. . . . Why? Why do I hurt?" My head rolls from side to side like my spine isn't strong enough. That must be the drugs too. They make the room spin, and I have to close my eyes again.

I try to remember Mama's face, but I can't. The drugs wore off and now I'll never see her again. I see someone else's face. She's fluffy-haired and muscled. She's black and red and yellow-cheeked, the colors of an apartment fire, and she smells like soot. She feels like my mother but she's not, and still I curl into her lap. That's also made of pain. I whimper.

"Aventine Colatura."

An old man is saying my name. He sounds so excited to meet me. . . .

"Do you consider yourself to be a special girl?"

It's a strange question, isn't it?

"I don't know what you mean," I mumble, opening my eyes—a bad idea. My head won't let me see anything straight. "Maybe? I haven't done anything very special."

The man pats my leg twice excitedly. He has the same face as Governor Voss, but through the haze I don't quite believe it's him.

"Ah . . . but you have, my dear. You have! The entire scientific community will soon know about you." He claps his hands together once. "And me," he adds.

What does he mean? I wonder, lifting myself up from the bed. It doesn't work; I collapse back onto the sheets, boneless. *Something's wrong. My arms feel wrong.*

The room continues to whirl like a pinwheel, toppling

sideways, then straightening itself out. I swallow my heart and look down.

Bare feet, bare legs . . . I'm in hospital clothes. I blink when my eyes pass over a spot of red. I try to focus on it. At both hips, a bandaged white stub. They're just . . . just lying there. Where my hands should be, they're not. I start to breathe so fast my lungs can't keep up. *It can't be.* I try to wiggle a finger, any finger, but nothing moves. *I'm wrong, I must be wrong.* Shoulder, elbow, forearm, wrist . . .

. . . blood on gauze.

A wave of sick washes over me. On the floor, a metal pail is waiting. *I have hands,* I tell myself, and I force open my eyes because this can't be real. It can't. *This is a nightmare.* My eyes won't open. They already are.

"Mama," I cry, reaching for her to come back—the real one.

There are so many tears now, each one slopping down my face faster and faster. "Why?" The word is blubber on my tongue, caught up with the crying. "Why would you do this? What did I do?"

The old man, thin as a shadow, hovers over me.

"Why do you think this is about you, child? You've done nothing wrong. This is not about you. Or, not just you, I should say. It is for *us.* Humanity. Science." His words are slow and they stretch and stretch like rubber bands, but I listen with both my ears and my eyes. I try to keep up.

I hear him say I did something for science.

"You see, Aventine, the medicine you were given, it's more powerful than you can imagine. It fixed your tumor, you remember. But I believe that's just the tip of the iceberg."

I'm not sure I'm listening anymore. A thing is growing inside of me. A feeling, like fire, is being born. This is how dragons must feel. *I want to burn him.* My insides are scorched for the first time. It's as though I've never known true anger in my life.

I'm shaking.

My hands. He's taken my hands from me . . . for science.

6

Lucas can't be following us. Sipu knocked him out good, and tied him up even better. But every time a damned mouse squeaks, I turn my head to check.

I almost killed Derek's brother. If it hadn't been for Sipu, I would have.

The realization stings. I don't like to think about what I'm capable of. It seems the better a person I become, the worse I become at *exactly* the same time. Doesn't being good kinda mean you're not being bad?

"We're close. The ladder should be coming right up," Derek says, shaking me from that depressing thought train. "What happens when we reach the top?" He's quizzing me, as if I might not remember. Normally I'd give lip, but not today, not now. Ain't the time for sore feelings.

"The ladder leads to an airlock. There, we'll change into our wet suits, you'll knock open the lock, and then it's swim practice all the way to the lab's basement. Since we're still a few stories below sea level, we'll need to hold our breath a ways. After we break surface, the old air ducts will be right there ready for us to crawl through. We follow those to . . . the shitter." I end with a grin he can't see.

"Hopefully that's not a metaphor," Derek answers. "And then?"

"Once we're inside, we'll set our comms and split up. Your distraction—"

"That's right," he says. "Let me show you." He reaches into the side pocket of his bag and pulls out an unlabeled vial of . . .

"Air?" I squint into the empty glass.

"Air-*borne*," Derek corrects. "It's a replica of the HBNC virus, minus the infectious genetic material. In case of a containment breach, the lab is equipped with viral sensors—they'll identify the protein makeup and go off. The switchboard operator will then order all staff to the lab's detainment area."

I stare even harder into the vial, amazed. "Easy peasy," I say, sarcastic. "How'd you guys get this? Or should I just assume it's another Tètai hat trick?"

Derek returns the vial to the side pocket and picks up the pace. "Kitaneh said she took it from a dead bird, guessing that's how the virus spread. Never really made sense, though. The protein shell supposedly dissolves after it releases the virus; she couldn't have pulled it from a dead

37

bird. Who knows." He shrugs, and a few moments later, pulls off the tunnel's main drag. "It works, though. We used it once before."

Metal claps against the wall. "Found our ladder," Derek announces, testing its sturdiness with a shake. "And after we separate, what next?"

"I search Basement A, find Aven. We all meet back in the first-floor bathroom and get outta dodge the same way we came."

"Perfect. And you're confident Callum will be waiting for us? Is there a chance he might not show?"

"No way. He's too reliable," I say, but Derek looks unconvinced. "Callum's not just the brainy, intellectual type—he's made of stronger stuff than he looks."

I don't mention his tiny, totally unrelated fear of water.

A twinge of something passes across Derek's face. Maybe he doesn't appreciate the glowing endorsement I just gave Callum. Which would mean he gets jealous, just like regular people. An interesting realization, but not one I've got time to dwell on.

Derek certainly ain't—he's halfway up the ladder by the time I've got my hands on the bottom rung.

I race to catch up, climbing at a straight vertical until we hit the steel airlock. Inside, a fluorescent light glows blue, buzzing as it flickers on and off. "Wet suits on," Derek says. We drop our packs in tandem, yanking out the awkward black flippers first. Next come the wet suits, still sopping from earlier.

I turn away from him. "Don't look," I mutter. Maybe I can

change during one of the dying lightbulb's off moments.

"How do you know I'm not already?" Derek jokes, and I can practially hear him grinning. Even so, I hop into the clammy wet suit like I'm on fire.

Last, I throw on goggles, resting them over my eyebrows. Without hair it's so much easier, but the realization comes with a pinch of regret—my crazy curls, lopped off on Callum's floor. It was worth it: my new look made it easier to break into Ward Hope so I could get the cure to the patients. But I still miss my curls.

Fully suited, I turn to face Derek. Already, I'm sweating up a storm under my neoprene. He hands me a mask with a rubber and mesh cup, and an attached elastic band. It makes me feel like we're entering nuclear bomb territory. I pass it back.

"It's a respirator mask, Ren. You should wear it once we're in the lab."

"I'm immune, remember?" He knows this—I ran into him at Ward Hope just as Aven was waking, and we had to escape via the contagious ward.

"You're immune to the Blight. But we're walking into an experimental laboratory. They could have a hundred disease strains floating around that we haven't even heard of." He passes me the mask again. "It's waterproof," he adds, "so just throw it around your neck for now."

I do as I'm told, though I can't help but wonder how necessary it is. Back at Nale's, kids sometimes got the flu or the pox, but not me. Never so much as a cold. Never a broken bone neither.

How awful would it be to catch my own incurable disease

after saving Aven from hers?

I ain't positive, but I think that'd be called *irony*.

"You can't get sick neither, right?" I ask. "You took some water with you? I heard glass in your pack."

Derek's eyebrows gnarl up. "You heard that corpse bit. I'd hoped, maybe, that you hadn't. Yes, I took water with me. Enough to last a while. I won't get sick."

Leaning over a keypad, he asks, "Ready?" His fingers look ready to punch in the code and unlock the metal door.

I lower my goggles and press on the plastic lenses. Once I'm sure all the air is out, I answer, "Ready," nodding and rubbing my palms together.

A wheel as large as I am rotates automatically. The metal door rises. A great green wave-tongue begins to swallow up the room. "We swim when it's full!" Derek calls out over the noisy roar. I couldn't swim now if I wanted—I'm cemented to the floor by a hundred tons of seawater crushing my flippered feet.

The dark, lime-green brackish water reaches my knees, then my hips. Too soon, it's past my collarbone, splashing under my lower lip. When it passes over my mouth and I have to start treading, I look to Derek.

He waves.

Nervy bastard. The water barely touches his armpits.

Kicking my fins, I glare in return and wait for him to catch up with the drowning bit. He steps closer and grips my hips with both hands—I don't expect it. In one quick motion, he lifts me up and sits me in the bent crook of his thigh.

"Easier, huh?" he says, wiping his face.

My cheeks burn despite the cool water. "Mm-hmm," I manage, looking away. My spine fits perfectly against the curve of his chest.

The room darkens as it fills with brack, and Derek flips on his cuffcomm's light. When the water's too high and he can no longer hold me, he drops his knee but doesn't let me go under. Still gripping my waist, mouths pressed to the ceiling, we take a deep breath, then push ourselves out of the airlock.

Derek shoots ahead, a long black fish nearly invisible in the water. The beam of light coming from his wrist ain't much, just enough to follow by. It casts itself against the remains of whatever this building was before the DI took over. Algae covers most everything—too much to tell what was here before.

As we swim higher, though, I spot a pattern in the architecture: vertical bars.

We're in a prison. Might've even been police headquarters, from back when the United Metro Islets was part of the Mainland, with an army and a police force and everything. Seeing how before the Wash Out the DI *were* the police, it makes perfect sense.

Air—the first ache hits like a hunger.

My heart seizes, but I press my lips tightly together. The ache will go away; it always does—I just need to keep my mind calm. Override the body's instinct to freak out. Choking the sensation down into my belly, I force my throat and jaw to relax so I can clear my mind.

It don't work. I'm revved like an overwound toy. There's no

escape in my head. Fear is tucked behind every corner. *He took her.* As if she were a thing to be experimented on, or a game piece he can move to get what he wants.

What would I do if he's already killed her?

My heart drums so loud, it becomes a rhythm in my head. My vision blurs. I can't stop it. I'm not swimming anymore. I don't know how to. *If Aven's hurt, I'll—I'll . . .*

Like a shadow that grows longer and longer, my fear begins to shapeshift until it's entirely unrecognizable. It becomes a dark, strange thing. An animal made only of teeth. There is one corner of stillness left in my mind, and I've found it. The dam I'd built between myself and the answer to that question comes undone, releasing a terrible truth by the tons.

I don't need to lie to myself. Don't need to pretend I'm better than I actually am. We can't all be as good as Aven—not when people like Voss exist.

I know what I would do.

I am necessary.

I will do necessary things.

7

AVEN
THURSDAY

The governor walks back into my room like a knife. Behind him, the door closes automatically, and it sounds like a vacuum being released.

Since the last time he left, I haven't been here in this gray prison. I've been off in my head, doing other things. Things I'll never do again. I've been braiding my hair and painting my nails. I've been racing a speed mobile, like Ren always promised. She said she'd teach me. *How will I steer if I can't turn the wheel?*

"Let's play science, Aventine," the governor says. As though science is a game played on the playground. "What does a lizard have in common with a starfish?"

I shake my head. I have no idea what he's talking about, and I don't care. All I care about is what he took from me and why. After he left, I cried. I did it for so long, I thought I was empty. But the moment he walks in, it's like I never cried at all. I'm completely filled up with tears again. I blink them back.

The governor ignores it, if he's even noticed. He crosses his arms behind his back and looks down at me.

"They both possess the unique ability to regenerate themselves. If a starfish loses one of its arms, that arm will grow back exactly the same as before."

What is he saying? Does he think . . . ?

I push the possibility out of my head. I'm not a starfish; I'm not a lizard.

"You are a slow child, aren't you?" he murmurs, half to himself, half to me. His gray hair reminds me of sharp metal. He is a thing that cuts; that's all he knows how to do.

I hate this man. I don't know that I've ever said that about anyone before, but I'll say it about him: *I hate this man.*

"Let's have a look." He lifts my arm up from the elbow, and I don't resist. I have no bones in there. Bones are for fighting. I don't know that I have any of that left in me, if I ever had it to begin with.

Slowly, he unwraps the gauze. I'm a mummy. It takes forever. When the hair on my arms prickle against the air, that's how I know the bandage is off, but I don't dare look down. I haven't been able to look down since the moment I realized what he'd taken from me.

Governor Voss *hmms* and *ahhhs*, then laughs to himself. "Don't you want to see?"

I force myself to open my eyes and peek in his direction.

"It seems you may in fact have something in common with the starfish and the lizard." He points to my wrist, to a scar in the shape of a perfectly straight white line. "This is where the amputation began. And yet, here you are with a good inch extra of bone, muscle, veins, and skin."

He's right. . . . The curve of where my thumb used to be is already starting to form.

"They're—they're—" I stammer, unable to choke out the possibility. "They're growing?"

"They are," he tells me.

This time I don't blink away the tears. I can't tell if I'm happy or angry. I think I'm both, but the tears look the same either way.

"I wouldn't have hurt you unless I thought you'd fully recover. I'm not a bad person, Aventine."

My cheeks are wet down to my chin. The thought of my hands growing back, that this might not be forever—it's too much.

"But you are—" Spit mixes with tears and I barely understand myself. "You are. How do you not see it?"

"They're growing back, my dear," he says, cocking his head, confused. "No harm done."

I don't know that I've heard such a loud, strange noise come from my mouth before. I don't recognize myself. Thrashing in my cot, "Get me out! I want my sister!" I bellow.

"Quiet!" The man drops my arm onto the bed as he stands. An arrow of pain tears through my shoulder. I bite my lip to keep from crying. The pain quiets me, not him. "Child, you have tried my patience long enough. Perhaps you'd like to find out just how well the medicine you were given works?"

Opening the door, he calls into the hallway, "The patient is unstable. We need some Dilameth in here, right now." Moments later, a team of nurses files into the room.

"After you have administered the Dilameth, you're to bring Miss Colatura over to Quarantine."

No one understands. They're watching him. They're hesitating. They're not touching my bed; they're not touching me.

His face takes on that cutting look. Ants crawl up my spine, tunneling homes through the nerves along my vertebrae. "There is so much about the medicine we do not yet understand. It heals, but we do not yet know if it protects against future infections," he explains. "Miss Colatura will remain in Quarantine for the next forty-eight hours to allow for potential inoculation of the virus."

It's like I've been kicked into outer space without a spacesuit. The weight of everything crushes my lungs. "I don't want to be sick again," I plead. "Please . . ."

Two women pin me against the cot, while a man with a syringe stabs my inner elbow. It happens the same as last time, only faster. "I hope there's enough of that medicine left in her system that she's protected," I hear someone say. A foghorn sounds off in my head, barreling into the distance and disappearing with all my thoughts. The world becomes one giant sinkhole, and soon that falls away too. This time, I smell no flowers.

8

REN
2:45 A.M., FRIDAY

In my chest, the pressure unclenches. Salty brack spills over my face, sweet relief. I take gasps of the dank air, dog-paddling to stay afloat, blinking away the seawater. When I spit, I also make sure not to swallow. The brack'll only make me thirstier, and the canteen is out of reach.

"You made it," Derek says, swimming closer. He pushes slick, reddish hair from his eyes. "What happened? You had me worried for a minute."

Me too, I don't answer. Derek's treading water, looking at me with those damned eyes of his. I don't know what to tell him. My fear spawned some monster I'm not so sure I'd care to look at just yet.

"There's our front door," Derek says, thumbing toward

47

an algae-coated, rectangular metal chute. It drops into the water a few feet off. "I'll go first." He ducks underwater, and moments later I hear his body bumping around inside.

I follow, swimming under the duct's mouth. When I come up for air, I'm hugged by Derek's chest on one side and metal on the other. Proper breathing is going to have to wait—the space is hardly big enough for us both. We're nose-to-nose, and that's putting it mildly.

Inside the duct, Derek shines his cuffcomm's light on two handlebars. "They're suctioned on—you can move them. I've got two more for myself. They should help the climb. You ready?" he says. I snort and shake water from my face.

He swims out of the duct so I have room to maneuver. Once he's gone, I grab for both handles, back pressed against metal. Bracing myself with my knees, I slowly make my way up. I yank the handles off and replace them as I go. Below, I hear Derek doing the same.

A few minutes in, the old, unused chute makes a T, where it connects with the newer one—a vast improvement as far as travel plans go. This one runs horizontally through the building's walls, so we no longer need to haul ourselves against gravity. I let Derek pass me, not knowing which way to go on my own. I store the turn in my mind.

We move in time with each other, sliding our knees simultaneously to cut down on the noise. I'm hoping against hope the neoprene of our wet suits sufficiently muffles our entry.

Soon, artificial light from whatever room we're passing cuts a dozen lines of shadow into the chute, and I know we're well inside the building. At the telltale gurgle of a toilet being flushed, Derek and I exchange glances. I stop breathing. Nothing like a little bathroom action to settle the nerves. A bit too much, actually. *Oh no.*

Laughter starts bouncing around in my gut. Like a Ping-Pong ball, it flies up into my chest. I can't give in. To be done in by toilet humor. Pathetic. I bite my lip and look at Derek. He just rolls his eyes.

I can't help it. It wants out. It needs to be released—I snort, I cover my mouth, I bite into my wrist, but it's already out there, wobbling around inside the metal duct, echoing like it came straight from the belly of a clown.

The shuffling in the bathroom stops.

Fear, acidic and sharp, washes over me, destroying every last ounce of funny. My laugh dies a quick, hard death, and we wait to see how bad the damage is.

A door swings open, a faucet runs. Footsteps. Another door shuts and the room quiets.

Whew.

Once Derek is sure the coast is clear, he starts grappling with the grate. It pops out and he slides forward, feetfirst, through the opening. I follow suit, but I'm not ready for Derek's hands gripping the backs of my thighs, helping lower me down. I gasp, my body turning rigid and tight. His hands make my nerve endings dance, though the moment means nothing. He and I can't mean anything, not now. Not yet.

My feet touch ground; he lets go.

Quickly, I reach for my cuffcomm and type Callum a message:

Made it in. See you at the duct.

I push send as Derek hands me two of the three white lab coats he's pulled from his bag.

"One's for Aven," he explains, throwing his on. Moments later, I emerge from a bathroom stall wearing the two coats, both many sizes too large. "Ain't no way I'm gonna pass for working here," I mutter.

"It'll do."

Now Derek reaches into his lab coat and pulls out a clear thimble, which he hands to me. "You'll need this to access the basement level. It's a—"

"A Print Mimic," I finish, ogling the thing. "Yeah, I know. DI banned these years ago. Pretty sweet score, I gotta say."

"So you know how it works?"

"For the most part. Just lay it over someone's prints and the gelatin makes a mold."

"Exactly. There's a scanner at the stairwell. You can pull the prints directly." Derek glances at his cuffcomm. "It's time. Ready to split up?"

"I am."

I've been ready since the night Voss took Aven.

"Be back in thirty minutes or I'll come looking. There's

another level below this—I'll head that way."

It's 3:00 a.m.—I set my own countdown clock.

"Don't forget the mask." Derek points to the rubber mesh cup thingy dangling, somewhat soggily, from my neck. Before I place it over my face, the two of us lock eyes.

I could write a book about what we say, and what we don't say, in those few seconds.

"This will work," he assures me, placing his own mask over his head.

I lower mine too, and he cracks opens the bathroom door, poking his head into the corridor. Then he signals for me to follow.

Derek turns right and I turn left, a new worry hanging around me like a shadow. We continue to walk in opposite directions, but the nagging feeling won't go away.

I spin around in the middle of the hall, only to find he's done the same.

He's standing there looking back at me. Tall, broad-shouldered, mussed hair and bear-brown eyes. The way he's staring . . . I take a mental snapshot. He cares about me, he does. It's on his face. I don't want to ever forget the way he's looking at me right now. Everything I need to know—it's all here in this very moment.

"I'll come after you too," I say in a husky whisper. "If you're the one who's late."

He takes a few steps backward. I don't see the smile under the mask, just a subtle lift at his jawline. Then, he turns away. And though we lost the rope back in the tunnel, I can still feel . . . *something*. It's tugging, pulling tighter and tighter—a line of connection immune to distance or time. Reality frays its edges but the line doesn't know how to break.

It doesn't want to.

9

AVEN
THURSDAY NIGHT

If the other room was too bright, with a cold sun stuffed into the lightbulb, this room is its opposite. I come to again, hardly able to see. Round, yellow bulbs dangle from chains in the ceiling. I'm sprawled out across one of many mattresses that line both sides of the room. Some are empty. Shadows move in the background. They're people. They're also ghosts.

A woman wipes my forehead, telling me to relax. She whispers *"Shh . . ."* in my ear. Her voice reminds me of hand-made lace, crocheted out of iron. "Gather your strength," she says, but she doesn't understand.

I don't have strength. I'm piecemeal.

I refuse to look down at my arms. *What if the governor's wrong and I'm like this forever?*

The only hope I have for getting out is Ren. *She* is my strength.

Just one time, I wish that weren't true. That I could do something strong for myself, without her help. But today's not that day. I have to hope she'll come. If I lose that . . . I lose everything.

As my eyes adjust to the dim light, I begin to make out the woman's features. If the moon had a skinny face, she'd be that moon. Her hair falls like chain metal, wiry and long past her shoulders. And for some reason, if I'm not imagining things, she feels familiar.

"I know you," I say, squinting.

The moon pushes a few strands of hair behind my ear and continues wiping down my forehead. "Do you now?" she answers with a smirk. The lines in her face are deep. Deeper than when I knew her, I think.

"I do."

"And how?"

Something about her brings me back to the 'Racks. I'm sipping on a bag of soup. I think it was this woman's goodwill that had brought it to the door of my one-room apartment with Ren. *Tomato, I think it might've been?* Cold, rehydrated, but oh-so-delicious.

"Mrs. Bedrosian?" I ask, wondering if Ren ever had enough extra green to leave her something nice in return. Probably not. We never had extra green.

"Yes, love." She laughs and leans forward, planting a motherly kiss in the middle of my forehead.

This simple act of love . . . I want to cry. Maybe it's the

drugs—I've been half-awake since they brought me here—but I remember her now, my mama. She came back to me. The governor made me remember her. Her white lashes, the way she smelled when I was in her lap, and the way she sounded. And though I forgot her face as soon as I woke up, I remember the rest. I remember her, and I miss her.

I don't want to miss her. Missing Ren is bad enough.

Without meaning to, I shrink away from Mrs. Bedrosian.

"It feels like forever since I last saw you," she says, and she brings a foggy plastic cup to my mouth. "Drink."

I drink. The water tastes dank and metallic; it's been through roof pipes. I finish in two gulps. By the time she takes the cup back, I know when I heard her voice last—that night comes back to me like a boomerang. *The Blues raid.* Chief Dunn, Governor Voss's military right-hand man—he'd paid Ren a visit, but that wasn't why he was there. He was making a Transmission Arrest. He was there for Mrs. Bedrosian. Someone charged her with passing on the Blight and so they took her.

Here. *Quarantine.*

She still has the virus, then.

A ball of anxiety settles in my stomach. I don't want to look at Mrs. Bedrosian how the other lady looked at me—like she's not human, but . . . *what if the water can't keep me safe?*

More of that night comes back, a jigsaw of screaming and begging. It fits together in a perfectly horrible picture. *Her husband*—he'd followed Chief Dunn into the hallway while Mrs. Bedrosian was being dragged off. He was pleading with the chief not to take her, and then—

The sickening thump of a body falling to the floor.

He never got up.

Does she even know?

I nod. Yes, it feels like it's been forever. But it hasn't. Not according to minutes and hours and days. Time shouldn't be measured like that. Those units don't work unless you've got somewhere to be. Time should be measured in change.

I lick my lips. The water she gave me wasn't enough. It never is. My skin is so dry it flakes against my tongue. "Do you know what happened after they took you?" I ask, swallowing.

Mrs. Bedrosian watches me closely. "What do you mean?"

My heart, the thing that's supposedly a pump for blood, feels like it's pushing concrete. I don't want to be the one to the tell her. So badly, I don't want to be the one.

But if Ren had died and I was never going to see her again, I'd want someone to tell me.

Now Mrs. B's watching me like I'm something awful. A bomb, about to go off. It's too late to change my mind. "Your husband . . . ," I begin, with no idea how to string together this hideous combination of words. "He was trying to . . . and Chief Dunn . . . he, he—"

I can't finish. I don't have to.

Mrs. Bedrosian covers her mouth, as if to keep something inside from escaping. "Don't say it," she croaks. I nod the rest of the sentence. She shakes her head, breathing heavy. She wheezes into her palm. When she drops her hand, there's red there, splatter painted against her skin. "No, no, no . . . ," she repeats to infinity.

The shadows gather closer. Everyone here knows loss. Another prisoner gently offers Mrs. Bedrosian his hand. His frail eyelashes carry tears for her, like an offering. Behind him, an older woman with a straight, stiff back and a steel bun rests a bony hand on Mrs. Bedrosian's shoulder. She turns, stands. The two lock together. "He's dead," she sobs. "He's dead."

They rock in each other's arms until more people approach. Squeezing Mrs. Bedrosian one last time before separating, the older woman looks down at me.

I realize . . . *I know her too—*

"Miss Nale?" I whisper, standing.

"Aventine Colatura," my old headmistress says, smiling—I think she looks proud, though I have no idea why that would be. She takes both my hands in hers.

"You're here too." I glance around Quarantine and Miss Nale's smile falters.

"It was bound to happen. I've seen too many of you children take sick." She pauses to cough into her shoulder. "Never thought I'd see you again after you ran off in the dead of night. Ren's idea, I'm sure."

I smirk and shrug. She's not wrong. "I'd started to show symptoms. You were going to notice any day. Ren didn't want me to go to a sickhouse."

I don't say that I ended up there anyway, after she got nabbed. Being at the sickhouse used to be my worst memory.

Now I have new worst memories.

"Are you two still friends? Excuse me," she says, catching herself. "Sisters, I mean?"

I nod.

"I'm glad. She was there, at my home, for so many years. She never trusted me, though. I would have thought of her as my own if she'd let me. I very much hope to see her again."

Me too.

Miss Nale squeezes my arms once more before returning to Mrs. Bedrosian's side.

Still parched from the drugs, I use my bandaged wrists to lift my cup from the floor, and I look for more water. On the other side of the room, three steel barrels with spigots sit on top of a table. I head for them, moving through bodies so skeletal that if it weren't for the tumors, I wouldn't know that they had skin. Misshapen lumps bulge out of necks, cheeks, kneecaps.

In the background, a radio is on. It's broadcasting some West Isle radio channel no one here cares about. It's just to distract us.

When I try to fill my cup, the barrels are empty.

"Orderly don't come until morning to replace them," a teenage boy says to me. His greasy black hair falls over one eye, and I see no tumors. I wonder if he has them in the lungs, like Mrs. B.

I stare into my cup and close my eyes.

Outside, a cure is waiting.

In my head, a thought no bigger than a seed firmly takes root. I know from this second it will never go away on its own—it needs to grow. Its roots are too deep. It wants to be something important.

We have to do something, I realize. *Ren and me, together. For them.*

The thought gives me fire.

10

High volts of energy surge through the soles of my feet, pushing me to *go*, but running would jeopardize everything. No one runs in a lab.

I walk slowly through a glass corridor, headed for the stairwell to the basement. As I pass each window, I look for glimpses of straw-colored hair, even though we don't think she's on this floor.

An old woman wheels toward me from the other side of the wing. She's chairbound with an IV dangling over her left shoulder. An aide pushes her along. The two talk in low tones, and our eyes meet. My feet stop, like they want me to get caught.

Act like you're supposed to be here, I remind myself, and continue on. As the woman and her aide near, I notice her features: skin darker than mine, but with a smattering of freckles over her nose and full cheekbones. Her hair turns out in every which way. I've seen that face before, but I don't know where to place it.

"Has the treatment kicked in yet? Are you feeling any better?" I overhear.

The woman rolls her eyes, and if I'm not mistaken (there's no one else in the hallway), she rolls her eyes *at me*. Like she wants me to laugh along.

"I'm old, boy. Find me a cure for that. Then I'll feel better." Her voice grates, crude and pissed off. Once upon a time it might've been a nice voice. Now it's just angry.

"Well, Mrs. Voss, your husband—"

Mrs. Voss?

She looks so much older now.

Back in the arboretum Governor Voss had shown me her picture—Emilce, he said her name was. Also said she was the only person he'd kill for.

"Don't talk to me about what my husband believes," Emilce Voss interrupts. She waves her hand, exasperated. "You're no better than him, keeping me here. One of these days I'll be gone and he'll blame you."

The aide snickers to himself. He finds her antics hilarious, clearly.

"I can only pray."

I like this lady, I think to myself as the hallway goes dark. Soft blue emergency lights flicker on, and a woman's calm voice sounds through the loudspeakers.

"This is not a drill," the voice announces just as I reach

the stairwell and the small, metal fingerprint scanner. "Attention, employees: evacuate immediately to Basement C Detainment Center. This is not a drill. Thank you."

The speakers crackle and go silent.

Derek's distraction worked.

A minute too soon—employees file into the hall, all heading for the stairwell to Basement C. The same stairwell as me.

Brack. I gotta work fast.

I slip on the Print Mimic. Pressing down on the scanner, I squish my finger around and linger there; it needs to pick up the entire fingerprint.

But I don't lift my finger soon enough—the scanner reads the unmolded jelly.

"ERROR."

Behind me, I hear lab staff approaching. They're murmuring to one another, asking if anyone knows anything about the evacuation. I don't turn around; it'll only look suspicious. I lift my index finger and press.

"ENTER," the door says. Its steel bolts unlock and I sprint down too many stairs to count. At each level, employees spill into the stairwell. I push past—it's an evacuation; I can afford to be pushy.

When I can go no lower, I throw open the door to *BASEMENT A.*

The corridor is dark, empty but for one, single lab tech. He's jogging, headed for the opposite staircase. Closing the door, I wait for him to leave. When I'm sure it's safe, I push it open again.

I race from one end of the corridor to the other, passing

only one room. Through long glass windows an operating table stands abandoned. *Where is she?*

I backtrack, spotting a second door.

There wasn't only one room. There was only one room *with windows.*

To the right, an ID scanner.

Irrationally, I begin to think I can sense her. Like maybe, we've been together for so long that I could let my gut be my guide. Some say that's impossible. Don't matter to me. Thinking something's impossible only makes it less possible.

Are you in there, Aven?

I shake my hand, resetting the Print Mimic. I press down on the scanner. This time, I'm faster, wiggling my finger around before lifting it away.

The bolts inside release.

"ENTER."

Holding my breath, I turn the handle.

I'm in the quarantine observation room. The green-tinted, two-way mirror gives it away. On the other side, men, women, girls, and boys. I can see them, but they can't see me. They're spread out along the floor, not two inches between mattresses. Some wear the hospital napkins. Others seem to be dressed in the clothes they were arrested in—coats or skirts or rags.

A different handle catches my eye, this one closer to the floor. I lift, but it's locked. I push a red, plastic button to the left that says *OPEN*. It sounds like turning on a vacuum. Air gets sucked out the other side and a metal bin pops open into my lap.

Crumbs of food gather along the sides.

This is how they feed the prisoners . . . like animals.

I stare in disbelief. An old man, toothless and whiskered, notices I've opened the bin. He sticks out his tongue. Behind him stands a middle-aged woman with a gaunt face and long, wiry gunmetal hair.

And right there, up against the far left . . . I spot her.

My Aven.

"Feathers," I whisper, using her old nickname. She's lying on a mattress, eyes closed, white-blond hair spread out like a fan of sunlight. I tap the glass, but I'm invisible. It's already 3:16—only fourteen minutes before we meet Derek. *I need to get her attention.* I glance between my wrist and the two-way mirror, and that's when I get an idea.

I type Aven's name into my comm. Then, after applying the projection setting, I unlatch my cuffcomm. I tilt its screen up against the glass mirror. Her name shines through. Holding my breath, I focus the image. Soon, the letters appear in blue-white light on the ceiling, for everyone to see.

A-V-E-N.

11

AVEN
3:16 A.M., FRIDAY

R ight before a lightning storm, the air starts to feel buzzy. Charged up. It knows something big is about to happen and it wants to be ready.

Here in Quarantine, it feels exactly the same. The electric energy in the room wakes my chest up first and my ears up second.

The room is abuzz with voices. . . . People saying something. A name, like a question.

Aven? Aven?

I hear it spoken a half dozen times before I'm sure this isn't some drug dream, where the only word that exists in the human language happens to be my name. Opening my eyes, I see people moving like bees, antennae twitching left and right, looking at the ceiling.

My name?

I don't understand at first. But then I notice a path has cleared between me and the observation room where the lab techs spy on us. Hope is a lightning bug in my heart, pulsing on and off again.

Renny? Could it really be her? I won't truly believe she's here until I see her. Writing my name in lights definitely sounds like a trick she'd pull, though. My brain sends a message to the empty space where fingers used to be, telling them to cross each other for good luck. When I can't do it, I worry that I don't have any luck left.

As I step off the mattress, I hide my arms behind my back. If it is Ren—if she's really here—I don't want her to see me this way, without hands for hugging her. Not just yet. She'll be so angry, I know it.

I don't want anger to be the first thing she feels when she sees me.

I walk toward the green mirror.

It's slow-going. My spine feels so old in my body. Once, at Nale's, we were shown an image of a long-necked animal with fancy lady eyelashes and spots all over. It always held its spine straight and tall. As I walk, I pretend I'm that animal. I fake grace.

Halfway there I hear: "It's me! It's Ren!"

That's all I need to believe it's true, that she's really come for me, and that soon we'll be away from this place. My eyes grow wet, and I smile for the first time since they brought me here.

"I'm going to get you out," she calls through the food bin,

and I wonder how she plans on doing it. I wouldn't be surprised if she just took a battle-ax to the glass and called it a day. "But there's no door to this room. We need a different one. How did you get in?"

I glance around the room, trying to remember where I came in from, but nothing jogs my memory. I was in a different room with the governor, and then he had me brought here. I shrug at her through the mirror-glass, frustrated by my own uselessness. Even if I could find a door, I wouldn't be able to open it for myself. My throat closes up.

If this were a fairy tale, I would be the worst heroine ever. I'd be Rapunzel, without the hair.

I start to cry, the not-good tears this time.

Ren presses her hand to the glass. I stand there, wishing.

"Don't worry," she says, voice muffled. "I'll figure something out."

Eye level with the bin, I remember my earlier idea—it nearly worked too. I dig my elbow into its handle, hard enough to open the bin. "Unscrew its nails, Ren! Use your penny!" I call through the opening.

Moments later, the metal bin is jiggling from the inside. It shakes and shimmies, and its nails drop to the floor—

Ren yanks it aside. "Climb through!"

A crowd gathers behind me, their voices low and rumbling as they watch. I hadn't noticed, but now that I see them I don't know what to do. They're jam-packed together, leaving me no space at all.

A little boy dodges in front of me. He throws his shoulders into the empty square. "I'm first!" he squeals. Other prisoners huddle closer, thinking they can follow.

"What do I do, Ren?" I cry.

The boy struggles as she tries to push him back. "You can't," she grunts frantically.

Someone grabs hold of the boy's ankles—"Foolish!"

The space around me widens as Miss Nale drags him off to the side. Towering over his stalky frame, she stands him up by what's left of his collar. "They have hardly any chance of escaping as it is. And when they are caught, the punishment will be far more severe than anything you've seen here in Quarantine."

The boy cowers under her grip, while the rest of the prisoners eye me. I slide in front of the opening, covering it with my body. "I'm sorry," I say weakly, unable to meet anyone's eyes. "She's right. But if we do make it—if by some small chance we aren't caught . . ."

The seedling idea that was in my head explodes—*kaboom*. I look down at the empty space where my hands should be. "We will come back for you," I tell them. "With every piece of me they haven't taken, I promise you, we'll come back!"

Silence. Not dead silence, but an alive silence fills the room. It's the breathing of hundreds of people. Thin, ragged, weak, in-and-out breathing. Together they make a tidal wave.

I . . . I can't believe I just said that.

My promise terrifies me.

"Ignore the two of them," Miss Nale says. "Here, we are alive. Out there, we are criminals. They may make it out, they may not. But they certainly won't with hundreds of us ogling, giving them away."

The crowd murmurs. A few pairs of eyes stray toward us, watching, but most head back to their mats and chairs.

Through the empty square, Ren gawks back at me. "You do realize what you just told them, don't you?" Then, shaking her head, she says, "We'll figure it out later," and anxiously waves me through the tiny square. "Hurry!"

But it's so small. . . .

Maybe I am Rapunzel, I think. *Maybe I don't have hair, but I have my smallness.* The very thing they took from me is the thing that will help get me free.

I go feetfirst. My shins, knees, and thighs make it, but not my hips. They bang against both concrete sides, and they don't budge any farther. "I don't know if I can do this, Ren," I say, shimmying myself back and forth, unable to squeeze through.

Ren lifts up my legs and twists me at a diagonal.

Then she pulls.

Even though I've been through worse, I still whine. The concrete scrapes my hips and shoulders, shredding my paper gown.

Then she sees my missing pieces.

"Aven . . ." Ren's face falls so quickly, I imagine all her freckles dusting away.

Her jaw locks and I watch as that single vein on her forehead works overtime. It only shows up when she's mad. "Voss won't get away with this," she promises, but her voice is a snarl and it doesn't sound like she's making this promise to me.

I tuck my wrists under my armpits. Maybe if she can't see

them, she won't be as mad. Spotting a pack of Virus Exposure Level tests on a shelf, something else occurs to me—

"Ren, quick. Take my blood."

Understanding, she opens up a new pack. She sticks the needle into my arm as gently as she can, but I still flinch. Moments later, the scanner beeps.

"Negative," she says, but we don't have time for relief. "Put this on," she says, unbuttoning her lab coat and handing it to me. I do the best I can, shrugging it on after awkwardly finding the sleeves.

Ren replaces the bin, leaving the nails on the floor. "C'mon," she says, but the moment she touches the door—

12

REN

3:30 A.M., FRIDAY

"**Y**ou're not supposed to be here!"

A lab tech in a plastic suit and a respirator mask barges into the observation room.

I swallow. To get caught *here*, now. Like this? I'd be ashamed of myself.

The lab tech ain't dumb—he sees an escapee in a hospital gown and realizes there's no containment breach. Pulling off his mask, he reaches for the wall, about to call for backup. Behind Aven, there's that metal bin, as quiet and unassuming as any makeshift weapon.

Only hard enough to knock him out, Ren.

His hand's on the dial pad. I don't wait for security to answer his comm; my window of opportunity will have become a mouse hole.

71

Grabbing the metal bin from the wall, I throw it into the triangle of soft skin under the man's chin. The tech's head whips back with a sharp crack. *His jaw*—I choke back a gasp. He collapses. Metal crashes.

The tech's face is bloodied, a gash under his neck spilling red onto the floor.

I look to Aven shivering next to me. Her mouth forms a perfect, horrified O. She's closed her eyes, covered them with her bandaged wrists . . . and I'm glad.

I wouldn't want to see myself do that either.

"I had to," I say, but I'm afraid. She's seen me feed her, bathe her, care for her. But she's never seen me care for her like this. Maybe she doesn't know how far I'd go to keep her safe.

Aven nods and drops her wrists, but her eyes stay closed.

"I don't think he's dead, Feathers. I know how to fight."

She opens her eyes and looks at me like she's assessing. Like she doesn't know what to think.

"We had no choice. . . ."

We. I want her to remember that I'm not doing this for my health—I'm here for her. Aven's never raised a hand to anyone; she's never had to. Her goodness may be innate, but it's also a privilege—one that I can't afford, because I love her too much.

Touching her forearm, I guide us back out the door. The corridor's blue emergency lights are still on—staff's still in detainment and the coast is clear, temporarily. If I'm right and security cameras gave us away, someone's gonna follow up real soon. "We have to run," I say, and I take off first hoping to jump-start her flight reaction.

Aven follows; we sprint up three flights of stairs. It's the most movement she's had in years. She keeps up, though, with her long, alien legs. Taller than me, she is. I'd forgotten, after so long in bed. Back on the first floor, we race through the glass corridor.

I knock once on the bathroom door.

Please be in there, Derek.

I push it open.

Empty.

I comm quickly:

Where are you?

"We can't leave without Derek. He got me in; I won't leave him behind," I tell Aven fiercely—irrationally—terrified that we may not have a choice. "One minute, that's all."

We don't get one minute.

The room goes dark. A siren wails through a speakerphone. In the far corner, a red light strobes around the bathroom.

Someone's found the lab tech.

For a moment, I forget that we're inside a dingy bathroom. Instead, we're in my heart, its chamber frantic with red flashing lights.

The siren howls for blood.

I can't leave him.

"Ren!" I hear Aven call over the noise. "We need to go!"

And . . . I can't stay.

Derek would tell me: keep moving, don't stop until you're

73

safe. But I wish I knew he was safe first.

The vials of water—I remember. *Without them, he'll die. He'll be a walking corpse by tomorrow.* I jump onto the sink, reaching for the grate. The putty we'd used to keep it in place stretches away like gum. Inside the air duct, Derek's and my bags are right where we left them.

I pull out five small vials and search the bathroom for a solid hiding spot—a place no one would look without reason.

I race for the last stall. Lifting the lid with one hand, I drop the vials into the water tank. They sink under the valve, mostly out of sight. One more time, I mad dash for the sink, jumping up onto it.

Quickly, I type into my cuffcomm:

Magic's in the toilet.

I don't say any more than that. He'll figure it out.

"Now we go," I say to Aven, sending the message off. "I'll lift you up, but you'll need to maneuver yourself in."

Aven bites her lip. She eyes her wrists like she's not so sure.

"You got this, Aven." My voice is calm. Reassuring. Mentally, however, I'm ripping Voss to shreds.

"Here," I say, and I hold her by the elbow. She jumps; I swing her onto the sink. Then, wrapping my arms below her hips: "One, two, three—"

Aven throws her elbows into the metal duct and hurtles

herself in. A moment later, she kicks her foot out. It takes me a second to realize what she's doing, but then I understand.

It's for me to grab on to. Even now, after everything, she never ceases to amaze me.

13

"Let's do this," Ren says, clambering into the duct. She taps my ankle twice.

I prop myself up on my bandaged wrists and make it ten feet before the hurt is too much. Instead, I drop back down onto my elbows. It's better, but everything still aches. *Ignore the hurt, Aven. Soon you'll be out.* I had a tumor the size of a Ping-Pong ball in my head for years. I should be able to ignore this.

"We're moving fast enough, don't worry," Ren says, probably because she can hear me dragon-breathing through my nose every few seconds. I'm annoyed with myself, and she knows it. "I'll tell you where to turn. We're looking for the earlier ventilation system that's no longer in use. Careful, though—it connects with this one and drops out just above sea level. That's where Callum's meeting us."

I don't ask who Callum is. If he's one of Ren's friends he can't be that bad.

The alarm continues hollering for us to come back, though it's duller here in the duct. I force myself to move faster.

A few minutes in—

"Ah!" I cry.

One second I'm crawling along, the next I'm dangling over the edge of a fifteen-foot drop. I heard Ren say this would happen—I just didn't realize the chute would disappear beneath me. My torso folded over the edge, Ren holds my feet, and I wiggle backward.

"*Holy brack*, Aven." She whistles her relief. Still breathless from the close call, she asks, "Did you happen to see a headlight on down there?"

Come to think of it—I look over the edge again to be sure. "I see it!" I point down the chute to the bright yellow glow of a headlight. Gasping, I can feel my fingers as they extend out toward him. *Maybe they're back! Maybe I'm a starfish, or a lizard. Maybe the governor wasn't lying.*

When I look, there's nothing there. Disappointment rips me in half. It's like losing them all over again.

"He did it!" Ren cackles, slapping the side of the air duct twice. Her excitement makes my disappointment easier.

"Okay," she says, scooting past. She pulls a rope from her bag and ties it to a handlebar that looks suctioned onto the duct. "I'm going first. If you hold the rope under your armpit and wrap it around one foot, it should be easier. Rest your feet on my shoulders if you get tired."

A gust of air blows up the chute, and I'm wearing a paper-thin hospital gown. I'm almost naked, I realize with a shiver.

"First things first," Ren says, awkwardly banging around in the metal box. She's peeling off her leggings—for me.

I believe in silly, childish things, like imagining my way out of places—but I didn't say a word; Ren just knew. I add telepathy to the list of things I believe in.

Ren pulls the leggings over my knees, and I wiggle in the rest of the way. "Good," she says. "That'll cover the important parts. You do not want to get rope burn *there*."

Now she's the one in her underwear. "I'll be fine," she assures me, and I don't doubt it. Ren can handle just about anything. I actually laugh from loving her so much. I'm not sure what she wouldn't do for me.

If she had to, she'd kill, I think, remembering the lab tech's face. The realization scares me. I wonder if I love her because of this truth, or in spite of it.

Would I do the same? Could I?

Ren lowers herself down the rope, inch by inch. When it's my turn, I take her advice. I tuck the rope under my armpit and twist it around my ankle. I want to do it all myself—at least start off that way. I push my muscles until they shake, but it's the chafing that hurts the most. My hospital gown shreds all around me.

I have to use Ren's shoulders. She takes some of my weight, and the rope burns less.

"We're here," she says, dangling under me. "We're gonna drop into the mobile together. Wrap your legs around my waist, piggyback style."

78

I look down the shaft, past Ren and into the mobile. "You want to jump into *that*?" I ask. The moonroof's opening is so tiny.

"It can fit two, don't worry."

"Okaaay," I say, shaking my head, not liking it. I monkey onto her back until she's holding all my weight. I don't know how she does it, where she gets all her muscle.

"On the count of three we're both letting go," she says, grunting, and I feel her fighting to hold on. Her hand slips, and we drop down a few inches. "Here goes. You ready?"

"Uh-huh." My voice wavers.

"One. Two. *Three*."

She does it. She lets go, and I let go, and we're meteors falling through space.

Callum's Omni catches us like a wormhole. It bucks from side to side. We land with a loud thump and Ren hoots, pounding the floor with her fist. "Guts of steel, this one!" She grins to the boy in the driver's seat like she's so proud of me. "I got no words. *Impressed* don't even cut it."

Ren pokes me and I look away, tucking my wrists away between my legs. I didn't really do anything. I just followed her the whole way out.

"Where's Derek?" Callum asks, giving up the front seat. He hardly has time to move out of the way, Ren propels herself forward so fast.

Through the rearview mirror, she shoots him a look.

She hates herself—it's written all over her face, and I can't help but feel guilty. *If they hadn't come for me . . .*

"He'll be fine," Callum tells her. "Derek knows more about

this city than the DI. He'll know what to do."

From her expression, I can't tell if what he said helped.

"Moonroof, closed," Ren murmurs. "Beamers, dimmed."

I'm in a mobile. The realization buzzes alive inside me. *My first time.* I'm terrified, breathing heavily into my knees, and my heart might jackhammer itself out of my chest, but . . .

I'm living.

14

REN
4:00 A.M., FRIDAY

"Everyone ready?" I ask, not expecting an answer. How ready can you be for a high-speed getaway from a government lab?

Lowering the Omni underwater, I flip on the beamers only for a second—otherwise I can't find a way out of the building. Spotting a window through the dark brown murk, I carefully steer us through it and into the Hudson Strait.

When I flip off the high beams, Callum hands me a DI-issued thermal-imaging visor. I know these from my DI training. Throwing it on, I get no time to adjust to the new way of seeing.

In the distance are three hot yellow blobs. Two southwest, one north. We've definitely got DI Omnis headed our way. *Brack.*

"Hang tight, folks," I warn.

"Reservoir dock, please?" Callum says to the VoiceNav system. Apparently he's *always* polite. Even now. To technology, when we're on the run.

A cluster of neon-green lines appear on the navigation panel, drawing us a map of the West Isle. Reservoir Dock appears as a small red dot northwest.

Meanwhile, the three hot yellow blobs grow exponentially bigger, according to the visor. My nerves balk at the odds. I swallow too much air, like a starved person. But I know what I'm doing, I'm no amateur. *In, out, in, out.* I give my breathing a pattern and force my heart to chill the brack out.

If there's anywhere I know what I'm doing, it's behind the wheel.

Then why am I so on edge right now?

Looking in the rearview mirror, I have my answer. Precious cargo. It's making me cautious, as well I should be. But I win 'cause my methods are unorthodox to the point of suicidal, some might say. If I start flinching at every mobile that bites my way, I'll never get us out of here.

The DI Omnis draw closer, but we have one advantage—they don't know where we're headed, so they don't know they're in our way. It's not a huge advantage, but it's something.

I wait for the blobs to get bigger, and then, when one of 'em comes a bit too close . . .

Pedal to the metal, baby.

I gun this beauty for all it's worth. We shoot forward. I stick to my seat and my stomach drops. Steering us directly over the nose of one mobile—

I bring us nose-to-nose with the second.

I set the Omni in reverse. A glimpse in the rearview, however, shows me a surprise: the first guy's pulled a 180. He's now headed for our tail. I swallow. *Okay, not that direction.*

Facing forward again—

"Ren!" Aven shrieks from the backseat. Her voice breaks with a fear like I've never heard before, and my insides twist up. The echo-location sonar beeps shrilly. On the screen, I see why. . . .

A red arrow is headed right for us. It's a net, attached to a harpoon. Or a harpoon attached to a net, depending on which you like less.

The arrow hurtles closer, until it's practically an Egyptian pyramid on the screen. I cut the wheel to the right, spinning us off at a ninety-degree angle.

There, suspended like a bullet in midair: a third blob.

"Will someone please turn off the sonar!" It should've been turned off soon as we made it out of the building, but both my hands are on the wheel, and Aven don't have hands, so that leaves Callum.

He flips it off and the beeping ceases, thank heavens. I'm the only one who needs to see the harpoons coming for us anyway.

"I hope nobody's worried," I say to the others, trying to cut the tension. "This is nothing."

They both side-eye me as I give the Omni more speed. The mobile strains, its engine grinding for more.

Of course as I say that, blob number three decides now's a great time to let loose a net. Through the visor, I see a new red arrow rushing toward us. Thankfully, though, this guy ain't much of a shot. I rotate the wheel just a few degrees and avoid it entirely.

According to the dash's schematics, I've got a turn coming up.

I wait until the last possible moment and swing a hard left. Aven and Callum groan in unison, thrown into the side of the mobile.

"Intentional!" I say. "I'm taking turns last-second, banking on how badly they suck at driving."

Sorta glad the thermal visor doesn't show you when someone's about to puke.

I look behind us and spot only two yellow blobs. We push past the remains of one old building and then another, but we're just not moving fast enough to lose them. And honestly, without Benny here to rig the speed, we're not going to outrace them either.

"How you doing back there, Aven?" I ask.

I wish I could split myself in two. That way I could be the driver *and* the sister. I could get us safely outta here, and I could reassure her that no one will ever, ever take her away again.

Each time she's in danger feels worse than the last.

"I'm fine."

That's all she gives me. In the past twenty minutes, she's said nothing else. When Callum saw her wrists, she wanted to talk even less.

"We're almost there." I glance at the map, knowing I have

to lose these guys pronto. Our dot is three-quarters of the way to the dock. I give the Omni as much speed as she can handle, but navigating through all these buildings, taking turns left and right—it's impossible to go full throttle.

Blob one releases another dart. In my visor, I watch the red streak get bigger and closer.

I swerve.

Metal rips through the Omni. Water sprays into the pit, a frothing white stream of brack shooting everywhere. The floor grows slick. I spin around to see a foot-long metal harpoon skewering the left side, just above Callum's knees.

"Ren!" he calls over the hissing water, holding his hand against it. "We need to get out!"

I gun the engine again, but it don't work—the dart's attached to a rope, which is in turn attached to a net. They're reeling us in easier than tuna fish. I watch Aven's face for signs of even more unrecoverable trauma, and I find her bracing herself, pale as a corpse.

"Callum. We're fifty feet from the surface. Even if we could make it by swimming they'd be up there waiting for us. Then what?" I tug the visor off and stand up, an inch deep in water.

He doesn't answer. He's reaching for an extra wet suit under the seat and ties it around the dart, to plug up as much of the hole as possible. Finding my eyes, he pushes his sopping, shaggy brown hair away from his face. "Even if we could lose the harpoon," he says, "the Omni will be slower than before, and with the heat sensors they'll still be able to follow us. There is no way out except *out*." He points to the airlock in the Omni's butt.

For a moment I believe him. My chest sinks hard. Maybe he's right. I've got Aven to think about. At least if we evacuate, we could split up. She might have a chance at not being found.

"Ren?" Aven asks softly, pale brows knotted. She looks up at the both of us, white hair slick against her skull and her hospital-napkin dress soaked through. She's so thin. She must be freezing. She leans forward like she wants only me to hear her. "What would you do if you were alone?"

I almost laugh. She knows how to get to the heart of it, don't she? "Well," I start, thinking it over a moment. "I guess I'd go out there and knife the net—"

"And then what?" Callum asks hotly. "They can still follow us, remember?"

I scowl, and though he's right to ask, I could do with a little faith.

Looking to Aven's small, pale face, I find nothing but faith. She's waiting for me to think of something, because she believes I will.

I close my eyes.

If I knife the net, how can I get them to not *follow us?*

Her teeth begin to chatter. She's cold. She needs a wet suit or something. She's been through too damn much to die from hypothermia.

I shake my head—*hypothermia.* The idea that comes to me is nuts. Any idea that starts with *hypothermia* must be.

And yet . . .

"What is it?" Aven asks. "You've got something—I can see it."

I feel like I've just swallowed a fish whole. This is a terrible idea.

Good thing I love terrible ideas.

15

Water fills the mobile, so cold it makes my teeth chatter. I'm as stiff as the dead, my arms pale and blue, and I'm fighting to stay awake. I'm just so tired.

"How much do you two trust me?" Ren asks, but the question is just for show. I know from experience. She's already decided.

"Thermal imaging," she begins. "It locates engines, 'cause they run hot. And you know what doesn't run hot? People underwater. Totally undetectable. Right, Cal?" She looks for confirmation. He nods.

"We're gonna trick their visors. We've got to stay underwater. But, since we're still too far from the surface, we need this engine to take us there quickly. First, I'll need to cut the harpoon free."

"You're flooding the mobile," I murmur.

"You'll have a wet suit."

A hard shell forms around my body. Suddenly I feel so young and so old at the same time. In the seat, I notice that I'm rocking back and forth, but I don't recall doing it on purpose. The water is rising, and I'm so sleepy it's hard to keep my eyes open.

Ren jumps over Callum's knees and kneels down next to me. "We're so close. Do you know how close we are?" She makes an inchworm with her fingers. "That's the distance on the map. It's nothing. You've got that much left in you, I know it."

I hug myself harder, tucking my wrists away. I'm not sure I do. She won't allow no for an answer, though. "I can't do the wet suit alone," I tell her.

"Well," Ren says as Callum pulls a spare out from under my seat. "I have two pieces of good news. Callum has hands, and he just happens to be experiencing a temporary bout of blindness. Lucky you, am I right?"

On cue, Callum closes his eyes. Kneeling, he holds the wet suit open for me to step into. I can't help it. I laugh and roll my eyes. Sometime's she's too much. I feel myself warming up a bit, just from Ren forcing me to move around.

Hopping past, she grabs a second wet suit from under my seat and then pushes a button on my side of the Omni. A metal wall rises. Ren disappears behind it.

When I look over at Callum, his eyes are closed, as promised. "Go on, then." He nods. "I'm blind, remember?"

Pushing my wrists against the waistband, I wince as Ren's leggings slide below my butt. True to his word, Callum's eyes stay shut tight.

The water is a full foot high now and Callum's no longer kneeling. He's doing a balancing act, holding the wet suit for me. I'm about to step in, but movement outside the window catches my eye.

It's Ren—she's already sawing away at the net, knife in hand. I watch her, totally frozen. Soon the fraying rope drifts from the harpoon and the mobile slows.

She slips out of sight, and I step into my wet suit.

Callum tugs the shimmering blue neoprene over me like fish skin, or a mermaid's tail. I like thinking about it that way. He peels me into one sleeve, then the next, and zips me up. Last, he dusts off my shoulders. We're chest-deep in the water. It splashes against my chin and up into my nose.

"Breathe normally," he tells me. "The harder you're breathing now, the harder it will be to fight back the hunger pangs."

"Hunger pangs?"

"Air hunger. Instinct will tell you to open your mouth, even though that'd be a very bad idea. You can ignore the air hunger a few times before it becomes a problem."

"Like passing out?" The thought alone makes me tired.

Callum nods and the metal gate that separates us from the hatch opens wide. A dripping-wet Ren swims back into the Omni.

"Done," she announces, spitting out brack. "We're free. When the whole pit's flooded, I'll fire up the engine and get us outta here. Even if they notice the rope's been cut and we're no longer in tow, they'll have no clue where are."

I tread water next to Callum, my mouth pressed to the roof. We're waiting until the last minute. I flap my arms, but everything is so much harder without hands. Swimming, they were like fins. I've got nothing like that now, so I kick my legs a hundred times harder just to do the same work.

Ren paddles into the front seat, holding on to the wheel.

The inches of air dwindle away. Soon they're gone.

Murky brown water wets my lips, and I let myself sink into the flooded mobile. It's easier now that I'm not fighting to stay afloat. Callum bobs next to me. He gives me an underwater thumbs-up.

Since I can't give him one back, I cross my eyes instead. Hopefully he gets the message. Just then, the water kills the dashboard's bright buttons.

It's so black we could be floating in outer space.

Through the window, DI headlights fade into the distance. They still haven't noticed. Once more, the engine grumbles on, a sleeping giant who never wanted to be woken up again. It kicks into gear, jutting forward quickly enough that Callum and I both float back into our seats. My mouth almost snaps open without warning. This is what Callum was talking about. The hunger. I want air so badly, I'm straining the muscles in my throat just to keep my mouth closed. My heart triples its pace. Anxiety spreads under my ribs, a chain saw whirring, blades spinning and spinning like it will never stop.

I need to breathe.

Callum grabs my hand. I watch his outline shifting in the black water. His body hangs so peacefully. Ren's too. I imagine I look the same, and in my mind's eye I picture the three of us: dangling, suspended in darkness. I wonder if this is what it was like being in my mama's belly. I let the thought calm me. It relaxes my throat. I realize I no longer feel it—the hunger.

A bright lamp shines yellow outside the window as the Omni's nose splashes the surface. Above us, Ren reaches for the moonroof. She braces herself against the wheel and pulls it open manually. The Omni tilts as she swims out, and Callum lets me through next.

My face breaks into the cool night, and I gasp and gasp. I take in so much air I make myself dizzy, thankful that air isn't like food or water, and you can't throw it up. Once it's in me, it's in me.

From the dock, Ren's hand reaches out. The yellow lamp looms directly behind her head—it's so bright. It reminds me of that light at the end of a tunnel people say you see when you're about to die.

Lifting my wrist, she pulls me through the water. We move together jerkily, her dragging, me kicking. I'm not floating, suspended anymore, like in those moments before being born. I wonder if that's what's happening to me right now, if I'm being born, one more time. I even gasped for air and everything.

92

It's with this thought in my head that I haul my body over the edge of the dock.

I guess I shouldn't be surprised that it's Ren who catches me.

16

Callum's Omni sinks a slow, watery death. It's too depressing to watch.

He and I both risk glances back across the strait, thinking the same thing: the DI must have figured it out by now. I'd give us an hour, tops, before they find the sunken Omni.

Still catching our breath, we gaze across the water. It occurs to me that I'm standing on West Isle territory for the first time. The Ward's gap-toothed skyline is dark, of course. Only a few lucky buildings, the ones with electricity, glow from the inside.

Turning around, I count five—no, *six*—skyscrapers on the West Isle. They're different from the ones back home, covered in a shining, mirrorlike metal. It reflects in a bazillion different directions.

Callum leads us, wet and bedraggled, over the swaying wooden pier. "Reservoir Dock used to be an actual reservoir. All brack now, of course," he says in his best tour-guide voice, passing his canteen.

We take it greedily, a few swigs for each. And maybe a few sips more after that. Callum's a West Isler, after all. He can afford it.

"Easy does it," he says when he sees we might just finish the canteen. "Drought season's coming. Weather forecasters predict especially low rainfall this year."

"But don't you guys just buy black market?"

Overhead, a solar-powered lamplight casts a soft blue glow along the dock. Callum exhales. "West Isle isn't as wealthy as you'd think. Not the way we once were. Black-market fresh adds up, and it's taken a heavy financial toll on many."

So, what he's saying is—they're *less* rich.

Got it.

Aven, nearly sleepwalking, stumbles over the planks. I'd like for us to be moving faster, but she's exhausted, and the gurgling strait is too tempting a lullaby. Dropping back, I loop my arm through hers.

Callum closes a gate behind us. "Are you cold?" he asks Aven, shrugging off his jacket. She doesn't answer, so he just lays it over her shoulders.

"I'm sorry I didn't wear two," he says to me awkwardly.

"No, no . . . this is nothing," I say truthfully, waving an arm. "It's warmer than any winter night in the 'Racks."

Embarrassed, he looks away. "Right." He nods. "No heat."

I don't like talking about my home with him. It's not that

I'm embarrassed about being poor—I'm not. I'm embarrassed by its side effects. Things like not being clean and not being able to wear different clothes every day.

"Hey, Feathers." I nudge her until she blinks at me bleary-eyed. I point down. Beside us, little spikes of green sprout up along the concrete slabs. *Grass.* Growing straight from the ground. We've seen it before, up on the garden rooftoops, but in the Ward it just can't grow like it does here.

Aven wakes up for this. Arms still looped together, she pulls me to the very edge of the concrete path. We stand there on tiptoe, dangling over the wild green abyss. "Count of three?" she says, grinning. *"Three!"*

She takes one wide step onto the green, dragging me with her. She lets out a squeak and starts swishing her feet around, smashing down one foot and then the other.

This is what I love most about my sister. Her default is happy. She's been drugged, lost her hands, told to keep her shit together while I flooded our mobile, and . . . here she is, smiling. Jumping. Flattening grass with her feet.

I don't know how she does it.

Callum leans up against a lamppost, watching and smirking. A moment later, he looks over his shoulder. I check the rippling, dark strait also. Dawn's begun to peek through the clouds, turning the sky a soft gray, and the water is clear.

I exhale. "We should go," I say, wary of being out in the daytime.

We work our way inland.

Callum steers us down a street paved with sloppy, uneven

stones. Nailed to the storefronts are actual paper flyers. They read:

A DAWN FOR DISCOURSE:
BEGIN THE DAY AS YOU WOULD SEE IT FINISH.
Join together for a peaceful assembly led by fellow UMI citizen Jary Kahn if you agree . . .
FRESHWATER FOR OUR NATION
MUST NOT BE OPTIONAL!

I wanna ask Callum about it—but then we're passed by a woman wearing a mask with a long, curved nose. . . .

"Uh, Callum?" I point.

"Just a mask," he answers quickly. "The Blight's made everyone more fearful over the last few months. The mask protects from the virus; it has a built-in air filter."

"But what about the cure? The governor stole so much of the serum during our drop-offs."

Callum rubs at a fluff of brown hair on his temple. "He's made some available to the public, but it's wildly expensive."

As predicted.

"The governor didn't give it to the prisoners, that's for sure," Aven tells us, carefully watching the bird mask pass us by. "They're still sick." She shakes her head, brows clenched. "Ren . . . we can't just leave them like that. We have to get them out."

Do we?

Now that I have Aven back, I can't muster the willpower

97

to sneak back there so fast. Not that I'm happy hundreds of sick prisoners are living in filth and squalor because the government says they're criminals, but . . . how the hell am *I* supposed to fix that? And why me? I got what I went in there for. Now all I care about is protecting her.

"Let's talk about it tomorrow. There's a lot we need to know before we do anything." I look to Callum for reinforcement. "Right?" An older sister telling her no has a lot less authority than a bona fide scientist.

"I'm in agreement," Callum says. "Let's discuss tomorrow."

Shouts fill the air, but we see nobody. *What's going on?* I wonder, glancing around the mostly empty streets. When we turn the corner, I get my answer.

In the middle of the road, a pack of people, all wearing the masks, stand around cheering. A man raises his fist. Nailed to his pulpit, a flyer: *A Dawn for Discourse.*

The man has the look of old wealth that hasn't seen an update in some time. "Now is the time!" he yells to the crowd, adjusting his black suspenders. Spittle flies from his mouth. "We must campaign Governor Voss for a Second Appeal Upstate!"

"Is he serious?" I ask Callum, boggled. *Why would anyone want another appeal?*

The crowd continues cheering, but they're silenced when the man holds up his hand. "I know what you're thinking— the First Appeal failed. Negotiation with Magistrate Harcourt, the leader of the Falls' government, proved unsuccessful, as did force.

"Four times a month, Harcourt auctions off their extra

water stores. Yes, my friends, *extra*! Sources on the Mainland say that they have a surplus. And four times a month, the UMI cannot afford to win these auctions! Well, hear this, fellow West Islers: the UMI *cannot* afford to lose! Not anymore. Our previous failure means only one thing: we must try again!"

Not that I think anyone here is interested in my opinion, but considering the death toll was somewhere in the thousands and we still didn't win—I'd beg to differ.

The man goes on, feverishly digging one hand into his pocket. "Only with a larger military do we stand a chance!" he shouts. Then he points across the strait. "Governor Voss's recent success in nearly eradicating the Blight is an opportunity for all of us."

I spit onto the pavement. "Bullshit." Looking at Aven, it hits me that she still doesn't know the truth. "*Callum* made that cure from the spring water, and me and some other racers got it to all the sickhouses. Now Voss is taking the credit."

"The Ward is no longer a place of disease, and those people need a calling. They need a mission. A purpose! *This is that purpose.* Too long has the UMI gone without a reliable source of freshwater. We must campaign Governor Voss and Chief Dunn to lead them to their purpose!"

The masked crowd roars, eating it up.

Wide-eyed, Aven looks at Callum and me. "He wants to make the Ward into an army?"

"Looks like it," I answer, kicking at a cobblestone.

"As I said," Callum says, gesturing to the sky, "drought season. People are protesting—it's the third 'discourse' I've seen this week. They'll have to rely entirely on rainfall, or go broke buying black market."

It takes all I've got not to point out that right across the Hudson Strait, we've been doing that same thing for years. It ain't easy, but we do it.

"It's them. . . ." The words shake out of Aven's mouth as she tucks her arms away.

At the far intersection, there are two men in telltale blue fatigues round the corner. They're headed down this block—

We duck under the awning of a boarded-up storefront. "No, no, no . . ." Aven repeats over and over. It's like watching a storm roll in. She tries to control it, but she can't.

I poke my head up. The officers are ten, maybe fifteen feet away. Aven watches me. Her bottom lip quivers, her whole body heaving. She can't breathe.

I can barely breathe too, watching her this way. *We need to hide.* I glance around for a better spot, but this is the best we've got.

"Help," I say, turning to Callum and gesturing to the wooden boards. He kneels closer and we grip the bottommost two-by-four. It pops off, dangling from a nail.

"In," I tell Aven. She slips under the wooden board, and when Callum and I follow, she doesn't look back. In a far corner of the clothing store, she balls herself up. White hair drapes round her shoulders, hiding her face.

She's crying.

Seeing her like this, I want to throw knives or something. Just when she's healthy, they mess with her body *and* her head. *I can't let this go.* When I met my other self underwater, all my teeth bared, I knew I wouldn't be able to. Now I'm doubly sure.

Voss can't exist.

"No one's taking you away again. *No one*," I whisper, crouching in front of her. She doesn't look at me . . . she just lifts her eyes to Callum.

He's peering between the wooden boards, and quiets us with the tiniest motion of his hand. A shaft of sun shines bright triangles onto racks of dusty, unworn clothes.

We freeze. The officers' muffled voices are coming from right outside the storefront. Their shadow steals the light away.

Seconds pass.

Callum drops his hand. The voices are gone. He turns slowly, and then he nods.

I exhale. Relief floods my body, but Aven's still glued stiff. "Let's get you something to wear," I say quietly, eyeing the clothing racks behind us. She needs a distraction, but she doesn't want to move.

Standing, I ask, "When have you ever seen a closet this big?" To tempt her, I begin rifling through the hangers. May as well look for myself too. I hate walking around in neoprene.

Like a turtle poking its head out from its shell, Aven glances around. She takes tiny steps toward one rack, then another. After deciding that we're safe enough, she smiles at me.

Even in here, in this dusty, abandoned store, her smile does a better job than the sun. Everything just feels warmer.

I leave her to explore and go meet Callum by the registers. He's gesturing for me to join him, wearing a fool grin on his face. I think for a second he's found green and wants to rob the place. But that'd be absurd. This is *Callum*, after all.

From under a register, he retrieves two bizarro masks, passing one to me.

Up close, I see it's not just a mask with a crazy long nose— it's a beak. This is funny, because—"Callum . . . birds are how the virus spreads, right?"

Even his snorts are gentlemanly. "You are correct. Interestingly enough, we're not the first nation to adopt this accessory. Hundreds of years ago, during the Plague, people wore them as well."

I slip on the mask, letting it dangle from my neck. "You ready, Aven?"

She pops out from behind a clothing rack wearing a fuzzy, light blue skirt, and a new tee. It reads *Suck it, Asteroid* over a cartoon of a burning meteor.

"Love it," I say.

Waving a hanger at me, she says, "This is for you. I'm all ready to go." She pushes something long and floppy into my face with a smile.

I don't know if I even want to see. Aven and me, we have very different taste.

I eye the garment, then look to Callum. He just raises both his hands. Boy's staying out of the clothing talk, apparently. It's black. That's good. And stretchy—also good. I hold it up and finally make out what it is. . . .

A jumpsuit.

A black, cotton, long-sleeve jumpsuit, *with* a built-in pleather belt. And a zipper up the side.

I laugh, holding it up to myself. It's a tad long, but that's no surprise. Easily fixed too.

Aven wins. "It's perfect," I tell her.

I lift the bird mask over my sister's head; her smile falls away. "We have to go out there again," she remembers.

I nod, smoothing her hair under the elastic band. "No one's gonna know it's us. We've got these awesomely creepy bird beaks—we're totally disguised."

I don't sound as sure as I would like to, though.

Truth is, I'm worried. The DI are out there. And Voss will never stop looking for me, not until he finds the spring.

"We're gonna make it to Callum's easy peasy. I mean, c'mon—we're birds!" I say, going for humor instead. "Eh, Feathers? Get it?!"

Aven rolls her eyes at me.

And then I watch her steel herself—in the way she sets her jaw and the furrow of her brow.

She's gonna be okay.

Don't mean all's forgiven, but my rage, for the moment, quiets.

17

I keep my head down as Callum leads us through the West Isle; Ren says acting normal is the best way to keep from getting caught. I try to focus on how wonderful streets are. Back home, everything sways—the docks, the boardwalks, the suspension bridges.

With the bird mask on, it's easier to pretend. I'm something with wings. I could fly away at the last minute if I need to. Some people might think it's silly—I'm fourteen, after all, still pretending. But I don't. It's how I survived. When you're stuck sick in one place for years, you find other ways to live. Even made-up ones.

Beside me, Ren is sending out comms left and right. "Just letting Derek and the others know we're safe, and we're almost at Callum's."

"Others?" I ask, hopeful. Ren winks. She knows who I'm really asking about.

"You'll see him soon enough," she says just as her wrist buzzes. Looking down, she reads the message. "Speak of the devil!" She nudges me twice with her elbow. "He says hi and that he can't wait to see you."

I don't care that I'm blushing.

As we walk, Ren fills me in on everything I've missed, from finding the Tètai family album and learning Derek's true age (it's in the centuries) to the night she and the other racers distributed the cure. The same night I was taken.

One block away stands a cream-colored castle-like building made entirely out of giant slabs of stone. "We're close," Callum says, pointing.

Ren's bird mask does a double take. "*That's* where you're taking us?" We both walk a little bit faster.

Swanky, I think, knowing that's what Ren would call it.

A humming noise grates in the air, growing louder the closer we get. "What is that?" I ask, covering my ears. It sounds like it's coming from a nest of electric bees. It doesn't hurt to listen to, but I feel it in my belly and it makes me even more anxious.

"Private turbine generator, for electricity. My entire complex pitched in to pay for it," Callum says, opening the building's glass double doors for us.

We follow him into a circular lobby filled with potted, dying green things. I don't understand why they have plants if they don't have the money to water them. Seems cruel to the plants.

A guard sits at a wooden desk. He's gray on top with whiskers like our old cat, and he's playing chess alone. When he sees Callum he waves, chess piece still in hand.

"Morning, Dr. Cory," he says with a nod for both Ren and me.

I can tell he's wondering about us. Who we are, if we really belong here. And we don't belong here, not really. It's a different world on the Isle.

I smile back, though, as wide as my cheeks can go from under the bird mask. Ren gives him the stink-eye. I'm not too surprised. Rich people always make her grouchy.

Except for Terrence, of course.

He's different. He grew up like us, orphaned by the Blight, and his new dad just happened to be rich. Thinking about him still gives me bubbles.

Callum turns down a carpeted corridor, still on the ground floor. He unlocks a heavy lead door and pushes it open. Inside his apartment, gray drapes keep out almost all the light, so we can't see much of anything.

"It's late," he says, turning on a small lamp. "Tomorrow we can discuss our next move. Before calling it a night, however, I have a surprise."

Whatever he's about to show us . . . it's good. I can tell. His face is lit up like he's been plugged into a magic power outlet somewhere. He walks us through the living room and down a narrow, dimly lit hall.

At a door two rooms down, he stops.

Seeing what's inside, I squeak, "They're glowing!" and run toward what looks like a fish tank. Except, it's not filled with fish. It's filled with algae-covered rocks growing neon-green mushrooms. A pump attached brings old water out and circulates it with new water. From underneath, burners heat the tank, throwing off tiny blue circles of fire. "What is this? Is this the water?" It's all too weird.

"That's the water, all right," Callum says with pride.

Ren grins. She tousles his already messy brown hair. "You never said you could grow more! Sneaky scientist, ain't we?" She lets him go and peers down into one of the glass bowls, her finger tracing the rim.

"That's because I *couldn't*. The mushrooms wouldn't grow."

"Why are the mushrooms so important?" I ask, eyeing their bright green hoods. "I thought it was the water that healed me."

"It was. But only because of the mushrooms. They have these chemical compounds, phytonutrients, with medicinal properties, some antitumoral and antiviral in nature. All plants have phytonutrients, actually. Just not in the same quantity or combination. And since the mushrooms grow in an underground hot spring, they release those compounds into the water. That's how the water cures the Blight."

"That, and *me*," Ren quips, pointing a finger at him. She taps the crook of her arm. "My blood. It made the serum work better, naturally."

I don't need to ask what she means: Ren's immune to the virus. Of course her blood would help. Ren never told anyone about it, though. At the orphanage, Miss Nale warned her not to. She was afraid the DI would experiment on Ren so badly, she'd end up dead. Which doesn't seem so far-fetched, now knowing what I do.

I turn back to the neon tank, mesmerized by the soft green glow. "So how did you keep the mushrooms alive, then?"

"I made a breakthrough," Callum says with a bounce, clearly happy I asked. "I realized I knew nothing about the cave's ecosystem. They can't just grow out of rocks, or water. Plants need soil. In the cave there wouldn't be soil, but I guessed that there might've been some algae growing on the rocks. I tried a few kinds and landed on the right one. Nothing special about the species, but without it, the fungi have no way to grow."

"So simple!" I laugh, though I'm sure it sounds much easier than it actually was.

"Not quite," Callum says, confirming it. "The fungi would seem to be growing, and just when I thought I'd succeeded, they'd die all over again. I was confounded. Until I had my *second* breakthrough."

Ren and I exchange glances, waiting for him to tell us. He leaves us hanging for just a few moments before the big reveal. . . .

"The fungus is parasitic," he says at last. "If the spore count grows too large, it will actually kill the algae."

Seeing both Ren's and my blank expression, he explains.

"Spores—they're like microscopic baby mushrooms. Given the right conditions, they'll grow. But with too many, the algae dies. No algae, no fungus. That's why it kept dying off; the spore count would get too high as the fungi reproduced.

In the spring's natural ecosystem—with fresh water flowing in and out—you've got a perfect ratio, always in flux."

"Okay," Ren admits. "I don't usually dig the science stuff, but it's pretty impressive how you just figured all of it out."

Callum grins sheepishly.

"A real, live Fountain of Youth," I murmur. "Just like in the stories."

"Well, I haven't found anything to suggest the water can reverse human aging, but as Ren learned, Derek's been alive for centuries."

At the mention of Derek's name, Ren glances at her cuff-comm. She stifles her sigh, but we both see how worried she is.

"Then why isn't everyone you gave the cure to immortal?" I ask.

"I filtered out any unidentifiable phytonutrients when making it. I left only the antitumorals and the antivirals, I was so terrified."

"Even if you hadn't, the immortality isn't a permanent side effect," Ren says. "Derek needs to drink the water every day or he'll turn into a corpse."

Callum lowers himself slowly onto the corner of his desk. "Unbelievable," he whispers, scratching his cheek. After a few moments of awe, he shakes his head. "Well, maybe they wouldn't have become immortal, but they would definitely have had a hard time dying—at least until the water was no longer in their system. I've identified more than one phyto-nutrient responsible for regeneration."

I nearly jump out of my skin at the word. Nudging Ren with

my bandaged wrist, I lean into her ear so only she can hear me. "Could it help? Would Callum give me some? Maybe if I drink more, my hands really will come back."

Ren turns and says, "What do you think, Doc? Can we give Aven a dose or two?"

"I don't see why not." Callum stands and pulls out an eyedropper from a drawer. He fills it with water from the tank, then pinches the water free into an empty vial.

He passes the vial to me. Too late, he remembers that I can't hold it.

Ren takes it. Bringing it to my lips, she says, "Drink up." I tip my head back and, slowly, she pours it into my mouth.

When it's all gone, I smack my lips together. "Yum." Just like when Derek gave it to me, I feel a jolt, a surge of electricity powering up my veins and my muscles and my bones. "Whoa," I say, going a little cross-eyed.

"What is it?" Callum asks, taking the glass back.

"Nothing bad . . . it gives me a buzz. I feel strong."

He replaces the glass in a drawer and turns to me. "The phytonutrients are going to work. I believe one of them switches on the chain of proteins responsible for regeneration. It's a good sign. Now, we just have to wait."

Callum yawns, shaking himself awake. "On that note, ladies, let me show you to your room?"

Ren and I share a secret look of excitement. Callum will have a bed for us, he has to—we won't be sleeping on just a mattress tonight.

He sees our not-so-secret look and grins, gesturing toward

110

the door. "After me," he says.

As he leads us out of the lab and back through the corridor, the water speeds through my veins. I feel invincible.

"We can talk about the prisoners tomorrow too, right?"

Ren sighs. "That's a pretty big conversation," she says. Her tone worries me.

"Aven, why don't you go ahead—last door on the right. Ren, if you're up to it, I can draw some blood now?"

"Fine," Ren heaves, hanging her head dramatically in the middle of the hallway. "Let's get it out of the way."

Callum chuckles as she kisses me on the forehead. "I'll be there in two shakes, but you go to sleep. Don't wait for me," she says.

"I won't." I peck her cheek in return.

At the last room I nearly faint. In the corner is a massive, four-poster bed topped off with clean white blankets. I rush for it. Plopping down and finding myself actually bouncing, I deem this mattress more than acceptable.

On the night table, under the lamp, lays a sleek black cuff-comm. Looking closer, I see my name's etched in gray on the back. *Callum got this for me.* I choke on my laughter.

I like this Callum guy.

Using my elbow, I flip the light switch and the room goes dark. I laugh again, this time at how easy it all is.

Getting to sleep, however, is another story.

Exhaustion tugs at my eyelids, but I resist it. I don't know how long I spend with my eyes wide-open, blinking at the ceiling. I last as long as I can, until I own the truth:

I'm afraid.

There are places in my mind where I don't want to go. There's a white room. And in the white room is a knife of a man. And in the knife-man's hand there are sharp tools. And in this place, I'll never be whole again. My memories are the opposite of lullabies.

You're safe, I tell myself. *It's okay to close your eyes.* But when sleep grips at me with both hands, I still fight.

I fight until I can't anymore; I'm too tired.

I don't go willingly to those places, but I do go.

White walls, the color of a body—a dead body. A new dead body, floating down the strait. I wake, but not really: the dead don't wake. And here, we're all dead. I am a star that died long ago. Death always catches up, though. The doctor wears white because even she is dead. This is a place only the dead go. Her needle is full.

A black bird circles the room.

The room stops being white. We're still dead, though. Dead in a dark, wide bowl, where hundreds of stars have been shoved into tiny lightbulbs. They don't fall for our wishes anymore. They're losing light, because their home is out there, somewhere in the universe. I want to help them fall. In the dark, wide bowl I make a promise to the dead stars.

I will bring you back to life, *I tell them, and they believe.*

The doctor locks both my arms together. I don't fight back. It's always been like this. I'm always lying, locked and looking up while the black bird circles.

112

A knife without a face reaches for my hand.

Why am I doing nothing?

Because you are dead, *I remind myself.* You were not born a black bird.

The knife has a voice that is also a knife. It makes my ears bleed. But that can't be right—the dead don't bleed. The knife doesn't care. You're dead, *he says, and then he tells me he's not even a real knife. He's just a toy knife, and toy knives don't really hurt.* He's lying, *I think.*

The toy knife that is not a toy comes down across my wrists.

The black bird shrieks.

Two white wings fall onto a white floor.

The wings flap, and I die twice.

I push at the air, the sheets, but I still can't make myself move. *Only Ren can do that.* And then I'm being shaken—

I shoot out of the bed, gasping for air, pushing her away with a gauze-covered stump. I'm crying and I can't stop it: there's a knife still in the room, because it's still in my head, which means it will never go away.

Ren sits at the edge of the bed, eyes big with fear. She reaches one arm out toward me, like I'm a ghost back from the dead.

I've scared her with my nightmares. "I'm all right," I whisper quietly, watching her chew on her knuckles.

She touches my shoulder with the hand she's not chewing. "Are you?" she asks, and I hate it.

My dragon anger is back, burning my insides and

everything around me. "I'm fine!" I yell at her, but I can't yank the covers without fingers. Instead, I bury my head under the pillow, wishing that I weren't made of glass.

I'm not.

I'm not broken.

18

REN
2:30 P.M., FRIDAY

Afternoon sun punches through the windows, beating me awake too soon. When I open my eyes, I find I'm holding a palmful of Aven's tangled hair, like I'd been afraid she'd disappear in her sleep and I'd never get her back. She frowns, snoring ever so slightly, while the sun threatens the room with light. *Don't you dare wake her up*, I warn. *She needs rest.* Especially after what I saw last night. So damn terrified. Even in sleep she can't get peace. Just thinking about it, I'm a lit fuse. The monster made of teeth comes back, full force.

How could Voss have done this to her?

It makes no difference that he thought her hands might grow back—*he's evil.* He tortured Aven and called it "science." Kept medicine from the prisoners. Threatened to eradicate every sick person back home, banking on the Tètai to bring them the water . . . *just so he could steal it.*

Every day that passes, I'm more and more convinced the world would be a better place without him.

Angrily, I throw on my new catsuit. As I strap on my blade, my wrist buzzes. I jump up and read so fast, you'd think the message was about to self-destruct.

> I'm safe, I've got a way out. Ter's meeting me on Castle Islet, at Sybil's Cave. Will comm again when we're headed back to the Ward.

"Derek's alive," I whisper, laughing to myself—he must've found the toilet water. *He's gonna be okay.* I draw the drapes tight so Aven can sleep longer, and step out into the hallway, searching for Callum.

"Derek's safe!" I announce, barging into his mostly dark lab.

A dim green light bathes the room. The tank he built to replicate the cave's ecosystem glows like a man-made universe. A smaller tank—a mini replica of the first—sits next to it. Everything inside is shriveled and dead. An unsuccessful experiment, no doubt.

I find Callum hunched over, peering through a microscope. He doesn't lift his head. "C'mon in."

It takes an eternity for my announcement to travel the infinite voyage from his ears to his brain. When it does, he forgets the 'scope. "I knew it!" he says at last, rushing across the room. "When did you hear from him?"

"Not five minutes ago. He's got an escape plan—Ter's meeting him at Sybil's Cave."

"Sybil's Cave is close to Voss's mansion; he must be taking the causeway," Callum says, inhaling. "It's quite risky."

"Risky, why?" I ask quickly. "What's the causeway?"

Callum closes the door and offers me a chair, which I ignore. I like to hear uncomfortable news standing up.

"It's an underwater tunnel that runs between the lab and Governor Voss's mansion. Originally, it just led to a submarine employee docking lot, but for his convenience, Voss had it extended. Derek's not just sneaking out of the lab, he's sneaking out of the mansion as well."

I shake my head. "Foolish."

Callum realizes he's just given me a new worry. "I'm sure Derek has a plan," he says, touching my elbow for just a second before pulling back. As if a second was too long. "Security will be tight, but with gala prepwork, his won't be the only unknown face around. Maybe it's not so foolish."

I nod, hoping he's right.

Callum returns to his microscope. Peering down it, he looks perplexed. "Ren—" he begins, voice even. But the expression he's wearing . . . my nerves fire off warning shots. "I want to show you something."

Callum slides the mini tank toward me. Inside, dead fungi and algae have sunk to the bottom. "Last night, after taking your blood sample, I got to work immediately on the serum.

117

"I used *this* eyedropper," he says, wiggling it between his fingers, "to move it into a petri dish. Later, I used the same one to withdraw some water. By morning, the pH in the tank was off, and everything was dead."

"And you think it's because of my blood?"

"Or blood in general, I'm not sure. But I'd like to run more tests, if that's all right."

"Go for it," I tell him. "Just let me down easy, if you find out I'm actually on death's door or something."

Callum rolls his eyes. "Don't be ridiculous."

"Hey," I say, glancing toward the hall. "Before Aven wakes up, I want us to be on the same page about this whole prisoner-break-out mission she's totally gung ho on. You know she promised— I mean, *swore on her life* promised— that she'd go back there and get them out?"

I collapse into the foldable metal chair and groan. "How the hell would we swing that? There are hundreds of 'em!"

"I don't know." Callum lifts his plastic goggles onto his forehead. "But I do believe we should try, at the very least, to consider getting them the serum—which we now have. After the eyedropper mixup, I followed the steps for the last batch exactly, adding your blood last. It's almost ready—I haven't yet filtered out the regeneration phytonutrients."

"Jeez," I say. "You must have been up the whole time!"

"There's an event I need to make an appearance at tonight. Thus, no lab work. I wanted to make sure it was mostly done."

118

Reaching out to poke his elbow, I ask, "What's the event, Mr. Fancy Pants?"

Callum hesitates. *He doesn't want to tell me. Why not?* A moment later, he gestures toward the window, where a golden square envelope sits atop a metal filing cabinet. "Take a look," he says, and hands me an invitation.

The lettering is emblazoned with swanky gold ink.

IN HONOR OF GOVERNOR VOSS

DR. JUSTIN CORY, you are cordially invited to an evening of merriment and gratitude. Please join us on Castle Islet at Governor Voss's home, where we will toast his recent success combatting the deadly HBNC virus. Water and hors d'oeuvres will be served. Black-tie affair. Seven o'clock.

I nearly choke on the bullshit. Voss didn't *give* the sick the medicine—*he stole it out from under their noses.* And now he gets a party?

Callum sees my disgust and rereads the invitation to himself. "I imagine he's hoping to curry the people's favor before drought season hits too," he tells me. "The governor is quite aware of the Isle's financial situation—I don't doubt he has concerns that citizens might start rioting. You saw the protest. I believe it's just the beginning."

I chuck the invitation back onto the filing cabinet.

"For the sake of discussion, say we wanted to free the

119

prisoners." Callum lets the idea hang in the air, warming me up to it before going on. "How do you think you'd do it?"

I guess I shouldn't be surprised Callum doesn't want to give up so soon. The boy is too much like Aven, needing to do good all the time.

I'd start by killing Voss.

The invitation catches the early-afternoon sun, setting the gold paper on fire.

There's my chance, I realize.

And it's burning up in front of my very eyes. Leaning forward, I say, "Honestly, Callum? I wouldn't even try. Getting the prisoners serum is one thing, but freeing hundreds from a high-security government lab? Where would we even bring them? Not only is it damn near impossible, but if you think about it—if you *really* think about it—that's not the problem. It's just a symptom of a much bigger issue."

"You mean the governor," he says, not skipping a beat.

I raise both hands like he's caught me saying something criminal. Thankfully, though, free speech is still kind of a thing—a civilized holdover from the Mainland days. "Getting rid of him? It's like that saying about the stone that kills both the birds. Except, instead of killing the birds, it saves them. And I'd count myself and Aven among those saved. Voss will never stop hunting the spring, or me, or her."

"Could you do it?" he asks. "Assassinate him, I mean?"

I could. If I had the opportunity, I could.

I don't answer Calllum—the beast made of teeth sets me on edge if I look at it too closely.

Out of the corner of my eye, I catch Callum watching me, wondering. It lasts only a second: he don't need a straight answer.

I think he knows I'd do it.

19

One single blade of sunlight carves between the drapes, slicing me in two. I wake fast and move out of its way. *It's just sunlight*, I tell myself. *Sunlight can't hurt.*

Looking around the room, I realize I'm glad Ren's not here. My nightmare woke me and now she thinks I'm broken. And for whatever reason—sheer stubbornness, probably— it makes me feel *less* broken. Like I want to fight back. Yawning, I lift myself up from the bed—

Something feels different. . . .

I lifted myself. I felt the bend of my wrists and the push of the mattress against my palms. I could be imagining it. It wouldn't be the first time. I almost don't want to look, but my fear isn't so big it stomps out my hope.

I scoot myself closer to the edge of the bed, and, using my teeth, I begin to unravel the gauze. It flies away from me, piling invisibly against the white sheets. *White wings.* The fluttering stops me cold as my dream—my nightmare—comes back, but the gauze is already off.

I gasp, dizzy.

I don't believe it.

Pale skin, blue veins, and lines of new muscle have regrown up to my knuckles. Brand-new knuckles. There, the bones end, with only a little bit of finger webbing between them. It looks funny, but I'm not complaining. Turning my hand over, I inspect my palm. That's there too, complete with life lines and death lines. *Love lines.* The thought puts my heart in my stomach, and I think of green eyes.

I've been given it back, all of it. Almost.

They could grow more.

I laugh into the soft padded flesh of my palm. The knife in the back of my mind dulls, and I remember my promise to the stars. *I can do it*, I tell myself. *I can go back there.* I don't want to see the white room and the black room again, but with Ren, Callum, and Dorek—I could do it.

I won't let my fear be the reason I don't keep my promise.

Jumping out of bed, I quickly grab my new comm. Using my teeth, I strap it to my wrist and run from the room.

"You guys!" I yell, throwing open the door to Callum's lab. I find him and my sister standing over the glass tanks, talking. "Look!" I hold two palms up to their faces, one for each.

Ren grabs my half hand with her full one. "Holy brack!"

123

she says. "I don't believe it!" She wiggles the soft triangle of flesh between my index finger and thumb, amazed. Then she rolls my hand over, tracing each new line like I just did.

"Do we think it'll keep growing?" I ask hopefully, trying to read my future. Some people say it's possible. I don't know if it works on yourself.

"I think it will," Callum answers, drawing another vial. "Let's make sure, shall we?" He hands it to me as if it were a glass of white water: bubbly stuff that Ren sometimes drinks at Tank parties in the Ward. I take it between my palms, and I drink.

After topping it off with one last chug, I breathe deep. The water buzzes through my veins. The lightning sensation is back, only a tiny bit weaker.

"So. You guys," I begin, my eyes bouncing back and forth between Callum and Ren. Fully supercharged with the water, my promise overrides all my fear. "Can we come up with a plan today? To get Mrs. B and Miss Nale and the others out?" I ask, throwing the words into the air like dice.

"Callum and I were just discussing it." Ren avoids my eyes, hesitating. I hold my breath. "He suggested we, at the very least, try to get them the serum."

I do a double take, not understanding. "Wait . . . are you saying we can't do it?"

She looks to Callum for backup.

"It would be quite difficult," he agrees, spreading his arms wide and sighing.

I can't believe what I'm hearing. "But difficult is not impossible, right?" I ask in disbelief. This is what being dropped from a skyscraper must feel like.

"Aven . . . ," Ren starts, rubbing the bridge of her nose. "Freeing hundreds of people from a top secret government lab ain't exactly a cakewalk. Honestly, I wouldn't know where to start. But getting them the serum? That we can talk about."

I bite my lower lip to keep from crying. *I have to do this. I said I would. And I can go back now. . . . I'm not broken. I'm strong enough.*

The tears come anyway.

"I'm sorry, Feathers," she says, softer now. "I'm just not interested in risking both our lives so soon. *Your* life, especially. I just got you back, remember?"

"Then what did you save me for?" I shoot at her. "If not so that I can live my life . . . then why? What if I want to risk it? You're not my mother."

Her face falls. Now I feel like I've just dropped her from a building.

She's not, though. I've been given a second chance, and this is how I want to use it. Except—

I can't do it without her.

It's too late. The damage is done. Red-eyed, tear-streaked, I shake my head, because I don't know how to give up. Ren taught me that. I hear myself pleading with her like I'm a fly on the wall. I sound like the child I'm trying to prove I'm not.

I can't stop myself. "But I made a promise—"

"Exactly," Ren spits, her forehead vein blue and pissed. "*You* promised. Not me. I didn't volunteer for this job."

I stop breathing. *I—I can't believe her.* Can't she see how awful it is? Everyone believed me. *I'm a liar now.*

Ren's comm buzzes.

I look away, pushing tears from my face, but I can't stop the crying. I already begged. I yelled. I'm still the child. Out of the corner of my eye, I see her spin around and do a little jump. She's happy.

"It's Derek," she says. Exhaling, she reads his comm.

Her smile disappears.

20

REN

3:22 P.M., FRIDAY

Leave—the DI are coming to talk to Dr. Cory. Ter's got his Omni waiting at Sybil's Cave, but it's getting late. DI security tightens at 5—they're closing Castle Islet to the public. You have to leave now, or it'll be too dangerous.

Callum should stay put, act normal. They have nothing on him.

"*Brack,*" I curse. Slamming my hand against the wall, I read the comm aloud. "We've gotta leave, right now, this minute. Please don't argue with me, Aven. Just get your things."

I half expect her to pull the "You're not my mother" card a second time. She's fourteen; I probably should've seen it coming. Instead, I was blindsided—and damn, I had no idea how bad it would hurt. My sister just threw my heart to a ten-headed, ten-jawed shark and she don't even know it. Thankfully, she leaves the room without a fight, and I answer Derek's comm.

Will you meet us?

His reply is instantaneous:

Don't wait up—I'll find another way off the island if I can't meet you.

"Where's your map, Callum?" I ask, looking around. "I need to find Sybil's Cave."

He doesn't hear me; he's breaking down the tanks, muttering to himself. "I'm sure it'll be fine," he says. "I was just one of Aven's doctors at Ward Hope. That's all this is."

He disassembles the ecosystem in pieces—algae, fungus, rocks, and water. He ties them in small individual bags, then all together in one large sack. Into a second bag, he pours the serum with my blood added. He lowers both in front of me.

"Map?" I ask again.

"Of course." He walks me to the closet door and points inside. It's massive. At the top, it reads, *The United Metro Isles and the Upstate Region (Southern Half Only)*. "Sybil's Cave," he repeats to himself, searching the West Isle side of the map.

Meanwhile, I inspect the rest. Instinctively, my eyes find Falls—the city that once supplied us with water. Only thirty miles north, we got slaughtered in the First Appeal. "A Dawn for Discourse" forgot to discourse that informational tidbit.

"Here we are," Callum says, finally dropping his thumb somewhere along the Isle's coastline. His index finger drags southeast over water. "And here's Sybil's Cave," he says. He traces the small green landmass of Castle Islet, and taps its far coast.

"How do we get there?" I ask, peering closer.

He taps the map, remembering something. "It's a stop on the historic ferry tour. My building's also on the route, as it's pre–Wash Out. Every hour, on the hour, weekdays nine to five."

I check my comm—next boat arrives at four. "We have twenty minutes to get there."

Callum hands me both bags of water. "We can't risk the DI finding them. And don't take the pathway to the docking area—exit out the back, you can cut through. Careful, though; the terrain is steep, and fairly wooded."

He looks at me, his brows heavy and his face pale.

"We'll make it," I promise. He nods, and I go for the hug first. I tackle his waist, crushing his abs with my cheek. "We couldn't have done any of this without you. I just hope we're worth the risk. I know how important the water is to you."

Don't know why I just said that. It's not about the water anymore; it can't be. He's got different reasons for helping us. *Maybe I want to know what they are. . . .*

Callum's first to pull away. He reaches for my penny charm necklace and tugs at the newer one—the one he gave me. "You don't really think it's about the water, do you?"

Shaking my head, I scoff. "Hell no. It's 'cause, secretly, you like living on the edge. I know the truth about you, Callum Pace." Twice I poke the bony spot right over his heart. "Don't think you're fooling me."

He hugs me again, presses his cheek to mine like I'm something warm and he's something cold, when really it's the other way around. There's a quiet in the room, but not because the room is actually so quiet. Burners are still hissing blue tongue flames, and different mixtures are bubbling in rows. It's the quiet of things better left unsaid.

"No, Ren. There's no fooling you," he says.

We both let it be true.

Exiting through the rear of Callum's building, Aven and I race across a brittle lawn—then lurch to a stop. "Link arms with me," I tell her, peering down a green, tree-veiled gorge that drops straight into the Hudson.

Aven doesn't say no, but she also doesn't say yes, 'cause now I'm the bad guy.

Instead, she steps into the ravine and takes off at a canter, sideways. One bag bounces against her back—in it, the cure with my blood. When she hits sunlight, her pale hair goes invisible, like she's got no hair at all.

Carrying two bags of my own—one with algae and fungus samples, the other a backpack filled with fresh from Callum—I take off after her. I dart around trees taller than some leftover buildings in the Ward.

Leaves underfoot, overhead . . . they block out the evening sun. We run through splotchy patches of shadow and brush, grass and fallen branches. "Careful," I say after nearly slipping. "It's steep."

Aven adjusts the bird mask flopping at her collarbone. "I can see that it's steep, Ren," she answers between huffs of air.

I slide down a pile of dead leaves like I'm surfing. "Hey," I say. "Don't hate me, all right? I didn't want to lose you twice. That's no reason to be angry with me."

Aven exhales. Farther down the gorge, she jumps off a rock and lands perfectly despite the incline. I bat away feelings of envy. The kid's two years younger, and inches taller. Her legs rival these trees.

"That's not why I'm upset, Ren. You know why I'm upset."

"Yes," I say, gritting my teeth. "I know why. And I'm asking you to have a little perspective. What you promised is downright impossible."

"You've done impossible things before, haven't you?"

"Well, now I'm tired and I want a break! Isn't that allowed? Since when did saving everyone on the planet become my job? I'd like to, ya know, get back to living my own life at some point."

Aven slows at a wire fence, dock in sight. She turns to face me. "I understand. I just never thought of you as selfish, that's all."

I stop. My heart is gone—it's a jigsaw puzzle and every piece is missing. Keeping Aven safe has been my life. Am I selfish?

I never wanted to be without her.

"Ren. Don't you even wonder?"

"Wonder what?" I answer quietly.

"*You* found the water. If it were meant to stay hidden—if that's the only way to deal with this miracle—then . . . why?"

Catching up to her at the fence, I groan. She knows I don't ask questions like this. "Aven . . . sometimes things just happen, and there are no bigger answers. I did my part."

"Yes, you did," she says, palms on her hips, sweat beading down her neck. "And I'll find a way to do mine."

I try to think of something snarky, but you know what? I'm glad she's mad. It means she wants something bad enough that she'd risk going back to that place. If she needs to believe in fate too, fine.

"I'm sure you will, Aven," I answer, losing the sarcasm for once in my life. "I'm sure you will."

21

" *All aboard!* "

A blue-and-white-striped double-decker paddleboat grumbles up to the dock. "Hurry!" I yell to Ren, irritated even though she's only a few feet behind. *I just can't understand her.*

First, I toss the bag of water over the fence. Then I throw myself over as best I can without fingers. Ren, however, jumps it so fast, it's like she's not even human. We lower our masks together.

"All aboard!" a red-haired girl behind the wheel calls a second time.

The dock bucks underneath us as we run, the way I imagine a horse would. One that didn't want to give you a ride.

Reaching the ferry, our young captain holds out her palm. "Twenty greens, please."

I glance at Ren, anxious. She digs around in her bag and pulls out a bottle of water, unopened . . . not even refilled: a gift from Callum, for the road. It's pure black-market fresh from the Falls, probably worth six times what the girl is asking.

"Can we afford that?" I whisper.

"Can we afford not to?"

The girl looks at us like we're crazy. She grabs the bottle, stowing our payment in a lockbox under the wheel. When we head for the empty lower level, she wags a finger. "Upstairs only." Ren and I pass each other looks—we would have rather avoided people, if possible.

As we make our way through the upper deck, half the boat stares at us from under long, beaked masks. A teacher and her group of students; an old man in a red bow tie and loafers. They must've seen us pay with the water, and now they're wondering how we got so much and how we could give it away so easily.

Two teenagers, masks up, kiss like they're each other's oxygen tanks. As we pass, they make slurping noises. They're the only ones who don't stare.

At the front of the boat, we take two red connected plastic seats.

"Thanks for joining us on the one, the only, *Historic Star* tour boat, where I, Cap'n Mirabel, will be your time-traveling guide into the West Isle's past! Ladies and gentlemen, children on field trips and children playing hooky . . ." Here, she looks pointedly at me and Ren, and at the teens still kissing.

"We'll start by waving good-bye to Troy Towers, one of the few remaining pre–Wash Out buildings still in habitable condition."

The paddleboat takes the scenic route south, passing through the nicest blocks. We make a few other stops: a flooded church, the remains of a pre–Wash Out school. Ren checks her comm three times in as many minutes. I check mine too.

"It's only fifteen after, Ren. We'll make it there before five."

She squeezes my knee, and we ride in silence.

Captain Mirabel takes a sharp left. "Before we reach Sybil's Cave, I'd like to draw your attention to the right. There you'll see the home of our very own Governor Voss. First called Stevens Mansion, it was so named for the university that once stood in its place, built in 1890. The mansion remains one of the few historic sites left untouched by the Wash Out."

The girl continues her speech, but Ren and I have stopped listening.

There they are—*the Blues*. They surround the governor's mansion like flies in dark uniforms.

"They're early," Ren whispers, and the *Historic Star* slows. On the sandy wooded coast, a small painted sign reads: *Sybil's Cave*. It points left, south. As we near, we see the Blues boarding docked boats, checking passengers' IDs.

"What do we do, Ren?" I ask, gripping her arm. *What if they find us?*

I feel the knife again. It slices over both my wrists and

draws its blade against the front of my mind. The hands I don't have still shake.

Water churns under the paddleboat as the girl at the helm steers toward Castle Islet. People crane their necks to get a closer look at the mansion, but trees block the view.

"Sybil's Cave, everyone," our chipper captain announces as she docks. "I'm sorry about the commotion, folks. I was told we could disembark until five. Let's see if they'll let us, so you can get a closer look."

A man waves us over. He's huge. He wears a darker blue uniform than the other officers. His mustache and eyebrows are black. I recognize him immediately, even though I've only seen him once.

He killed Mr. Bedrosian.

Ren freezes. She grips the rail at her side. "Dunn."

The DI chief stands on the shore, hands at his hips like a statue of a Roman warrior. I try not to panic—*it's gala security protocol*, Derek warned us.

The tour boat sidles up to a docking ramp, and its engine cuts out. Chief Dunn boards the *Historic Star*—we watch his every movement from under our masks.

Ren doesn't look at me. She doesn't even flinch. Kicking her bag under my feet, she says under her breath, "I'm jumping. Keep your mask on. Don't disembark until he's actually following me and I've got good distance. Then run, swim for it—do whatever you need. Just get to the cave."

She gestures toward the sign. "Left, and you'll hit it. It's not far. I love you. More than anything else, I love you."

That's the last thing she says before hurtling herself over my seat. She dives into the water, north off the opposite side of the boat. Away from the cave. She never looks back. She's a black arrow in a catsuit. The water doesn't even splash.

I'm alone.

22

Chill brack curls up around me, all too familiar.

Did I just do the worst possible thing?

I don't know, and I won't until the choice has played out.

A low rumble travels underwater, but I can't tell where it's coming from—the sound's too muffled. There's more than one Omni purring out there, that I know.

A white spear—a dart—cleaves though the brack, headed straight for me.

I imagine getting skewered and my heart about stops. I paddle backward—the dart crosses in front of my nose. Its net billows past, narrowly grazing my knee. I gasp.

Water pours into my mouth and I swallow accidentally, gagging as it rushes up my nose. *I have to get air*—I kick myself to the surface, spitting, breathing hard through my nose, and when my vision clears, I see the giant, steaming heap of brack I've landed myself in.

Dammit.

They're everywhere—in Omnis and in regular ole boating mobiles. A pack of silver-blue metal hulls peel toward me, forming a circle. *I'm surrounded.* I gasp again, spinning. Nearest land is Castle Islet, about a hundred and fifty feet off.

I duck, ballooning my lungs so I can make the swim—but underwater, the sloping, sandy floor changes color. It lightens as I close in on the coast.

In an all-black catsuit, I may as well be wearing a target.

First, I need to lose them—I need to swim *impossibly* far.

Pulling back, I cut right and frog-swim up the coastline. I set my goal. *Five hundred feet—that's impossibly far.*

I keep going and going, so fast my legs are hot, powered up with adrenaline fuel. *Don't stop.*

The first air-hunger pang strikes, so I swallow it down. I could get gold medals for holding my breath. Still, it's harder when you're being chased. Plus . . . Aven.

With all the worry and the chasing, my heart blows up in my chest, making me want even more air than normal. I find a rhythm to my movement, something to distract me.

Push, glide, push, glide . . . I make the seconds pass like they don't add up to distance and safety. Swimming around one coastal bend and back again, the second air-hunger pang hits—

I clench my fists and grit my teeth, all the while keeping

my lips tight, but my body's exhausted. Just imagining air does me in—*I need it. Now.*

I don't know if I made it the impossible five hundred feet.

Floating upward, I flip onto my back, allowing only my nose and lips to break the surface. I swallow mouthfuls of air and get my bearings—I've managed to swim as far as the northern tip of the islet. The helis' rumbling grows louder and fainter in turns. From the sound, they're maybe four hundred feet southeast past the bend, searching for me in circles.

This is my shot.

Keeping low to the strait's muddy bed, I hold my breath and wait.

The growling dulls—they've turned away.

I don't broach the surface as I frog-swim for Castle Islet. When I'm nose-to-nose with the sandy floor, I launch like a rocket for the wooded area.

Propellors change directions tearing up air—they grow louder as I run.

23

AVEN
4:30 P.M., FRIDAY

"**H**er!" Chief Dunn barks, pointing at Ren's shape as she glides through the water. He races off the *Historic Star* and follows Ren along the coast. "Get her!"

The inside of my mask grows wet around the eyes, but I can't cry—I won't give myself away so easily. I glance around, panic building in my stomach. I'm torn between worrying about myself and worrying about Ren, but *she's* the one who always makes it out alive. Scrape by, barely making it out at all.

Everyone runs to the side of the boat.

I'm left here, looking around stupidly.

I have to do *something*—now's my chance.

Holding both bags of water, I stand and walk to the back of the boat. Here, the girl Mirabel is clipping her nails over

141

the rail, somehow bored despite the commotion. I can barely swallow.

Can I do this?

I tried to escape from the lab and I failed. The water is heavy in my arms. *I have the cure*, I realize. *I have no choice.*

When no one's watching, I go for it—like I'm escaping the first gate of hell, I scurry down the stairs. I jump from the docking ramp onto the rocky shore. The sign for Sybil's Cave points left, down a narrow path that circles the islet. I follow it, sand kicking up as I run.

In the distance, I hear a mobile engine getting closer. Its propellers smash the water. *Don't look back.*

"Stop where you are!" a voice commands through a megaphone.

Aven, you don't even hear it. I pretend my feet are made of motors, big ones, like the ones the Blues have in their mobiles. They move so fast—*I* move so fast—I'm actually invisible.

About fifty feet away, hidden in the brush, I spot a second sign—a white arrow pointing to an obstacle course of gray fanged rocks.

They jut out at every angle, trying to stop me. *Nothing can stop me.* I skip over one, then two. *I slip*—their edges bite at my ankles, so I crab-slide the rest of the way. At the bottom, greenish-brown mud sticks to my calves; I'm knee-deep in a tidal pond.

To my right is Sybil's Cave, its mouth so black, it could be a gateway to outer space.

"Ter?" I call, and wade out into the water.

First, I see bubbles. Next, the shiny red paint of an under-water mobile breaks the surface. Its moonroof opens and out pops Ter's head. "Get in!" he shouts, waving me over.

Seeing him . . . I'm so happy I want to cry. "Ter!" I shout, clobbering through the water. I reach his mobile and throw both bags into the moonroof.

Ter taps his comm. "Say hi to Benny," he says. When he grins, I get to see his perfect, smiling teeth. "He's listening on the DI channels, giving me alternate routes so I can avoid border patrol and islet security. Couldn't have made it here otherwise."

As he looks out onto the strait, his smile drops, hiding his perfect teeth.

"What is it, Ter?" I turn, following his gaze.

Racing toward the cave, three metal sharks. Their engines groan as they splash through the waves. *They've found me. I wasn't invisible after all, and now I've put Ter in danger.* I grip the moonroof, watching the world crack like glass. It takes just one tiny nick. Each fracture starts with me—it webs off in a dozen different directions, like everyone who's risked their life to get me to here . . . Ren, Ter, Derek. Eventually it has to shatter.

The third shark swims into the cove. It faces directly toward us.

Is this how everything goes to pieces?

The Omni surfaces. Its blue hull and its DI emblem—a white shield—reflect the sun. The roof slides open.

"Benny, what do I do?" I hear Ter ask, half inside the pit.

My other half is still outside the mobile. I can't help but

watch. Something feels off. . . . *It's just sitting there.* This isn't how "getting nabbed" is supposed to look. Not according to Ren, anyway. It was always, "Shoot the net, drag 'em off."

The DI Omni sways with the tide.

"Are you guys stupid?" a voice yells, and a girl emerges from the Omni. She doesn't sound like DI, and she doesn't look like DI; she's no older than I am.

"You'll never make it past them." The girl shakes her head. Her dyed blond bob catches the sun, looking white like mine. Even whiter, because she isn't so pale.

"Who the hell are you?" Ter asks, his head now out of the moonroof.

Comparing mobiles, the girl is probably right—hers looks exactly like DI property.

"I'm a friend of Derek's," she says, waving us into her mobile. "Comm him if you don't believe me. I'd suggest being fast, though."

Out over the strait, the white trails of two DI Omnis speed closer.

Terrence looks at me. "Derek doesn't have friends—he has family. And last I checked, his family had a hit list with our names on it. I don't trust her."

I glance back at the girl. She's anxious, rapping against the side of her mobile, watching the water. She seems genuinely worried about us being caught, but there's something else—I can't put my finger on it. I want to believe her.

"We *are* trapped," I say aloud, weighing both sides. "Could she be worse than the Blues?"

Ter's silence makes me wonder.

"Let's get a move on," the girl says, and the conversation is over—Ter squeezes through the moonroof with me. Together, we hustle aboard her Omni.

The roof slides closed over our heads. Inside, the mobile is aglow with as many buttons and screens as the space allows. Ter and I settle into the seat behind her, and she lowers the mobile underwater.

"My name is Sipu." She doesn't shake our hands. She's too busy flipping on that thermal visor thing. "You're Aven, you're Terrence," she says, finishing the introductions for us.

"Can you take us back to the Ward?" Ter asks.

Sipu's eyeball sockets go really wide. He must've asked something crazy. "Do you see what's between us and the Ward? I'll take you someplace else. Somewhere safe."

Where is it safe?

Everywhere we go, Voss follows.

24

Sand flies behind me as I tear up the Castle Islet coast-line. I slip between its trees, sopping, and weave deeper into the woods. Overhead, branches bend from wind or from props—I don't know, but I don't slow an iota.

Thick brush whips against me as I go. It stings my arms, ripping my new catsuit. In here, everything's a mess of ancient green and brown shadow. Only a few holes of evening sunlight break through.

When I'm sure it's the wind that's blowing the treetops and not a heli, I crouch low to send Ter a comm—Aven couldn't reply, even if she were safe. Balancing on my knees, I type:

We got separated. Tell me you have her?

I shiver, remembering Aven's face, the moment before I jumped. Under her mask, she was terrified.

Again I left her alone. I grit my teeth and let my anger warm me. This time, I'm not blaming myself. I'm blaming him. *Voss.*

I hit send, but a new noise stops me cold.

More engines.

I stay low and listen. They ain't like any engines I'm used to . . . they're different-sounding. I squint deeper into the forest. About a quarter mile off, I can make out the white stonework of Voss's mansion. Nearby, anchored and bobbing in his moat, I locate that engine I wasn't able to pin.

It's a truck—a shipping boat. That's why it don't sound familiar. Nothing ever gets shipped to the Ward. It ain't gonna tackle me, that's for sure.

I keep on, twigs cracking beneath my shoes. The islet might be dense, but it ain't wide. Less than two hundred feet farther, I land with an awkward splash in Voss's man-made moat.

The governor's home sweet home is *mammoth.*

My feet fumble in the mud and I duck back into the brush, leaving my gaping jaw behind.

I'd seen images from DI training, surveying maps and the land and whatnot, but up close, it's a different beast. You can tell the building is pre–Wash Out. Gray stones piled high between layers of orange brick, arched gothic windows, and the official UMI radio tower like a dunce cap atop the building's head.

Through the trees, I scan the island, looking for a way off. It immediately becomes clear that this ain't an option. I have no mobile; I can't take a ferry.

I'm not sure I want a way off, either.

Voss is here, a voice reminds, leaving me queasy with guilt.

Derek too, a different voice adds. It also leaves me squeamish, but for very different reasons. I reach for my comm.

Are you through the causeway? DI were early. Aven and I separated. On Voss's property now.

Three truck boats drift down the moat, docking between both banks. Repurposed tires surrounded their metal-box bodies on all sides, keeping them afloat. *Elite Isle Servers + Catering*, one truck reads, and another: *Catskill Fresh.*

Voss, you've done it again, I think, scowling. I'd like to throw rocks at his house. Just when I thought he couldn't get worse, he goes and does this—illegally buys freshwater when the UMI can't cough it up at the aqueduct auctions.

I spit in his moat.

Behind the Elite Isle truck, a group of girls my age stand in a long line. One by one, they approach a heavyset woman with square glasses and wrinkled lips. She rifles through a trunk, handing out black-and-white uniforms.

My cuffcomm buzzes. It's Derek:

Not through yet. Can you hide safely? May need assistance later.

I could hide. . . .

I could also hide in plain sight, I realize, watching the girls take their uniforms to the back of the truck. When they come out, they're wearing cream-colored aprons over black dresses and funny little doily crowns on their heads.

My own wet, grimy catsuit sticks to my body.

If I'm going to stand in line with a bunch of West Isle girls, I'll need to not look like a wild forest beast.

Using the truck for cover, I wade through the moat and swing right into the changing room. Inside, four girls pause to give me the up-down . . . just like the racers' girlfriends back home. One throws her old sweater into a clothing cubby: *bingo.*

I make a mad dash for the bathroom and wait for them to leave.

The girls snicker. Maybe they think I have to blow it up, 'cause soon the changing room is silent.

I take this golden opportunity to rummage through their cubbies.

A moment later . . . *presto*! No longer a forest monster. Wearing someone else's cleanish button-down shirt and oversized jeans, I return to the servant line.

The girls here are exactly as I'd pictured: round pink cheeks from having enough food. Clean, well-brushed hair. I must look like a bona fide rat in comparison.

I step up to the lady.

"Name?"

Of course there's a list. I don't have an answer for her, and she examines me like maybe I'm mute. "You don't have any no-shows?" I eventually ask.

The lady laughs heartily at my joke. "No-shows? For a gala held at the governor's mansion?" She pats her belly, still laughing, because I'm just so damn funny.

"But . . . I really need the money," I say seriously. The girl behind me puts her hands on my shoulders to move me out of the way. I spin around. *Who the hell does she think—?*

"Don't turn her away, Imelda," the girl pleads. Cradling the woman's palm, she sways side to side, like a sweet, excitable puppy. "Lorelai never shows. Just use her uniform."

Imelda eyes me like I'm pond scum.

"You gave me that exact same look, once upon a time." The girl throws her glossy peach hair over one shoulder like she's famous. "But just look at me now!" Behind us, a group of her friends giggle and hide their faces. It's faux embarrassment, though; they obviously adore her.

I, however, continue to exist as pond scum.

"I'll make sure she cleans her face."

Heat rushes to my cheeks. I turn away, rubbing at my skin. My fingers come back brown.

Imelda watches. She furrows her brow in a motherly sort of way. Sighing, she begins to search the trunk full of uniforms. "Name?" she asks, but it's just for show at this point.

The girl kisses Imelda's cheek. "Lorelai Gates," she answers.

Imelda side-eyes her and hands me a black dress with a

funny paper crown pinned to the collar. "Here you go, Lorelai," she says, totally monotone. To the girl, she adds, "You were never that filthy."

Dumbfounded, I ignore the insult and stare at my uniform.

A few moments later, my West Isle savior pulls me aside. "Lorelai's dad *totally* made her take this job because they're rich, and she's a teensy bit spoiled. Don't tell her I said that. I love the girl to death. I'm just saying: She. Never. Shows. It's rude, you know? This is a really good gig, and you obviously need it way more than *Lorelai* does." Her face drops and she covers her mouth. "*Brack*. I didn't mean it that way."

I'm so busy trying to follow—she talks so fast—it takes me a moment to catch up to the offense. When I do, turns out I'm too grateful to care.

"Look," the girl adds quickly, blushing. "It's tough out there, that's all I meant. My parents? They *both* work two jobs and we still end up short. I was even stealing fresh from shipping boats and selling it for a while. That's how I met Imelda. . . . Don't tell her I told you that."

This girl? *A thief for the black market?*

That's when it hits me . . . how little I know about the West Isle. They have their rich folks, like Callum, and they have their not-so-rich folks. I doubt this girl's had it as bad as me or Aven, but poor don't always need to be a competition. Tough is tough.

"Now, not to be mean, but . . ." The girl clasps her hands together, begging as she walks me to the changing room. "Please, please, *please* don't screw up? Imelda will kill me.

Okay?" Smiling, she holds open the door.

"Spigot's in the back. Hand towels right beside it."

I forget to smile, say thank you, anything—it all happened so fast.

I stare at the girl too long, and she nudges me into the changing room.

I'm in.

25

AVEN
5:03 P.M., FRIDAY

"You can leave your things in the Omni," Sipu says, turning off the engine.

As Ter and I watch the water in the airlock drop, a faint blue light flickers on in the metal room. Soon, there's no water at all.

The moonroof slides open, and Sipu hops out first. She grips the wheel on a circular steel door, spinning it a few times. As soon as it swings open, she rushes away, forgetting about us.

"She's off fast." Ter and I glance at each other, confused. His cuffcomm buzzes. "It's Ren," he says, typing a reply. "She's just making sure we found each other."

He comms her back and shimmies through the moonroof. For a moment our kneecaps touch. I don't mind if I'm blushing; it makes my cheeks pink.

Ter offers me his hand. So much has happened, I'm not thinking. . . . I give it to him. Quickly, I remember and pull away.

But . . . *I felt something*, I realize. A leftover tingling, like clingy static.

Resting against his palm, I find five half fingers. Wrinkled skin has grown around a second set of knuckles. *It's working! They could come back*—a bubbly feeling in my chest makes me want to laugh.

I bite it back, though.

My hands are ugly, I think. They don't mean to be, and I know it's not my fault, but they are. I don't even have fingernails. They look like alien hands, or the hands of a monkey. With this boy standing in front of me, I want to hide myself.

I should be grateful. *I am grateful*. But I see the ugliness, too. Curling my knuckles away, "Don't look," I tell him. "The water isn't done working yet."

Ter's seen, though; it's too late.

He doesn't pull away. He just lets me take my hand back. "They did that to you at the lab?" he asks, green eyes inches from mine.

I've never been this close to him before . . . not since Miss Nale's, when maybe we'd eat lunch together if Ren wasn't around. I always knew his eyes were green, but now that I'm so close, I realize I was wrong. That's not the right word for them at all.

Once, hunting pennies, I found this crayon . . . it was called *electric lime*. I've never had electricity, and I've never seen a lime in real life, but it fits perfectly.

What were we talking about?

I've forgotten everything: my hands, my fingernails, the dictionary definition of ugly. I only know that I'm standing here, and a boy—*this boy*—is standing with me.

"Lucas! Are you happy now?" Sipu yells in the other room. We whip around at the noise.

"Yes. Very," comes his muffled answer. "You think you can pull a stunt like that in the tunnel, and I wouldn't find out? Didn't you wonder how I knew Derek and that girl would head through there in the first place? Holo cams. And Kitaneh agrees knocking out your husband isn't very nice; now you'll have to earn your right to the springwater. I doubt she'll even let you into her apartment until she trusts you again. *If* she trusts you again."

A crinkle of worry forms between Ter's eyebrows. He helps me out of the mobile and pulls open the heavy steel door.

A boy, red-haired and very muscular, sits at a desk. *He looks just like Derek*, I realize, but I know it's not him. This one's too angry.

Sipu slams both hands down on the table. He ignores her. "Here you go." She gestures to Ter and me. "I've captured the maimed girl and her friend. You can do the rest," she shouts.

Captured?

Lucas pushes a button under the desk. The steel door sucks closed, locking with a heavy *chink*.

I gulp as the red-haired boy, Lucas, stands. He makes me want to bolt for the door. He moves so slowly, like those holos from science class of wild cats stalking in the brush.

Not saying a word, Lucas reaches into his pocket and tosses her something.

She catches it with both hands. Fingers fumbling, she pops off the cork to a small glass tube and tosses it aside. Then she chugs.

It's the water. . . .

"You lied to us?" I ask Sipu, whispering.

When she's emptied the vial, she drops it onto the floor—the glass explodes like a dying star. Sipu can't meet my eyes. She lets her blond bob hide her face, drying her lips with one sleeve.

She didn't want to.

"Why'd you bring us here?" Ter asks, putting himself between me and Lucas. His voice is cool. Like we're having a friendly conversation, but also like he might be my bodyguard, if necessary.

"Tie them up," Lucas tells Sipu.

"I said you could take it from here," she spits.

Scowling, he kicks his chair. As it screeches to a stop in the middle of the room, he grabs a line of wire from his desk drawer.

He stalks up to Ter, who backs away, hands raised.

I don't breathe. I back away too, until I'm pressed hard against the airlock. Lifting my cheek from Ter's black T-shirt, I peek under his armpit—and duck just in time.

He throws a punch, nearly drawing his elbow into my face. When he lets his fist loose, it connects perfectly with Lucas's shoulder.

Lucas shifts an inch, maybe.

Instantly, he throws a hook under Ter's chin, knocking his head against the steel door. A line of blood trickles down the nape of his neck. He doubles over. I reach for his hand—"Ter?" I ask as he staggers onto his knees.

I shouldn't have opened my mouth. . . . Lucas sees me. Grabbing my wrist, he drags me across the concrete to the other side of the room. I wince as Ren's leggings roll away, and the floor scrapes off a layer of skin at my hips.

He passes the line of wire over and under my palms, like it's a cold, hard snake. If he notices something is wrong, that my hands aren't all there, he says nothing. He ties the line so tight, I can feel the blood squeezing, aching through my fingers.

The ankles are next and I begin to lose hope. I can't expect Ren to come for us—she has no idea that we're here. I don't even know if she's okay, much less able to save me. For the billionth time. Curling myself up into a corner, I lay my head to the concrete. This time I don't cry.

Tied up beside me, Ter's barely awake—there's only the smallest sliver of white in his eyes. His head droops like he's sick. I lean against his shoulder, wanting to comfort us both.

Sipu paces back and forth, across the room. She's fidgety. When she looks at Ter and me, I try to harden my face.

I can't.

I should resent her . . . hate her for lying to us and bringing us here—but deep down, I just feel bad for Sipu. Lucas, her own husband, blackmailed her. She'd be dead if she hadn't listened. When she looks at me again, I give her a weak smile.

Not a friendly one—one that says *I understand.*

Projected onto the brick wall in front of Lucas's desk is a holo of the governor. He's standing on a balcony, talking to a roomful of reporters. Lucas's eyes and ears are glued to the image. "We knew this guy was bad news," he says. "Kitaneh better not screw up this time. Things are only getting harder for us. He's getting desperate. He knows finding the spring is the only way to avoid a Second Appeal."

When they show a close-up of Governor Voss, I close my eyes.

"Exactly," Sipu agrees, then pauses to face Lucas. "Which is why we cannot be stuck in the old ways. We've never dealt with a situation like this before." Under her breath she mutters, "Why do you and Kitaneh not see this?"

"Sipu, if we were doing things the old way, they'd be dead already," Lucas answers casually, throwing his thumb at Ter and me. "Kitaneh and I have always seen eye to eye . . . on a lot of things. Not just this."

Sipu's breath catches in her throat. She stiffens.

Seeing this, Lucas drops his eyes. "The old ways worked," he goes on. "Hundreds of years, the spring stayed hidden. Nobody was killing each other over it or using it to start wars. We never saw immortality doses in the streets. Nobody was getting rich off it. Then comes this guy." Lucas nods to the holo projection of Voss. "And her friend Ren—" He's pointing at me. "Now? It's all over."

How can he say that? I can't stop the words from coming out of my mouth—"But so many people aren't sick anymore," I tell him. "For us, nothing's over. It's all just begun. Right now, Voss is keeping hundreds of people in a prison waiting to die. *They're* the ones it's over for."

Lucas lifts himself from his chair.

I shouldn't have said anything. My heart beats so fast, I feel the blood pounding against the wire snake around my hands. They ache.

Lucas drops to a knee right in front of me. "Oh, kid," he says, snorting, squeezing my cheeks until they hurt. "It's over for you too. You're alive for one reason: so your friend Ren will come and find you. That way, we won't have to find her."

He jerks my head back and forth, and Sipu rushes to stop him. "Lucas—let her go. She's just a girl," she says, gently trying to pull him away.

Lucas releases me, but Sipu backs off too late. He glares at her, teeth gritted, and raises his hand—*he's going to hurt her.*

His open palm hangs in the air.

26

The kitchen, where I've been assigned (technically, Lore-lai) is hot, bustling with movement. Other girls from the line, also wearing black dresses and ridiculous paper crowns, fill flutes with a seemingly endless supply of freshwater. Gallons upon gallons Voss is giving out for free—a slap in the face to everyone, even West Islers, I'm beginning to understand.

I glance around, looking for someone to report to, when I get a comm from Ter.

Got her. Sipu picked us up.

Sipu? That wasn't part of the plan. . . .

A girl, short with long black hair, pushes me a silver tray. "Take this," she says.

I nearly drop it.

Backing away, I see her face—dark skin, round face. Wedded eternally to Derek. It's as if all movement in the kitchen slows down—steam from pots of boiling fresh pause their billowing, and no one moves. We're the only ones in the room.

"Kitaneh—" I breathe.

Our eyes lock. *"You."*

We look around, neither knowing who's gonna make the first move. *Would she try to kill me? Right here, in this kitchen?* She's in disguise. She won't want to give herself away. . . . *I hope.*

Kitaneh points a chopping knife at me. "Why are you here?"

"Why are *you*?" I say, no knife, though.

Her jaw stiffens and her eyes go cold. The other girls look at us. Kitaneh lowers the blade and begins violently carving carrots.

I understand the servant getup—*she's here to kill him.*

"Do you feel guilty at all, girl?" she asks. "Now that Voss is so loved by everyone, he will come after you, and us, more determined than ever before. This is because of you and what you have done, handing out water to the sick like it's some kind of drug." She continues chopping, harder now.

I step closer, not caring—she's here for Voss; she won't blow her cover on me. "And what about you? Don't you feel guilty at all, *girl*?" I say. She doesn't get to play holier-than-thou because she's ancient and I'm not. "A cure for the Blight existed right under your damn basement, but instead, you let people suffer. Guilt-free, you are," I scoff, sarcastic.

Kitaneh drops the knife onto the cutting board and turns to me. "You have *no* idea what you're talking about," she says, gripping the counter. "I do what is necessary, but I am not without conscience. I'd die tomorrow and give up this 'calling' if I thought humankind wouldn't destroy itself."

I wanna call bullshit; Kitaneh protects the spring with more ferocity than a rabid dog. Then again, that kind of fanaticism tends to run deep—kamikaze deep.

Kitaneh turns to scrape the extremely well-chopped carrots into a metal bowl. "I don't even care why you're here." Dismissively, she waves her knife. "Voss isn't the only one who won't live to see morning," she whispers.

Then, Kitaneh smacks my arm with her wrist. "What are you doing standing around? Take it, I said!" She's handing me the tray, and everyone's watching.

I do as she says, her threat ringing in my ears, and hurry out the kitchen. The glasses of fresh wobble in my hands, and I just about fall directly into the main ballroom. The party hasn't even begun yet—*who the hell am I supposed to be serving?*

I steady myself, putting on my best servant face, and get my bearings. I'm in a long room with a new window every five feet. The ceilings are so high, they could fit ten of me standing. At the center, a wide, winding stairwell opens up to the dance floor blocked off by men and women also in black. They're not dressed like us servers, though. They're sporting jackets and ties, mics and holocams. *It's a press release, or an impromptu State of the UMI*, I realize, cursing my luck.

Governor Voss steps out onto a balcony. Everyone hushes.

With no mask, I'm a sitting duck. I weave through the crowd, back turned to the governor as long as possible. A woman in a wheelchair dressed entirely in black sits beside him. She's hunched over, her face covered by a black lace veil.

Emilce Voss . . . his wife. It must be her.

"Thank you all for coming," Governor Voss begins. He looks over the room, occasionally making eye contact with some of the media. I, however, avoid his eyes like the Blight. "My wife and I are overjoyed to have you in our home, documenting the new developments that have taken place in the UMI—more specifically, in the Ward. Hopefully by now you've come to learn that my medical team has found a cure for the HBNC virus. And, if you haven't, I'd advise you find yourself a new career."

The journalists and reporters offer an anxious but well-timed laugh.

Voss pauses, smug and self-satisfied up there in his ivory tower. "The HBNC virus, nicknamed the Blight," he begins, "has ravaged the UMI's poorer neighborhoods for years. Finding a cure for the virus was the only way to reunite our nation of islets. And, after years of hard work, we were finally rewarded. The cure was distributed and, one day later, the virus had been eradicated among the population by nearly seventy-five percent." He looks at the closest camera, dead-on. "I thank each and every citizen for your support these past few years. Without your faith, this day would never have arrived."

The governor pauses, turning. "I'd also like to thank my beautiful, supportive wife, Emilce. She's stood by my side while I made the eradication of this plague my priority, sometimes overshadowing all else."

Emilce stays utterly still. Everyone looks to her for a sign, a gesture, something to show she's heard him, but she gives nothing. Voss sighs. With one final exhale and a tip of his water glass, he toasts to the room. Everyone mimics him, tipping their glasses. Quickly, I raise mine, so I don't look like the odd man out.

One man mumbling notes into his cuffcomm raises his hand. The governor's jaw locks. "I hadn't planned on taking questions today—"

"Wouldn't be much of a press conference if you didn't!" the reporter quips back, laughing. "Now that you've got a handle on the Blight, will you consider a Second Appeal, Governor Voss?"

A hundred pairs of eyes are on him, not including the cameras. Those count for everyone watching on the West Isle and the few with holos in the Ward.

"Right now, my priority is to continue the search for viable freshwater aquifers *within* the UMI."

I almost choke on my drink, 'cause I know what he really means—"viable freshwater" is code for the spring.

If he thinks that he can stamp out that question, though, he's mistaken. Someone else, a blond woman, raises her hand, though he's clearly not calling on anyone. "What if it doesn't exist? You've exhausted the original budget for this search. When will you do what's best for the UMI?"

"Chief Dunn, what are your feelings on the subject?" another member of the press interrupts. My breath catches and I shift deeper into the crowd—I hadn't even seen Chief from here. "What's the point of having a military nation if the military has no say in decisions that affect us all?"

The room goes silent. Chief and Voss exchange glances. Voss nods and Dunn steps forward, the trunk of his torso nearly taking up half the balcony.

"I support Governor Voss."

That's all he says.

But as he disappears behind the banister, Dunn gives Voss a death glare to end all death glares. And he keeps his hands behind his back like they're actually tied together. Like there's nothing he can do.

Chief Dunn wants a Second Appeal.

The room devolves into a chattering mess. Reporters hold up their mics and shout over one another, determined to be heard.

"Before the Blight hit, Chief Dunn once mentioned enlisting the Ward in a draft. Is that still a possibility?"

"You could offer incentives!"

"But they should *want* to fight for the cause!"

All the hairs on my body stand tall, and my muscles tighten. I want to make human punching bags of these people. *They really believe we're disposable.* Then I remember the protest, and that I shouldn't be surprised.

Gripping the banister with both hands, Voss looks down, his skin sallow and shadowed. Even under the chandelier's soft light, his cheekbones form cutting angles. He stands at the white podium, waiting. The room settles.

"The First Appeal devastated our population and Magistrate Harcourt *still* refused to reopen the aqueduct. Chief Dunn agrees that a search for a local water source is of preeminent importance."

Translation: Voss will never stop looking for the spring.

I knew this was true, but to have him say it to my face? I have no choice. I could let Kitaneh do the job—if I thought for a minute she'd succeed. Considering how the Tètai have had over a hundred years to bury this guy and he's still here . . . well, I wouldn't put my money on them.

I have to do something. *Now.*

Dunn ushers a visibly agitated Governor Voss out of the spotlight. The two disappear abruptly behind the balcony.

Sometimes opportunity presents itself. Sometimes, you have to hunt it down.

Time to hunt.

I discard my tray on a table next to a decorative bowl of nice-looking rocks. *Where did he go?* I can't see Voss wanting to rub elbows with the reporters, not after that show—educated guess says he's still on the second floor.

Backtracking, I scan the banquet hall for another way up. At the far end, past the kitchen, I find a second stairwell. Though it's been blocked off, it don't even look like it's trying. A thick, velvety rope droops across the banisters. I hop over and race up the stairs.

At the top, I find a drink cart stocked with bottles of liquor. Voss's personal stash, I imagine. You don't drink the stuff if you don't got the money or the means to rehydrate yourself later. And Voss has the money.

Wheeling it down the hall, I peek into room after room. They're all empty. I pick up my pace. At the final room—the one closest to the balcony—I hear a voice. I crouch low and listen.

"Ungrateful—I'm finding it for *you*," a man growls. *Voss*.

I slip inside the room.

It's long, with a rich burgundy ceiling and gold molding. In the center, a glass chandelier hangs. A mirror hung horizontally above a set of drawers gives the illusion of an even larger space. I lower myself so I can crawl in. The silk rug gives nothing away. I don't even allow myself the luxury of breathing. My chest is brick-heavy, clenched and tight.

Could I really do it?

At the sound of a woman's voice, I go stiff—*he's not alone*. I scurry past the drawers, toward a plush armchair tucked into the corner. Sliding behind it, I arch over the armrest and listen.

"Can't you just be patient? I'm doing this for us," Voss continues, insistent. In the center of the room, the woman dressed in black, his wife, lays on a cot. She looks more like she's about to attend her own funeral than a gala thrown in her husband's honor.

He's gripping her ankles like she'd run if she could.

A nest of plastic tubes connected to an IV snakes out from her forearm. Inside the IV bag, a muted greenish liquid drains into her body. *It's the serum he stole.*

Governor Voss picks up one of her hands, but he may as well be holding a corpse.

Actually, a corpse would be indifferent to his touch. Her hand tightens into a fist. "Old age is not a disease," I hear her rasp. *"Let me die."*

The governor drops her hand, backing away from the cot.

From the bar in the corner, he pours himself a drink the color of caramel, which he downs in one sip. The crystalline glass drops like a hammer onto the table. Without offering his wife another look, he strides toward the door—about to pass my hiding spot.

I reach for my blade—I'm too slow. Been wasting my time, listening to their pathetic saga. *Can I still do it?*

Slipping back behind the plush ivory chair, my heart beats so fast I can barely feel a rhythm at all. Hilt in hand, I wait until Voss faces the door. He lays his hand on the knob, about to turn.

I could do it like this, a blade in his back.

Except . . . I'm a statue. Worse than that—I'm wallpaper.

I don't move. I don't know if it's fear or a random bout of morality kicking in, but I *can't* move.

The door opens.

The door closes.

The governor is gone.

27

ill he do it? Will he hit her?
Eye-to-eye in a standoff, neither Sipu nor Lucas shows any weakness.

Lucas lowers his hand.

When Sipu turns away, I catch her wiping the corner of her eyes. They're red from tears she won't allow, but her face is feral. Wild, unforgiving.

"I'm getting our prisoners some water so they don't die before we kill them," she says abruptly, shutting the door behind her.

Lucas returns to his chair, but the press conference is over. He fumbles with some buttons on a remote, and it plays again from the start. I wish I didn't have to watch. I don't like seeing that man, even when he's made of pixels and light.

Groggily, Ter lifts his chin. He shakes his head and forces his eyes open, then winces. Glancing around, he asks, "We're really still here?"

"We are," I say under my breath, wiggling my new half hands. The snake wire is too tight—it's cutting off my blood. I rotate them around but have to stop a moment later as Sipu walks back into the room.

"Kitaneh's asking for you on the wall comm upstairs. She wants to talk," Sipu says to Lucas, canteen in hand. "Something to do with . . ." Her voice trails off and she nods in our direction.

"I didn't miss any messages," Lucas says, checking his cuffcomm.

Sipu shrugs.

He crosses the room, watching her. "I have the water. Don't forget that, Sipu," he says.

Lucas leaves the door open behind him.

Kneeling in front of Ter and me, I spot the knife she's holding behind her canteen. She brings one finger to her lips. "Get in the Omni," she whispers, taking the blade to my wrists first, then to Ter's. The wires burst open and blood rushes back to my hands, numb by now.

Under Lucas's desk, Sipu reaches for a button. Ter meets my eyes—we share one second of hesitancy and reach the same thing. The steel door gasps open.

We rush for the airlock.

Upstairs, Lucas crosses noisily from one end of the floor to the other, stampeding for the stairs—*he's caught on.*

Sipu races behind us, spinning the airlock's wheel closed.

I hop into her mobile first, followed by Ter. Sipu is last. She jumps into the front seat, and as the moonroof closes, she lowers the Omni underwater.

Red lights flash all around us, but the airlock's filling up—the door can't open, or the basement will flood.

Lucas is too late.

Sipu steers the Omni through the strait without even turning on the high beams—she knows the waters by heart. We veer through underwater alleys and parks, slowing down only when she's sure we aren't being followed.

"I'm sorry," she says as she lowers the Omni onto the Hudson's muddy bed. She flips on the lights inside the pit. "When I brought you there, I thought I had no other choice. I was wrong—I had two choices and liked neither."

Outside, seaweed dances in the current. As it grazes the windshield, I lean closer to her. "Why did you decide to help us?"

Sipu sighs. "Is guilt an answer when it doesn't change anything?" she says, leaning back against the headrest. "There are things I wish I never knew. For years I did nothing, when the water was right there . . . right under my feet. And I would have continued, had Lucas not raised his hand to me. I could have waited for him forever. Now I see, he belongs with Kitaneh."

Her answer is too vague to understand completely, but the word *guilt* is clear—she wishes she'd done something with the water.

Sipu pauses and lifts her head, as if remembering she's

not alone. "Where should I bring you?" she asks. A current gently sends the Omni sideways, and both bags of water roll over my feet.

My promise.

It comes beating back to life inside of me.

"What if there's something we *can* do?" I say, and both Ter and Sipu pause. "The FATE Research Center. We wanted to get the cure to the prisoners in Quarantine." I hold up a bag of water for them both to see.

Sipu takes the bag from me, turning it around as she inspects it. "Leftover stolen goods," she says.

I shake my head. "Callum, Ren's friend, made more."

"You're mistaken," she says, passing the bag back. "The spring's ecosystem is impossibly delicate. It would take years of trial and error to re-create it artificially. I know. We tried. We gave up."

"Okay," I say. "Then this must be apple juice."

She takes the bag again, this time inspecting it even harder. As if it could speak to her and prove what I'm saying.

"Look," I say, showing her my hands. "Voss cut them off . . . at the *wrists*. Now see?" I wiggle all ten of my half fingers.

That must be proof enough—Sipu laughs into her palm, brushing aside a few blond strands. "You were going to bring it to the prisoners?" she asks, when something else occurs to her. She narrows her eyes at the bag. "But there isn't enough. Four people, maybe. Not hundreds."

Of course, she doesn't know about Ren's blood—and I don't know if I should tell her. "Callum found someone who's immune," I say instead, "and he added their blood to the water. It works in one dose now. It's the same cure Ren and the other racers got out to everyone in the Ward."

Ter leans forward, elbows resting against his knees. "With all the doctors and scientists invited to the gala, the lab *will* be half-staffed," he says. "But . . . it could also be doubly guarded because of your escape."

"These prisoners . . . ," Sipu says. *She's actually considering*—I bite my lip. "They were arrested for transmitting the virus?"

Ter and I nod.

"And they wouldn't be in there if they themselves hadn't contracted it?"

More nodding.

"You're sure?"

I don't know why she doesn't believe us. "I was in there with them. . . . I'm sure."

"If that's true," Sipu says finally, "I want to help you."

I bite my cheeks to keep from grinning too hard—she wants to help *me*. I'm not just asking her for help . . . *she's asking me to let her.* Like *I'm* the mastermind. I feel brighter than a dozen roof-garden fireflies.

"Wait," Ter says, deep in thought. I whip around to find him eyeing me warily. "Ren expects me to keep you safe, not hand-deliver you to the same people responsible for doing *that*."

I flush, angry and embarrassed, hiding both hands from him. "Well, that's your problem. Maybe I don't need to be kept safe. And even if I did, there are more important things to worry about. Like this. Getting a cure to Mrs. Bedrosian and everyone else. You know Miss Nale's in there too?"

Ter exhales and drops his eyes. I think he agrees, he's just afraid. "So, do we have a plan, or are we gonna wing it? 'Cause I vote plan," he says, raising his hand.

"I have a way in."

"Really?" Ter and I say together.

We're sitting in a DI Omni . . . of course she does. This can't be the only trick up her sleeve. She nods and smiles weakly. Helping us hurts. She's lost her family for us, *for this.*

"Yes. I know how," she says at last.

My promise beats louder. It's so loud, it's a hundred heartbeats in one. Hundreds of heartbeats trapped in a prison cell made out of ribs. They're in there, waiting to be let free.

We're getting them the water.

28

"**D**on't need to see you, child, to know you're there."

I curse from my hiding place, silently (or not so silently) punching the armchair. *How'd she know?*

"Closer," Emilce Voss says, exhaling. "Come closer."

I should make a run for it—things just got a whole lot trickier now that I've been found. And yet I don't run. I push the chair out of my way and walk toward the woman on the cot. I watch her black veil rise, and then fall against her face. Her dark, clawlike hand trembles as she lifts it away. But the lace is too heavy. With one weak tug, it falls to the side, and I can see not just her features, but the outline of her entire skull.

Ashen, papery dark skin. Dark freckles. The smattering

of spots along her cheeks stands out like dirt. Veins line her neck like waterway maps. Her insides may as well be wrapped in brown plastic.

I try to hide my disgust, but I don't know that I can. In the one day since I saw her at the lab, she's turned into the walking dead. "How—" I stammer.

"Time, it seems," she says weakly, "is finally catching up with me."

I can't help myself—I glance at the serum.

"You know about that, do you?" Emilce nods. "Then you know it's not the *real* stuff. It's a serum my husband *retrieved* by some means or another. But it's been altered. It's effective against the virus, of which I have been cured, blessed be." She brings her hands together in fake prayer. Even in her condition, she's managed to keep a healthy dose of sarcasm. I can't help but laugh a little.

"Its other properties, however, are . . . diminished. Nonetheless, he keeps pumping the stuff into me. Nothing can turn back the clock. Even the unaltered water is merely a pause button. I would like to remove the batteries." Here, she laughs. It's an unnerving sound. Like hearing Death laugh at his own joke, but he's the only one in the room.

"If you wanna die so bad, why not just kill yourself?" I ask, calling her bluff. It's a harsh question, but I'm curious to know just how serious she is.

"Give me something sharp, and strength enough to pick it up, and I will."

I swallow. "So he's just keeping you here? Like this?"

"I'd call him a monster," Emilce says, her voice full of nails, "if I hadn't loved him for so many years. He claims to love me in return—that's why I'm still alive, if you were to ask him. So he can find the spring . . . for *me*." She rolls her cloudy eyes. "But it's not for me. I'm his last connection to humanity, that's all. He's afraid to lose himself."

Emilce wavers between anguish and hard-edged anger, like she can't decide which should win.

"So he puts the water into your IV?" I ask, eyeing the plastic bag at her bed.

Emilce squeezes air between her fingers. "Tiny drops. Enough to keep me alive. The rest, he saves for himself." Her hand falls, exhausted from such a small motion. She looks at me like I'm the last person on earth and she's already gone.

Glancing back toward the door, my hands instinctively turn to fists. The more I learn about Governor Voss, the more I understand the word *hate*.

"I had no idea what he'd become, how finding the spring would affect his mind. We've been married over a hundred years, you know? Once, he was a good man. *This* is how he loves me now: he damns my body, though I've damned my soul." Now she's rambling, in the way old people do. They'll tell you their life story when you haven't asked for it.

Emilce Voss pauses. Narrows her eyes, focusing on me. "So you're one of the Tètai girls. Here to murder us, I assume?" Blinking, she shakes her head, just barely. "No, you're not. My husband and I would both be dead by now if you were. You're not here for me. Who are you, then?"

For a moment, I consider the truth. Saying my name. I want to tell her the many ways her husband made my life hell. From contracting me to be a mole in my own city to stealing the serum to kidnapping and torturing my sister. All of it. I want her to know.

Before I can say a word, her face goes bloodless.

"You're her. . . . You're Renata," she whispers. Her old eyes grow wide, watering a little. "From the Wanted notices—you worked for my husband. He told me about you. He said you'd found the spring. Your friend, the girl—he took her, I know. You are Renata, yes?" Emilce reaches for my hand, gentle at first. Nodding, I stiffen, and she feels it. She grips my fingers anyway. She doesn't let go. She only clings harder. She holds on to me like she's falling. Like I'm falling too. I swallow, confused. I want to pull away.

"My husband has hurt you and your friend in unimaginable ways," she acknowledges, wiping her eyes. She loosens her grip. "I tried to stop it, but it seems fate cannot be avoided."

Fate had nothing to do with it.

"So, child. Is it revenge you're after? Or . . . perhaps you're bigger than that. You're saving the world from a greater evil?"

This woman is good. Too good.

"Both."

Emilce sighs. It sounds like giving up. "Good." She points feebly toward the library behind her. "Over there is a book with no title. Bring it."

I cross the room toward the bookcases, confused. Still, I scan the shelves like she's asked. Never before have I seen so many books. Dozens of sizes and shapes and colors. A few are so ancient, their leather bindings have chunked off into pieces on the shelves.

Bottom row, smack in the middle—I find the book with no title.

It's black. I pull it from the shelf and see immediately it's not actually a book. It's made of wood. Finely carved too. With a shiver, I remember the aboretum. The governor whittled a miniature Trojan horse for me to give to the Tètai. It was a message. A threat. And, as it turned out . . . a trick.

The book is a box, I realize. *And Voss made it.* On the black-painted "cover," carved in script, I read two words—*Bellum Pestilentia*—and my gut twists. The Trojan horse . . . it had similar writing: *Bellum Exterminii*, "War by extermination" in Latin. That's what Callum had said. Tracing the carved letters, I translate easily this time, no help needed.

Bellum: War

Pestilentia: Pestilence. Disease.

War by disease . . .

"Bring it to me."

Unable to breathe, I walk the box back and place it in Emilce's lap. She tugs at something under her collar. A gold chain necklace falls over her shoulder, a melting halo. A key dangles from its end.

"Open it."

I rotate the box and search for a lock. Between its hinges, I feel a sliver of empty space just wide enough for a key.

Reaching for her necklace, I fit the key into the keyhole—the box unlocks.

"Murder isn't the only way to destroy life," she whispers.

Then she lifts the latch.

29

S ipu plays with her cuffcomm until neon-green rect-angles and squares light against the glass windshield. "Here is the governor's mansion," she tells us, pointing to a rectangle facing west. She moves her finger to a square below it. "And here, the FATE Research Center."

I trace over a short green line between both buildings. "And this connects the two? How far is it?"

"The causeway is only a mile," she says. "Not a long walk from the lot."

Ter reaches for a different square smack in the middle of the two but farther into the strait. "And what's this building?"

A grin tugs at one corner of Sipu's mouth. "A secret labora-tory needs a secret docking lot, correct?"

Ter shakes his head in a *duh* sort of way, and laughs.

"Makes perfect sense," he admits. "A hundred mobiles outside doesn't exactly scream 'secret.'"

"The docking lot connects to the causeway, only accessible by fingerprint ID," she goes on. "We'll follow the causeway to the lab, also accessible by fingerprint ID."

Looking down at my own hands, I wonder, *How are we going to get that? I don't even have fingerprints to fake.*

Ter asks the obvious question, and immediately Sipu reaches under her seat.

Opening up a metal box, she says, "We'll use these." She lays something rubbery in both our palms. Under the reflected green light is a clear thimble made of gooey, jelly-like plastic.

I fit it over the stub of one knuckle and ask, "This is going to give us fingerprints?"

Ter ogles it, laughing. He already knows what it is.

"They're called Print Mimics. We bought them for my sister and her husband to use on a recon assignment, extras for the rest of us. The assignment bombed, though." Sipu pauses here, stiffening. Her voice drops like she's holding something back, and her face is unreadable. "We haven't used them since."

"And then what?" Ter asks. "How do we get the water into the quarantine area?"

Flipping off the projection, Sipu, in total darkness, says, "That I don't know." The mobile rocks like a baby's cradle in the deep tide.

"You don't have a map of inside the lab?"

"I have many things, Terrence. I have DI uniforms, lab

183

coats, and yes, a map of the lab. What I don't have, however, is an invisibility shield," she says, turning to face us. "How we plan on carrying a sack of green water around unnoticed, that's up to us."

"I have an idea!" I say, bouncing in my seat. "In Quarantine, there were these metal barrels filled with water that we drank from. Every day, they were replaced. If we can find where they keep them, we could swap out their water for ours, right?"

Nodding, Ter leans forward. He looks at me. "That could work," he says, and he taps my knee. "That could work."

"It's perfect!" I insist. "And we were given these plastic cups to use. They were tiny. If we made sure to tell everyone to drink half a cup, it'd be about the same dosage that Callum gave me."

"This is good," Sipu says. "I like it. How many people were there? Do we have enough water?"

"I don't know how many people, honestly. . . . A ton? The room was as big as Nale's roof, Ter, and the mattresses were pushed together with no room between. There were people everywhere."

"Whoa, that's, like, hundreds. Max, we're talking five."

I begin to do the math in my head—since Ren was never so good at it, I actually kept track of our money, until I got too sick. "The tube Callum gave me was about two ounces. So, that times five hundred is . . ." I pause, figuring it out. "A thousand ounces. Maybe seven gallons? About one bag. We won't even need the second," I say, patting it gently.

"We'll have to figure out where they store the barrels. The

lab's rainwater-collection system wasn't built to accommodate that many, so they must be bringing in outside water," Sipu says.

Ter snaps his fingers. "Then shipments would come into the lot, right?"

"You're right. And they wouldn't keep barrels of fresh in the lab—it would be too tempting for the employees. I bet there's a supply closet accessible through the lot as well, where they hide the used barrels needing to be refilled."

We all inhale and look at one another wide-eyed—the plan that's taking shape might actually work.

Sipu calls up another projection—this one of white square outlines within other square outlines. "Here's a map of the lab."

I'm able to show Ter and Sipu the quarantine room even though it's not labeled, just from memory, by tracing my escape with Ren backward. Then, peering at the schematics, we memorize our route—the ID access point leads into the main hallway. That connects to another hallway, and the only way into Quarantine is by first passing through an entry station.

"We can't all bring them the barrels," I realize, sinking into my seat. "Only one orderly came to change them out. Never three." So badly do I want to be the one to give them the water. I want to watch their faces as they begin to feel better. I can't, though. It's not even a bad idea—it's just plain silly.

"I'll do it," Ter offers. "It's a manual-labor job. Those usually go to brawny men like myself anyway." He makes a muscle for me.

Eye roll. I push him playfully. *I'm flirting,* I realize. *And I think I'm doing a good job.* I smile to myself in the dark. Then, a second later—

Wait. . . . *Did he start it?*

"Good. Aven and I will hide here," Sipu says, pointing to an inventory room. "I think we have a plan, you two." She taps the steering wheel, excited. "We'll enter the lot, take prints. Then, we locate the supply closet and swap waters. Make it through the first and second access points. And, while you bring the barrel to Quarantine, Aven and I will be waiting in the inventory closet. Anything missing? Are we ready?"

"Ready," Ter says.

I gulp. My throat is dry, but my palms are clammy. *Am I ready?* My fear could take over and ruin everything.

And then, something hits me: Maybe there's no such thing as "ready." Maybe you just do it—or you don't.

"I'm ready," I answer. The truth doesn't even matter.

30

REN
5:55 P.M., FRIDAY

Inside the box is an empty glass vial. The white label stuck to it reads *HBNC*.

I'm shaking—*this can't be true*—but it's all coming together, and it don't matter that every bone in my body, every hair, muscle, sinew, and pore resists it. *Bellum Pestilentia— War by disease. Pestilence . . .*

Blight.

Light pixels throw themselves onto the air. They form a holo of the governor himself, cropped from the shoulders up. In the image, he's holding the very vial that's sitting in this box. He looks directly at me, and he speaks.

"This is a message for the Tètai:

"Hyper Basilic Neoplasma Contagion—that is what I've named this virus, and it's taken me years to develop. Do not for a moment doubt my intentions. This is a deadly biological agent. Hear this: If you will not provide me with the spring's location, I will release this virus, and then I will wait. As long as it takes for you to provide me with the cure, I will wait. The dead will be on your hands. It is within your power to stop this from happening.

"You know what I want."

The holo repeats on a loop and Emilce drops the lid closed.

I turn nuclear. My insides go radioactive. I'm like the power plant upriver that infected everything. *The virus. Voss created the virus.* I can't breathe, I can't think, I can't swallow. *I can't . . . I can't . . . I can't—*

"Why do you have this?" I ask, doubled over next to Emilce's cot, about to be sick. "Your husband sent it to the Tètai. How did you get it?"

"It was sent back, by one of them. A girl . . . Kita something," she says nonchalantly. "Their way of spitting in his face, maybe."

Now I'm really reeling. *Kitaneh knew.* She knew Voss would release the Blight, and she did nothing to stop him. *Does Derek know? Do Lucas and Sipu know?* Did everyone know, then sit back and watch as it all happened?

Emilce lowers the lid with one hand. "Take the box. Use it for your vengeance or your vigilante justice, I don't care which. Just use it."

I'll use it. The beast made of teeth bares its jaws. I'd forgotten it was still inside me, but here it is. Ready. Waiting. I take the box from her hands.

At the last moment, she pulls away.

"On one condition." Emilce looks at the IV, watches as it drips the serum and a minuscule dose of everlasting life into her veins.

"You want me to kill you." It's not a question. I already know that's what she wants.

Emilce nods. "Guilt," she begins slowly, "is uniquely powerful. Some, it motivates into action. Others, like myself—steadfast inaction. By the time that girl had sent back the box, the virus was out. It was too late . . . if you believe in too late, and I did. Fear helped. How do you destroy the man you love and continue on, both of you alive?" She stops there and looks away. "I'd like to be dead when he finds out."

I inhale, my palms wrung together in worry or in prayer, I'm not sure which.

I examine what's left of her body like a poor surgeon, unsure if I'm fit for the job. *This is also murder*, I realize, no longer breathing. But if I would kill the governor for vengeance, then I should have no qualms killing for mercy. She wants death. I should want it for her.

"All right," I whisper.

I reach for her far arm. There, the tube's been taped and tucked under a loose flap of skin. "What's going to happen to you?" I ask, touching the inside of her elbow.

"I've never done this before. I couldn't say."

She's made me laugh, this woman. I inhale, trying to keep my fingers still for her sake. Don't want to cause her any pain . . . beyond what's expected, that is. I pull, and the wire slips out. Around the hole, her flesh sags. A thin spot of dark blood pools against her skin.

"Perfect symmetry, isn't it?" she says, and I pause, curious. "I was the first to do nothing, and now I am the last." Then, her breathing thins.

I watch as her eyes glaze over. A choke bubbles up from my throat. I don't let her go. "I'll stay," I offer, because no one should have to die alone. Not even a monster's love.

"Special child," she whispers in a daze. "Someday . . . forgive us." Then, like burning driftwood that spits out sparks before it dies, I feel her reaching for me. Her arms pry at mine, gripping my shoulders and elbows. Begging, she croaks, "Find Miss Nale—she knows . . ." but the sentence collapses in her mouth.

Miss Nale knows what?

Emilce's body caves into the cot. Deep lines begin to form across her face, hard crags in the skin. Sunspots bloom on her cheeks. Her skin loosens. Her chest sputters weakly up and down. *She's still breathing.* "What does she know?" I ask, patting her hand gently. Emilce doesn't answer.

Her chest rises. It falls.

It doesn't rise again.

31

AVEN
6:20 P.M., FRIDAY

Sipu's Omni slows—*we're here.*

The docking lot takes shape in the dark water, an outline of a massive concrete box. Behind it, a glass tube—the causeway that connects Voss's mansion to FATE—runs north-south along the coast. Red fluorescent squares of light glow inside from the flooring.

We hover in front of a garage door for a moment when, to the right, a red eye glints on. A beam fans up and down the Omni, flooding the cockpit with blood-colored light. "What's it doing?" I ask.

A very excited Ter answers first. "It's checking the mobile's bar code."

For a split second, I'm worried.

"You didn't just paint this thing, right?" Ter asks Sipu,

joking in a serious kind of way.

The red light clicks off, answering for her, as she says, "Oh, it's real." She pats the dash like a proud parent. "It's from one of our early run-ins with the DI. The driver didn't make it, but we salvaged the wreck. And Lucas did a little hacking, to give it a different bar code." Sipu's jaw tightens as she says his name.

The garage door slides open sideways. She steers the mobile into an airlock as Ter examines every one of the Omni's nooks and crannies, like it's suddenly a brand-new mobile. Water drains away, leaving just enough to keep us afloat, and we enter the lot.

Behind us, the airlock closes.

For docking, a concrete plus sign divides the lot in four. Walking paths wrap the walls, leading to the causeway's entrance—the first ID checkpoint. The whole left is filled with mobiles of shapes and sizes I've never seen before— that side must be reserved for lab employees. To our right, one corner is filled with delivery truck boats. The other, closest to the checkpoint: DI Omnis. A pack of officers stand around, taking up space on the walking path.

"That's not good," Ter says, also seeing them.

Sipu steers us past the delivery lot. It's filled with white boxes kept afloat by a necklace of inflated black rubber balloons.

"I think that's it," Ter says, pointing to a door on our right, painted the same concrete gray as everything else. "It'd make sense to keep it near the delivery boats, and I don't see any other closets."

Sipu slows the Omni. "I agree. Looks like it could be it." Instead of continuing on toward the DI reserved lot, she swings right, bringing us between two white truck boats. "Ter, Aven, I'm dropping you off here," she says, handing us a pair of scrubs and a DI uniform each. "Scrubs first, uniforms over them. You two fill the barrel, and I'll meet you in the lot up ahead. Seeing how many officers are here, I think it's best if I play escort. Also, make sure no one looks too closely at the ID cards on your uniforms." She pauses, then holds out her hand. "Give me your Print Mimics—there are too many officers; you'll look suspicious. I'll pull prints for all of us."

I hand her mine, Ter hands her his, and then she throws on her own DI uniform.

Squirming into the back, I glance over my shoulder. Only when I'm sure no one's watching do I layer up. I emerge, fabric chafing fabric, like a blue starchy butterfly . . . except if butterflies turned into caterpillars and not the other way around. "Girls are hardly ever DI," I say to her, worried, eyeing my blue shirt and pants. "I don't think I've seen one in my life."

"There are some women at the base, in the offices, mainly. But . . . you're not wrong. We'll have to be fast," Sipu says casually, opening the moonroof.

Ter climbs out first. Hugging the plastic sack, I'm next, looking so ridiculous in this DI uniform—I'm *fourteen.*

Sipu reverses out of the delivery lot.

With his head lowered, Ter tells me quietly, "Don't look. There's a camera by the ID check. Keep your back to it."

I freeze awkwardly. With no fingernails, I bite into my thumb knuckle instead. Ter nudges my elbow toward the gray door.

I stop suddenly on the walkway. *I'm cold*, I realize. *I'm in three layers and I'm shaking.* Yellow bulbs dangle from the ceiling. They're attached to loose wires, just like—

I'm back in Quarantine.

Every point of light becomes a pinprick. At the back of my mind, a steel blade traces a line down my neck. It's like I'm looking through the eye of a needle—my fear's made everything small. I can't feel my heart . . . my lungs don't work. *Why did I come back here?*

"What's wrong?" I hear Ter ask, but he sounds so far away. He's shaking me, but I'm someplace else. Somewhere he can't get to.

You came to bring them a cure, I remind myself. *You came to get them out!*

Since the blade is steel, I know what I have to do.

I have to turn myself into steel too. Maybe, sometimes, it's okay to fight fire with fire—*Ren isn't here to do it for you.* I pretend I'm the knife. Ignoring the cold, I cut the fear with myself. I cut it in halves, infinitely.

I make it too small for microscopes.

When I open my eyes again . . . the shivering has calmed. Over us, the bulbs are just electricity burning up. I breathe, in and out, to remind myself that I can. *Whoever said make-believe didn't work?*

"I'm fine," I tell Ter in a whisper I can barely hear myself. "It's over. I'm okay."

Ter eyes me, wary as he tries the handle to the storage room. It doesn't budge. "Gimme some cover," he says, and pulls off the fake ID card tagged to his front pocket. I move between him and the officers, and the camera.

Even though I'm faced away, I can still feel them standing behind me. I can feel the ID check, and the security cameras. My body is a living, breathing target. I might have cut my fear into pieces, but there are things bigger than myself—now, I'm afraid for *us*. What we're trying to do.

In the corner of my eye, the men in blue take final swigs from their canteen. "Break's over," one says, before heading to the ID check. I hold my breath until they're gone, but the feeling of eyes on my back doesn't leave with them.

Ter continues wiggling the card between the door and the lock, jamming it up and down, until—

Click.

It unlocks. When he looks back at me, he's wearing a wide smile. I can't force myself to smile back, though. *If someone were to recognize me . . .*

I turn the handle first and push past him into the dark storage room.

I'd be the reason we get caught. I'd be why we failed.

I shouldn't be here.

Just as Sipu's maps predicted, inside the room we find steel barrels upon more steel barrels. They're stacked as high as the ceiling. I watch, unmoving, as Ter brings one down. *I shouldn't be here*, I think again. He pops off the lid. Without saying a word, we pour the water. The bag jiggles in our hands until it's totally empty.

It's anxious too. It's ready to finally do what it was put on this planet for.

My heart sinks. *The water needs to make it to Quarantine.* That's the most important thing. Not me, and not the promise I don't know how to keep.

Ter drags the half-full barrel onto a dolly. "Scrub time," he reminds me, and I touch his arm.

"I think . . ." My eyes prickle with saltwater. "I think I shouldn't go. The security cameras, the officers—"

"Are you serious?" Ter cuts me off. "You can't be afraid. We couldn't have come up with a plan if it hadn't been for you. . . . I'm not leaving you behind. No."

He doesn't get it.

Shaking my head, I say, "That's not even it, Ter. What if I'm recognized? What if we get caught and no one gets the water, all because I had to come along? It's more important that you and Sipu make it to Quarantine. I'm too big a risk."

Saying those words . . . my chest aches knowing they're true.

One thing. Here I am, healthy for the first time in years, and I can't do this one thing.

32

REN
6:15 P.M., FRIDAY

I close my eyes to Emilce's lifeless body, fighting off a lump in my throat. *Voss has hurt so many people. When does it end?*

Still holding the box, I realize, it ends now.

I walk across the room and prepare myself for what I've gotta do. I need to make it to the radio tower. Then, find some way out of here before the news spreads. And damn, this news will spread . . . *fast*. As I reach for the doorknob, my wrist buzzes. I read the comm—it's from Derek.

> I'm through the causeway. Come to the security room. Basement level, last door on your right. Will need you to distract the guard.

My feelings balance like a seesaw on a rooftop playground. I'm tight with unknowing, unable to reach a verdict about whether I should hate him. After what Emilce just told me— if I find out he knew what Voss was planning, it'd be hard not to.

And yet, in the back of my head, a tiny hope has survived the blow: *Kitaneh might not have said anything.* There's a chance. I'll show him the box, and the instant that he sees it, I'll know. His eyes will tell me everything.

I slip the wooden book into my apron pocket.

Rushing out into the hallway, I head for the stairwell reserved for the mansion's peons. I take it down one flight, then two more before spilling out into the basement. There, I fold my hands in front of me, trying to look the part. I do it how I imagine swanky ladies serving *even swankier* ladies might, and casually swing right down the corridor.

This level is most definitely out of bounds. There's no carpeting down here, no fancy-man furniture. Just dull concrete and enough light to see your feet by. I walk past a dozen locked doors. They look like they're keeping secrets.

At the last one—right where Derek told me to stop—I stand on tiptoe and peer through a small glass window.

I see a guard. He's leaning so far back in his chair, it's strained to the max. Flat glass screens surround him on all four walls: seven for the island itself, about five inside the mansion . . . I squint—

Main entrance. Ballroom. Some art gallery room. A cigar room and a sitting room.

Thank god, I confirm, exhaling. *Public spaces only.* Don't need footage of me assisting with his wife's death floating around. Just one more thing he'll come after me for.

Three screens show different angles of a tubed hallway, definitely the causeway. Two more for an area I don't recognize—some kind of docking lot.

And there in the corner, there's a circular door. If this is the right room, that must be the way in and out of the causeway. To its right, I notice some kind of ID code system, but from here, I can't tell how it works. I imagine Derek's got something planned, though.

Quickly, I type:

About to provide a distraction. Get ready.

I can think of only one way to distract the guard: *Emilce Voss.*

"Help!" I yell through the window, pounding on the door with both palms until they sting.

The guard nearly drops onto the floor, he's so surprised. He bounds out of his chair and runs to me. "What's wrong, miss? What's the matter?"

Kinda love that he just called me "miss." This uniform is indeed swanky. I put on my best fancy-maid-lady voice and cry, "I was clearing glasses in the ballroom and I could have sworn I heard a woman crying upstairs! She sounded like she was in pain. . . . You have to help her!"

I guess a story about Emilce Voss dying ain't so far-fetched, 'cause the guard appears to buy it. He lifts his comm to his mouth: "Security to personnel: We've got a potential problem on the first floor. Anyone up there to check it out?"

Static fills the room while he waits for an answer.

Not good. Not good at all. I need to get this guy out. It's not a distraction if he doesn't leave the damn room—

"Sir," I begin, sounding (ever so slightly) appalled. "Someone could be in pain, or worse, *dying.* Do you really think this can wait? What if it's Governor Voss's wife? She's up there, isn't she? He'd be devastated . . . especially if there were something that could have been done about it!"

The guard's face drops, his chubby cheeks drawing low into jowls. He makes for the door. I open it for him and follow through the corridor, all the way to the first floor. At the top of the stairwell, I say, "I hope everything's all right!" and let him run the rest of the way on his own.

I race back to the security office to find Derek inside, sporting a white lab coat and a simple disposable mask. He pulls a clear rubber-glove thing from his finger, and the door closes behind him.

"How'd you get through?" I ask, hugging him so hard I'd probably crack a rib—if he weren't immortal and all.

My eyes struggle to avoid the triangle of his chest that's wisely decided to free itself from his button-down shirt. He don't look half bad in a lab coat neither. He rocks it, in a hot doctor sort of way. I push the thought aside, remembering the box.

Derek waves the clear finger glove as we leave the security room behind. "Handy Print Mimic. I still needed the distraction, though, so thank you for that; the only people entering the mansion at this point are on the guest list."

We walk through the corridor, headed for the stairs. "And the help," I say, remembering my kitchen run-in. "Kitaneh's here to kill Voss."

Derek's face darkens. "Well, maybe this time she'll be successful."

Doubtful.

By now, the weight of my conversation with Emilce has started to feel like a boulder inside my chest. *Did Kitaneh tell him?* I have to find out. Taking the wooden book from my apron, I lift it up for him to see. I hold it like it's something unholy but also precious.

It is *precious*—it's the thing that will bring Governor Voss down.

Derek's copper eyebrows scrunch together, his whole face quizzical as he cocks his head. In that instant, I have my answer. I throw my arms around him, breathless and smiling. I rock him back and forth. "You didn't know," I whisper. "You didn't know."

He don't understand what I'm so damn happy about. Now, I have to be the bearer of the news.

Pulling myself away, I step up a few stairs so we're eye level. "Derek, you need to see this," I say, and pass him the box. He reads the carved words. Puzzle pieces of understanding begin to fit together. He lifts the latch.

This is a message for the Tètai. . . .

The audio plays on.

When he sees the vial's label, he lets the lid drop. The message is choked off, silent.

"Voss . . . he made it. So that we would give him the cure,"

201

Derek breathes in a dead, dry voice. "And Kitaneh knew."

He says it like it's the nail in the coffin between him and the Tètai.

Passing the book back, he asks, "What were you planning on doing with the information?"

I point up to the roof. "Radio tower?"

"We could piggyback on whatever channel they're using to broadcast the gala. Everyone in the UMI who's watching a holo will know."

"Everyone who gets news updates to their comms too," I add.

Derek holds out his hand for me to take. "Let's do it."

Palms clasped, we race to the fourth floor, where we can't go any higher. Swinging right with Derek flying at my heels, we see it—dead center of the corridor, a winding black staircase to the radio tower.

I run for it, driven by critical weight—every step brings me and Aven closer to a new, different life. One where we can wander round hunting useless copper pieces for luck, or anything else we damn please.

A life without waiting for Voss to catch up.

33

AVEN
6:31 P.M., FRIDAY

Ter knows I'm right, and he hates it as much as I do. Still, he mulls the dilemma over, exhaling and rubbing his scalp.

With a grin, he pops off the barrel's steel lid.

"Take off your shoes."

I don't move. *Could this work?*

"Get. In. The. Barrel," he says, sterner this time.

Without hesitation, I shove off my loafers and roll up my scrubs. Ter lifts me into the barrel, and I hug him so tight our cheeks stick together. *"Thankyouthankyouthankyou,"* I whisper, knee-deep in water as Ter pops the lid on over my head.

I'm sealed away in darkness.

To wheel the dolly, he has to tilt the barrel—I fall backward onto its side. If I turn around, I can lean with gravity against the steel and not end up swimming. I'm wheeled along the walking path, until I feel us slow, and then stop.

Outside, I hear Sipu's voice. "Where is she?" she whispers, and Ter explains.

"She was right," she answers. "It's better this way—the lab might be light-staffed, but the causeway is definitely on high alert after their escape. We've got guards at both entrances now to deal with. Here's your Mimic."

I'm wheeled to the checkpoint, where I come to a complete stop—this must be it. *Please work*, I pray, crossing my fingers.

And—they actually cross . . . *I can feel it!* I press the padded end of one against the other. No fingernails yet, but definitely another knuckle and at least a centimeter more of skin and bone. I whisper a silent "Thank you" to the air. I can feel the barrel's steel sides against my actual, real-live fingers, and it's amazing.

"ERROR," a robotic lady's voice says.

It isn't working?

"What's going on?" Ter asks.

"ERROR. ERROR."

"Brack," Sipu curses. "The Print Mimic has a ninety-nine percent unlock rate."

"ERROR. ERROR. ERROR." The robotic voice is starting to sound mad. I bite my lip, unable to do anything but listen. *Work, work, work*, I pray from inside the barrel.

"Try Aven's," I hear Ter whisper. "Quick, before an alarm goes."

A moment later, in a much calmer mechanical voice—
"ENTER."

Relief washes over me, though I'm still shivering.

When a second *"ENTER"* follows the first, I want to jump, but I know we've only made it past the first checkpoint.

The barrel's moving again, wheeled left into the causeway. "Names?" I hear a guard ask in a gruff voice.

Sipu answers for the both of them, with names that are *not* their real ones. I bet they're real, though. If you're actually trying to assassinate the governor, you do the research to get past his security.

"You know, shift change ended," the guard says, and taps the barrel. "You're late. You better get a move on."

"Yes, sir," I hear Ter answer. "There was a delivery issue, and the guy called the DI to resolve it. Officer Lane here was kind enough to escort me so I don't get any flack for it."

"I heard nothing about a problem with any deliveries."

"Then we're doing our job right," Sipu answers, and she snaps her fingers.

I don't hear any more conversation. *One checkpoint down*, I think as the barrel tilts backward. From the map, I know the causeway is about a mile long, end to end. But, since we're in the middle, that'd make it only a half a mile . . . about a seven-minute walk.

Even though Ren doesn't believe in luck, I still cross *everything*: my fingers, my eyes, my toes . . . every last one of my nose hairs. I don't cross my legs, because I don't want to fall over and give us away. But everything else?

Crossed.

Finally settled in for the haul, I close my eyes (still crossed), and wait.

About fifteen minutes later—"Out you go," Ter says, popping open the lid.

He places his hands under my armpits, which makes me squirm. I was clammy the whole ride, wishing I had fingernails just so I'd have something to bite off—I don't want him touching *there*.

The next time, both Print Mimics worked perfectly, and Sipu repeated the same story to the second guard. But we did have one real scare—a nurse yelled at Ter for being so late to the shift change. He had to start running, or it'd look like he was being lazy.

I got bucked around in the barrel like a ship tossed at sea during a storm.

When Ter lifts me, I flush and squeeze my arms tight so he doesn't have to feel my armpits. If he does, he doesn't say anything. He sets me down in the inventory closet, a puddle of water at my feet. "All right. This is it," he says, making double fists like he's about to enter a fighting ring. "Anything I need to know?"

He's looking at me.

"Don't forget, tell them *half a cup only*. We want everyone to get some. Also, warn them that it'll make them feel stronger almost immediately. That's normal. If they're suspicious or anything, you should tell them it's from me. Tell them, 'Aven's trying to keep her promise.' Okay?"

"You got it," he answers, wrapping his arms around me.

I squeeze him tight. "I wish I could go with you. . . ." I breathe into his chest. "I'd like to see their faces."

Ter pulls away, his hands on both my arms. "You can! I'll turn on my comm's vid. You'll both be able to watch from here." He pushes a button on his wrist and a tiny red light turns on. My comm lights up too, showing it's receiving the image. "Ladies," he says, opening the door. "I'll be right back."

"Good skill!" I whisper back breathlessly, hoping he's not wrong.

34

"We can't just go in," Derek says, peering up the winding stairwell.

I follow his gaze to a glass-bottomed window above us. Beyond, a neon-red sign affixed to the ceiling of the tower reads: *BROADCASTING.*

"We need to clear the room," he says, leaning against the rail.

"How? I'm not up for a brawl right now, if that's what you're thinking. I just want people to know the truth."

The truth . . . "I'll show it to them, Derek," I say, pulling the box from my apron. "They're newspeople, after all. They'll eat it up."

Provided they don't mind losing their jobs if this backfires horribly.

"It will only raise more questions," he counters. "Ones we might not want to answer."

"True. But broadcasting the holo will do that anyway."

Our eyes meet. Derek takes the first step up the twisted staircase.

At the top, he pushes the glass door.

The room is tiny, one wall glowing with red and blue buttons and another with glass screens lined up like ducks. One shows the guests making their way in through the entrance, all happening in real time. That must be on the main channel. The other screen replays the press release. The camera is on his face like a zit. And age is catching up with him. He looks older. Every day, older.

A half dozen people turn to stare. One woman wearing a fuzzy pink cardigan looks disgusted when she sees me, but *I'm* not the one in the fuzzy pink cardigan, so the joke's on her.

"You can't be here," she says, grimacing at my uniform.

"I'm going to show you all something," I say, ignoring her as I pull the book from my apron pocket. The newscasters eye me. Seeing Derek, they say nothing. I sense that a man in a lab coat is calming.

The message plays.

Their faces shift from suspicion to disbelief, belief, and last, to devastation.

"I'm checking if it's a fake—hand it over," a man wearing glasses and suspenders says. I hand him the box, and he fiddles around with its wooden connections. A silver disc pops out, which he slides into a black box.

We watch the glass monitor as the disc scans.

"It's not a fake," Derek insists, but our word against a computer is nothing.

"Who are these Tètai people?"

"Why was this spring so special?"

"How did you get this? Who are you?"

Derek and I fight off their questions like mosquitos on a hot night.

"None of that matters!" he finally yells over everybody. "Did you not hear the most important part of the message? The people need to know who we're cheering for tonight. A man who 'cured' the Blight? Or a man who *invented* it?"

Ding—the silver disc ejects.

We wait for the verdict.

"If it's a fake, it's a damn good one," the man in suspenders says, handing it to the woman in pink. "According to our software, the disc hasn't been tampered with."

She uncrosses her arms reluctantly and takes it from him. She looks like she might hate herself for doing this later. "News is news," she says, dropping the disc into a computer tower built into the wall.

A pixelated blue bar pops up, overlaid against the image of guests entering the party. They're laughing in their colorful ball gowns and black suits. The bar fills from left to right as the disc's contents transfer. . . .

Seventy-eight percent . . .

Ninety-two percent . . .

Ninety-nine percent . . .

Ding—the video is ready. Everything's been uploaded. Only one button left to push.

BROADCAST.

35

O nto the floor of the inventory closet, between two used laundry bins, I project the video from Ter's comm. He wheels the barrel right, down a blindingly bright hallway, then stops at an unmarked door. The entry station, according to Sipu's schematics.

To his right, an ID print check.

I hold my breath.

Ter quickly rolls the Mimic around on the scanner, pulling the print. I grab Sipu's hand, and we listen for the necessary double click.

The door opens.

He wheels the barrel into the entry station. Inside, a half dozen employees sit at their desks; they're all watching a holo in the corner. Only one person turns. Seeing nothing of interest in Ter, he watches the glass screen again.

"What's on the holo?" I ask, squinting.

"Live feed of the gala. We passed a few screens broadcasting it in the causeway. Bet these guys are pretty unhappy right now too, left to staff the place while everyone else is at the event."

Ter walks between the desks toward a door at the opposite end of the room: *QUARANTINE*. He's about to lay his Print Mimic on the ID scanner, but just short of it, he stops.

Why?

Another employee is saying something. I bring the comm between my and Sipu's ears. We listen, hugged together—

"Someone already did that, buddy." The man shakes his head, thumbing back at the door.

"I was told something different," Ter says quickly. "Right from the boss. Extra rations for the prisoners, tonight, courtesy of the governor himself."

"He's incredible," I say to Sipu, marveling at the recovery.

"I wasn't notified. Hold on."

"Go ahead, check the system. It's right there."

"Don't speak too soon." She taps the face projected between our feet.

He doesn't look like he buys it. Returning to his desk, he swipes a finger back and forth across a glass screen. He shakes his head. "I'll have to comm the head doctor to check. Sorry. Protocol."

"That's fine," we hear Ter answer. "But if he's at the gala, you think you'll be able to reach him? My ass is kind of on the line here."

The man types like the wind at his wristcomm. He looks up. "What's your name?"

"Elton Cavanaugh," Ter says, repeating the name Sipu gave him.

A few seconds of silence pass.

"Man, I'm a brand-new hire too," Ter complains. *He's really playing it up.* "I'm gonna end up losing my job over this, I just know it. All because someone forgot to send a memo." He pauses, again waiting for a response. "Look. It's just an extra ration of water, mister. Not even a full ration." He wiggles the barrel around so the man can hear it sloshing. "Just let me do my job? Please? I'm begging here."

The employee checks to see if anyone's watching, but no one is. Their eyes are on the holo. Finally, he gives a brief nod. "I better not get slammed for this, though. Then I can promise you'll definitely be out of a job." Reaching for the comm on his desk, he presses down and says, "Station to Observation Desk, we've got extra rations tonight. Orderly coming through. End."

"He's gonna make it," I whisper.

Ter lays the Print Mimic against the ID scanner. He rolls it around and presses down. The door clicks open.

"He's in!" I clap and shimmy against Sipu.

"It's not done yet," she says, and rests her palm on my shoulder. "Let's hold off on the celebrations until we're all safely back in the Omni."

She's right. *But still.*

As it turns out, Ter's not actually in Quarantine yet, anyway—he's in a sanitation room. Air vents hiss in the corners. The room fills up with gassy white clouds. When the fog settles, we see him reach for a yellow rubber suit hanging from a hook on the door.

Ter puts it on. We don't see that part—he's angled his cuff-comm so it faces away. I giggle, wondering if he's just being modest or if he's embarrassed. My cheeks are hot, and I'm glad we're in a dark room.

He opens the next door, *now* inside Quarantine.

I don't breathe. The loose wires, the yellow bulbs. Mattresses. I'm not even there, I'm just watching through the comm's holo, but I feel the bite of fear in my chest. I swallow.

I'm the knife, I tell myself. I can't undo the hurt Voss has caused me, but I can make it stop for others. *My own personal rebellion.*

In the observation room, someone's watching us right now. Ter lowers the barrel onto a long, foldable table. "Extra rations tonight!" he calls, yelling over a scratchy radio announcer's voice.

A line quickly forms, wrapping all the way around the room. Our first taker is a young girl. A small tumor grows from her neck.

"Extra rations," he says again, back to the observation room. "Care of your friend Aven."

The girl eyes him, unsure. She holds the cup to her lips letting it rest there. "Aven gave this to you?"

"Yeah, she did. She said she was trying to keep her promise."

As Ter fiddles with the barrel to buy himself more time, the girl slowly lights up. "Now, pour yourself half a cup *only*. It's not just water. You're getting something different tonight—something that will make you healthy. You'll feel strong afterward. That's normal," he whispers.

The girl smiles as though Ter's a genie who's just granted her a dozen wishes. I bite into my knuckles again, about to cry. The girl drains her cup and scurries off. As she moves down the line, she passes along Ter's message. In the background, the radio announcer gives a play-by-play of the gala going on only a mile away. It's a different world they live in.

Soon, people begin to catch on. It's like being on a rooftop, a hundred lightning rods all pointed toward a stormy sky. The room quiets—as much as five hundred people can. One by one, the prisoners approach the barrel and pour themselves half a cup.

I watch the way their faces change as the water courses through their body. Their glossy eyes seem clearer. An easy smile lifts the corners of their lips.

It's as if the entire universe, every planet and all the stars, the black nothing and time itself, came together to bring me right here to this very moment.

This has to be why Ren found it—why I was taken. To bring them *the water.*

I would have given up both my hands if I'd known this moment was a ripple at the end of the pond. I can't believe in meaninglessness—*not now*. This somehow made the pain worth it.

Ter turns away, leaving Quarantine behind.

He walks through the sanitation room and into the entry station. The man who just gave him a hard time nods as he passes.

Then Ter's back in the inventory closet, and right before our eyes, the door opens.

"It worked—it *actually* worked," he breathes, as shocked as we are.

Sipu pushes herself up from the floor. "And now," she says, "we get out. Fast. The observation staff might've already caught on." She hands me the Print Mimic. "You're going to need this at the next checkpoint, Aven. I'll pull mine off the next scanner. I doubt I'll be that one percent twice."

Taking the jelly thimble from her, we swing left out the door and into a hallway. We bolt down it, and at the far end, push through a second door leading to the main corridor: the one installed with bright bowl-shaped lights every five feet. Here, at the lab ID checkpoint, a holo screen hangs on the opposite wall, where a DI security guard has turned his chair to face it. Into his cuffcomm: "Special Lab Security to Base: What the hell is going on? Is this a joke? Out."

He pays no attention to us at all.

This is too easy, I think, and Sipu walks up to the scanner. *He's not even looking. . . .*

On the holo, the governor holds up a vial, speaking into the camera. His voice loses nothing through the audio—he only becomes more threatening. Given a hundred mouths on a hundred screens, he's larger than life.

Then the video loops from the beginning: *This is a message for the Tètai: Hyper Basilic Neoplasma Contagion—that is what I've named this virus. . . .*

We listen to the rest of the message, frozen.

Voss invented the virus?

The guard's wristcomm coughs static, then it clears. A voice crackles through. "Chief Dunn to all officers, Chief Dunn to all officers. About five minutes ago, information was released, potentially implicating Governor Voss in the creation of the HBNC virus. Until I know more, we can expect high-risk situations, civil unrest, riots—the whole nine. At this time, I'm asking that officers prioritize crowd control. That is all. Out."

The ground beneath our very feet shakes. . . .

I'm not imagining it.

A dull rumble grows from back the way we came. Next, we hear the crashing of glass from the hall, down by the observation room. With the glass shattered, the earthquake is no longer behind us, but in front of us. The door to the observation room swings open—

Prisoners pour out into the hall, floodwaters rising.

36

REN
7:17 P.M., FRIDAY

D erek touches my shoulder. "We have to go, Ren. It'll get ugly pretty fast. We're not safe." A moment later, we hear footsteps clamoring up the staircase.

"Window," he says, opening it for me.

I step onto the windowsill. Wind sucks into the radio tower, blowing up my servant dress. When I look down, there's no place to stop. The tower's roof ends right below our feet, then goes completely vertical. *Unless.* "Below the window, there's a drainpipe," I say. "It wraps around the tower, but over there, it's climbable. We could follow it down, then jump onto the mansion's flat roof?"

Derek gives me the thumbs-up, and I step backward out of the window. Holding on to the bottom sill, I walk along the drainpipe to cross the tower. Here, I monkey myself down the horizontal pipe until I can grab the vertical one. Derek's close behind. Gray, gritty shingles slide under the pipe, jettisoned over the edge.

Don't look down.

Being in a mobile flying off roofs is one thing. Dangling off a roof from both arms . . . different thing.

I'm glad I went first, I think, clutching the pipe with both hands. Derek would be getting quite the view right now. We slide together, and in the distance, a heli's props rattle the air.

The news is spreading.

The drain ends. It's only a two-foot drop from here. I hop onto the roof, and to my left I see a tall, arched window. I reach for it, thinking I can get it open—

A troop of officers passes in front. I duck to the side, hugged against Derek's warmth.

"Maybe we should just try to get off the island instead," he says, now standing next to me on the roof. He steps closer to the edge to survey the property. "Dammit."

I lean over the edge too, and spot a team of big guys in blue jackets. They stream out of a back exit I didn't even know existed. When I check the front entrance, I find more DI. Assuming there are other exits I don't know about and the DI are exiting out all of them, getting off the island ain't gonna happen.

"Not anymore," I answer. "The whole property is swarmed."

Derek's inhale is so loud, I can hear it over the wind humming through the drainpipe. "Ren, I'm out of options. I think we're in the safest spot we're going to find at present."

"So . . . we just wait?"

"Yep." He lowers himself onto the roof. "We just . . . wait."

I sink down too, hugging my knees. We watch the Blues comb the forest and the number of helis growing in the distance. We sit in silence a few moments before he gently pokes my shoulder. "You know, I'd be dead if it weren't for you," he tells me.

Derek gives me a second, and then it dawns on me—

"You mean the water?"

"That was smart thinking," he says, "leaving it in the toilet tank." Derek pauses, and I can feel him watching me. Up here, there's a soft wind. It tousles the leaves, but I feel nothing. Not with those eyes on me. "Thank you, Ren. For remembering." He sounds so plainly surprised.

East of us, the moon rises over the islet. It catches a fistful of his hair, turning it bright copper. "Well, I couldn't have you dying on me, Derek. Not *now*. You're one of the good guys," I tell him, with a goofy, playful grin on my face.

On a day like today, he's still makin' me smile. . . .

Derek laughs quietly, then looks at his shoes. "And here I always thought girls *liked* bad boys. All along, I've been doing it wrong." He glances at me, then away, then back again, suddenly a bashful little boy.

I shoulder-check him, 'cause apparently, I think roughhousing sends the same message as flirting.

"Oww," Derek says, rubbing his side, though we all know he's faking. "That wasn't very nice. I happen to like good girls, you know. Now that I'm a good guy, it only makes sense."

Getting up in his face, I say, "Then you, sir, are barking up the wrong tree," and I poke his abs this time—any excuse to go for the abs, really. "I never said I was a *good girl.*"

Then, like magic, he's wrapped his hand behind my neck. "Whatever you are," he answers, pulling me closer, "I like it." And then . . . he just holds me there like that, waiting. His breath is warm on my lips, and he's looking at me, at every bit of my face—*what is he waiting for?*

He's waiting for me.

Now I'm the one who does the magic. I bring my mouth to his, my body pressed close, and like two sides of the same coin, our lips meet. There's no fear this time, no hesitancy. He nips at my lower lip, and I take his upper one—it's as though we're made from the same mold.

They say the only way time can warp is by messing with speed and gravity. Well, here we are—it's a damn high roof, the world around us is spinning fast into entropy, and we are perfectly still. Time slows. It warps and bends with the push and graze of our lips, until it stops completely.

37

AVEN
7:20 P.M., FRIDAY

"Lab Security to Base," a quaking guard says into his cuff-comm. "Lab Security to Base. *The prisoners are out*, I repeat, *the prisoners are out.* I need backup immediately!" He pulls out his baton, knowing it's useless against these numbers. Still, he takes a fighting stance. "Get back!"

"You can't keep us here! Not now!" one man at the front cries, lights haloing his black hair. He has a bulldog's face and is the largest in the room by far. "We heard the radio-cast." His raised fist is bigger than my head.

Behind him, more prisoners flood the hall, a nonstop current. The strongest are first, men and women neither old nor young, but somewhere in the middle, where the sickness doesn't strike as hard. Their breathing is heavy. Tidal. No one wheezes, and there's not one tumor between them. They push toward us, fists swinging.

If the strongest are at the front, leading the charge, then the ones farther back are just waking up, snailing into motion—they didn't break the observation glass, they just walked through it. The water works right before our eyes: it shrinks their tumors, leaving flaps of stretched skin behind, then taking those too.

Some are holding each other and hugging, weeping into rags.

Some are angrier than that.

As the comm's clock ticks on, they grow stronger.

"We want to see the governor!" a woman yells, her voice singing with challenge. She steps forward—the overhead lights flash against her dark cheeks, and she looks sharp, like broken glass.

Somebody recognizes me—

"That's her," I hear a voice say. "That's the girl who said she'd come back for us." It's an accusation and a hope wrapped all in one.

Everyone's looking at me, expecting me to keep my promise. But . . . it wasn't supposed to happen like *this*: a mob out of the history lessons, crying for their king's head on a stick.

From a second stairwell past the observation room, at least two dozen men in blue fatigues and black boots tear through the corridor, more still behind them. "Back! Back into Quarantine!"

Officers run toward the flood, small black spheres in their hands, which they loose into the crowd. The things hiss, releasing puffs of chemical gas. We cover our eyes as the prisoners retreat from the smoke-filled hall.

No, I think, adrenaline lacing my blood like a drug. *They're not sick anymore.*

I cough out the gas, eyes stinging, and reach for the ID scanner. My Mimic hovers over it.

"Don't open that door!" the guard next to me barks. His baton swings in the air. "Remove your hand from the scanner and step away." My spine sends off sparks, each vertebrae itching with movement.

They deserve to see the governor. *We all do.* I feel around behind me for the scanner. *They can't go back.*

I lay my finger down, and then I press.

The door clicks twice, opening into the wide glass tunnel. Ter and Sipu grab for my scrubs through the smoke, and together we bolt. The causeway stretches on for a mile. An alarm sounds all around us, roaring like an animal in our ears. As we run, the floor panels light up red ahead of us.

At our heels, five hundred.

They cover their eyes and jog through chemical smoke, headed for the tunnel where the air's clearer. The first of them will hit the governor's in ten minutes. Less, possibly, with the water running through their veins. They dodge the fumes, then trample the checkpoint. Their gait is unbalanced as they pick up speed. But the longer the water has a chance to work, the faster they move—soon, the glass tube is packed with bodies. It groans under the weight of a thousand feet. Some are running. Others, still too weak from dehydration or not enough food, lag behind.

All just want to get away, get out.

On our right, we pass the door to the lot. We run between an underwater forest, dead, shrouded in dark green algae. We pass ghost cars and old, toothless buildings, seaweed swaying out their windows. In the distance is the door to the governor's mansion. . . .

It's thrown open, and a pack of Blues comes flying through, at least a dozen holding shooters—how Ren was netted.

But the Blues weren't aiming to kill her.

Us, however, they probably are. Ter and I freeze, but Sipu pulls us close to the glass, pressed there like it's the safest place to be.

Smart, I realize. She must think the guards won't fire into it and risk flooding the tunnel.

The DI hold, waiting for the stampeding five hundred. They're not worried about us anymore—there's a flood coming and they've got to hold it back. When the gap closes, they release the darts, cracking in the air, finding homes in shoulders and thighs and stomachs.

The woman with the broken-glass face is the first to fall, metal piercing her collarbone. I stop breathing.

Is this why I let them out? So they could die like this? I'm spinning in circles and everyone is falling. I see the little girl—the one Ter was talking to. She crumples to the ground three feet away.

Somewhere in there is Mrs. Bedrosian and Miss Nale. . . .

I close my eyes. Ter huddles over my body, protecting me like a shell. I hear someone crying.

I think it's me.

Then a hush fills the air, and I hear people murmuring to

one another. Through my knees I see the first woman who fell. In her hand she's holding a bloodied dart. She spits, and she throws the dart on the floor. Her shirt is painted red all the way to her waist. Winding her arm up like a toy, or a pitcher, she flexes her neck from side to side and keeps on walking. And she's not the only one—others pull darts from kneecaps and necks, blood fountaining onto the floor. They howl with the pain of it, whimpering on the ground, until it stops.

The water—it's closing their wounds.

No one understands, because there isn't time to understand. They look to one another, to the causeway's glass ceiling—they cry into the red, lit floor.

They understand only two things: they're *alive,* and they can *fight back.*

Standing, the prisoners aim their darts at the officers.

"Officer Hardy to Chief Dunn: The situation has not been contained. *We need more backup.* The darts aren't working; I repeat, the darts are ineffective!"

The dog-faced man with the black halo raises his fist to the air. "*We will* not *be contained,*" he growls. His voice is a spark.

"We will see the governor. You have no way to stop us."

"To the governor!" someone else shouts.

The DI faces flush with fear; they hold the shooters with a perfect army stance, but their barrels shake. They fire anyway, again and again. But everyone knows you can't poke holes in a dam. It only makes the water mad.

The gates are open. The prisoners cannot be stopped.

Tattered rags force themselves against blue uniforms—and the Blues don't stand a chance.

They trample the first DI troop, still firing off rounds that slow, but don't stop them. When they hit the ID checkpoint, someone drags a fallen officer to the scanner. They press his limp finger down, and the door opens.

"To the governor!" they repeat.

It's a battle cry.

38

REN
7:40 P.M., FRIDAY

Time and speed and gravity all catch up to us at once.
Inside the mansion, it's become *impossibly* loud.
When I check my comm to find it's only been about
twenty minutes, I'm floored. Derek and I separate, no longer
able to ignore Earth's pesky planetary rules. Looking through
the window, the coast seems clear, but the window's locked.
I reach under my dress for the knife still strapped to my
thigh and use it to whittle away the frame, creating a hole
around the metal bolt. Soon as it's big enough, I dig my finger in and I push the bar aside. The window pops open, and
Derek and I jump through.

Even from the servants' stairwell on the fourth floor we
can hear the people yelling. Shouts fill every one of the mansion's crevices, growing louder as we follow the stairs down.

At the first floor, Derek slows.

"Bring out the governor!"

"We want Voss!"

"Find him!"

This is *not* how I'd expected a hundred wealthy West Isle folks to uproar.

I knew they'd be upset, but in a righteous, moralistic sort of way. This is different. There's real anger out there, hot-blooded and unrestrained. The sound of people taking it personally, like *they've* been the ones getting sick because of Voss.

Pushing me up into the stairwell, Derek whispers, "Back, get back. Voss is right there."

Sure enough, Voss stands at the end of hall, the balcony behind him. He's surrounded by a group of officers, outside of the same room where I'd left Emilce dead in her cot. My stomach turns. He whispers something to Chief Dunn, and in the dim hallway lights, Voss's eyes are glistening and red.

He knows.

"Bring him out!" voices call from the ballroom. "Where are you, Voss?"

Will he do it? Will he face everyone?

He makes his way to the balcony. His footsteps are as slow and purposeful as a dead man walking the plank. There, his guards split up. Four cut off the stairwell that leads to the balcony, and the remaining two flank him, one on either side. Dunn's out of sight, way to the left.

Voss raises his hand to the crowd. "Quiet," I hear him say over the shouting. "Quiet, please."

The yelling subdues but not enough for him to speak—Dunn steps in. "Silence in the room!" he barks through a megaphone. That does the trick. The people quiet.

"First, I ask of you all a moment of silence for my beloved wife, Emilce. She passed away not thirty minutes ago. I understand your anger and confusion, but please . . . a moment for the dead. *All* of the dead." With that, he bows his head.

In the building's deeper recesses, I can still hear angry voices. But here in the ballroom, they're silent. It makes me sick, but I gotta give him credit for knowing how to capitalize on sympathy points.

After a minute, Voss raises his head. "By now you've seen the broadcast, wherein I appear to admit having created the Blight."

Appear *to admit? He's gonna deny it?*

"People!" he cries, pointing to the room where Emilce died. "My own wife is dead, a victim of the virus just as you are!"

The convenient lie rolls right off his tongue, but then I wonder—*who is he even speaking to?* Victims of the virus? Not too much of that here on the Isle.

So I can get a better look, I crouch past Derek. "Ren, don't," he warns, grabbing my arm and holding me back. Both my fists ball up. If I were a fly on this gaudy gold wallpaper, I'd see he's right. In some smart, objective corner of my mind, I know it's true. But I'm not a fly. I hear Voss lying, always lying, and I'm not human anymore.

"People!" the governor cries. "I am not responsible for the

death of my wife! I did not create this virus!"

Grinding my teeth, fists tight, I jerk myself free of Derek's grip. Our eyes meet. He blinks, confused. Shocked. I back away.

The blurring hallway calls my name.

I'm sucked underwater, where all sound dies except for my beast made of teeth. I thought I'd never have to see it again. I thought I could get rid of it by ruining him. It never went away, though.

He can't go on, it insists, gnashing for my lungs and for my heart, and then I'm not me anymore—I've been consumed from the inside. I'm running toward the balcony, and I don't know if Derek follows. I don't know anything beyond the shrieking need for justice and vengeance, and for the return of every moment where Aven and I suffered.

It's like I've been unplugged from my very self; the wires of my muscles won't connect to the wires in my brain. I feel my feet pounding through the corridor, and to my left, the leaves of a potted tree shivering at my ear. They're red. Star-shaped. Blood in my periphery. I feel my hand reaching for the blade still at my thigh. Then there is a hilt in my hand. I watch as the balcony nears. People see me now. They see the steel and its flashing promise.

I watch everyone watching me. They're in ragged, browned clothes, not Isle finery. Tucked beside the silk white drapes, I recognize a face. A girl, an old racing fan; she gave me fresh just because she liked me. Standing deeper in the crowd, the homeless guy who always hit me up for green to cover his Dagger addiction.

These are not *guests*, I realize. *They're the prisoners.*

I imagine a flash of moon-yellow hair, but that can't be—

And then . . .

Miss Nale?

"No!" she hollers, lunging for me from the bottom of the stairwell. Her graying hair loosens from the same bun she always wore. I freeze as she tries to push past the DI.

The ballroom falls silent.

"Don't! He's—"

Her face contorts like wet clay. "He's your—" She repeats it over and over, unable to finish.

He's your, he's your . . .

My ears hear nothing.

Then, after a dozen incomplete sentences, her mouth forms the final word.

39

en?

Watching, my vision blurs. I grip Ter's hand—an officer chases after her. She rushes for the hallway, and I lose sight of them. As I cover my mouth to keep from crying out, the prisoners raise their hands and cheer. They wouldn't have minded seeing the governor die then and there.

"They won't find her . . . there are too many people," Ter reassures, and I hope he's right. The cheering continues, and someone throws something into the balcony. It misses, landing in the crowd with a crash.

"He's lying," Sipu says, weary. Sinking against the wall, she pulls a hand through her hair.

"How do you know?" Ter asks.

"Think about it. What might he have to gain from creating a deadly disease?"

"The cure . . . ," I whisper, covering my mouth.

"Exactly. He'd sent it to Kitaneh as a threat, thinking she'd tell him where the spring was. She did not. She did not consult me, nor Derek, nor Lucas. I only found out later, when other things she'd said didn't add up." Sipu grimaces at the chaotic room.

Now I understand why she wanted to help . . . why it was so important that these prisoners be sick with the Blight. The Blight itself is what she feels most guilty about.

More people have taken to throwing things into the balcony: Silver forks sail between the banisters, landing at the governor's feet. He ducks as empty water flutes miss and shatter in the air like glass fireworks.

"Control them!" Governor Voss commands, fever-pitched over the crowd.

A foghorn sounds.

Above us, the glass chandelier shivers. A dart cracks as it's fired into the air, sailing for him. The whole room falls quiet, watching, as it lodges itself directly into his chest.

Voss, clutching his side, sways on the balcony. In that moment, his face ages a hundred years. The lines in his skin become deep, ancient caverns. His flesh sags even lower, as though his face were just a mask.

"Get him out of here!" Chief Dunn barks to the closest officer.

Like turning a volume dial up all at once, the room roars. Cheers ring out, people's fists lift into the air. Chief Dunn steps behind the governor, catching him as he sinks to the ground. Only half of his collared white shirt is still white. A thick red stain spreads from under the fabric, just over his rib cage. He's wheezing, gasping for air. A trickle of pinkish foam runs off one corner of his mouth.

I pull my eyes away, unable to look.

"Kitaneh," I hear Sipu breathe behind me. I follow her gaze to the back corner of the room. There, a black-haired girl in the servant uniform has dropped an empty shooter onto the ground. Smugly, she watches as Voss is wheeled off the balcony, coughing up red.

She senses us, and raises her head. Our eyes meet.

Voss might be dead, or dying, but nothing in her look says she's done with any of us.

40

REN
8:00 P.M., FRIDAY

I understand the word. I understand its shape as it leaves Miss Nale's mouth . . . and I don't. I cannot speak or think it. The word is a curse. It sinks like an underwater warhead in my mind. Soon it'll go off, even if I can't see it.

Both guards turn on the stairwell—

I have to hide.

Heart pounding, I pull my eyes from Miss Nale and retreat into the hallway. There, I find the blood tree. It's a weeping tent of dense red leaves, wide as three of me.

I slide behind it.

Spine pressed to the wall, I peer past branches and watch the guard. He holds his shooter in one hand, while I hold my breath. The long, thick barrel aims down the hallway. I imagine a dart being released into my gut, and the net packed behind it shocking my flesh.

Because I'm shaking, the plant does too.

The guard jerks the barrel toward the tree. I close my eyes. I force my mind clear. I bring myself back to a good day, the day Aven sat with me at lunch after I'd agreed to be her friend—the first offical day. She interrogated me about the race, then gave me her protein slop. Hot mystery "meat" meant to keep us healthy. She said I'd need it if I was gonna be a racer now.

Thinking of us like that calms me . . . the plant too.

From the opposite end of the hall, someone clobbers down the servants' stairs, making too much noise.

Derek—it has to be. He must have stayed there in the stairwell, waiting for me. Watching along with the rest of them.

The guard repositions his shooter and takes off at a run. I exhale, pressing my hands into my eyes. I hope he heads for the ballroom, where it'll be impossible to find him. *Thank you.*

In the background, the crowd's still jeering.

A foghorn blows—

He's your . . . I turn her words over and over in my mind, like a penny between a magician's white-gloved fingers. At the same time, I refuse it. The last word she said . . . I didn't need to hear it; I saw the shape of her mouth. The word pumps through my veins, and I wonder, if the guard had shot me, would I be bleeding black right now?

I duck out from behind the tree, hugging the wall, and I backtrack. Instinctively, I find myself stopping in front of Emilce's room—*I can't go back in there.* But my veins give me no choice. I open the door, then shut it quickly.

Inside, I wither. I slide all the way down the door, landing with my head gathered between my legs.

She's still here, I realize, glancing at the cot in the back of the room. Her body's been covered with a pale blue blanket. Someone should be coming to take her away soon. Or maybe not. . . . It's total chaos out there. Who's gonna try moving a dead woman through hundreds of rioting prisoners?

I stand up, wipe my eyes. I walk toward her body, steeling myself for what I might find. I circle it like a hawk afraid of its prey, realizing it's caught something else entirely. In one quick motion, I peel the blanket away.

I scrutinize her features the way an artist might do it. Their color, their shape—

Her hair's buzzed short, like mine. And for whatever reason, her deadness doesn't keep me from wanting to reach out and touch it. So I do. My fingers graze the grayed, flat kinks.

Different color, same texture.

Her nose is flattish while mine isn't, but her skin is a pale sort of dark, and covered with a smattering of freckles. I wonder how many she has. I tried counting mine once before. I made it to eighty-three, but only if I included the smallest, most barely visible ones under my eyes.

I see myself in her, and as soon as I do, I'm back in the ballroom, knife in hand, a crowd of hundreds at my ears. I'm watching the shape of Miss Nale's mouth as she yells a deaf word: *father.*

Next, I see the way Emilce looked at me when she said my name . . . how her eyes watered and how fiercely she gripped at me. I'd put it down to her being old and strange. *Find Miss Nale*, she'd begged. Now I know why.

My whole body convulses, seismic. I can't stop the damned shaking. *I killed . . . I killed the very woman who gave birth to me. Emilce is my mother. Was my mother.*

And Voss . . .

Voss is still my father.

My stomach heaves, and I stagger backward. I curl over myself, nearly fetal, tailbone dragging against the bookshelf. I gag, my body rejecting the truth straight to the core. I bury my head in a corner—I vomit. Over and over I try to push the contents of my body—*my very genes*—out from me. . . .

My eyes are wet, and then I'm sobbing, trying to claw apart my self from myself. I'm chewing at my nails until I can taste the familiar iron tang, and I know my hands are bloodied. *I need to be free*—I need to drain away the generations of bloodshed from my own blood.

I need to get him out.

41

AVEN
8:20 P.M., FRIDAY

Kitaneh sees Sipu. They lock eyes. The room parts to make space for their gaze. *Traitor*, Kitaneh mouths, before disappearing into the throngs. I exhale, while Sipu watches the empty space where Kitaneh just stood.

"You think she'll stick around?" Ter asks.

"She'll find a place to hide so she can assess the fallout. We don't know if Voss told anyone else about the spring. Chief Dunn, for example. Kitaneh doesn't like loose ends."

Turning, I spot a boy's familiar head of floppy brown hair. He's tall and lanky, but he's pretty cute in his fancy black suit. I squeeze Ter's arm. "Look!" I point toward the kitchen. "Callum!" I yell, but he's deaf to me. There's too much noise.

"I'm going to get him." I let go of Ter's arm, but he grabs me by the hand. Craning his neck to get a good view of the crowd, I can tell he doesn't like this idea. When our eyes meet, though, he sees he's not going to win this one.

"Fine . . . but be quick. This place is a madhouse. I don't want to lose you."

I navigate through everyone the way I imagine a dancer would—stepping forward as they step back, spinning on my heel as someone turns too quickly. When I finally reach Callum, he gives me a quick hug before we huddle into a corner.

"What on earth are you doing here?"

"Long story," I answer as Callum glances from his cuff-comm to the chaos, then to the balcony.

"It's Derek," he says. "He wants me to find Ren—second floor, room farthest from the servants' stairs. Says he distracted an officer and now the level's been blocked off, but he believes she's still up there."

"Where do we think the servants' stairwell is?"

Callum does a 360 and walks up to a girl in a black uniform hiding away from the fray. She's blond and ruddy-cheeked, fiddling with her comm. He asks her a question and she points over his shoulder, back toward the kitchen.

"Through there, left down the hall," Callum tells me when he returns. "And it is blocked off."

We follow her directions and sure enough, two DI officers stand in front of the far stairwell. "What now?" Callum asks, hands in his black suit jacket, trying to look casual.

Think like Ren, I tell myself.

"A distraction?" I offer weakly, when a thought comes to me: *Kitaneh just killed the governor. They'd probably like to find her, right?*

I whisper the idea into Callum's ear.

"What was she wearing?" he asks, and I tell him.

A split second later: "That's her!" Callum cries at the top of his lungs, pointing toward a random head in the crowded ballroom with hair dark enough to be Kitaneh's. "That's the one who killed the governor!"

Immediately, both DI stand at attention. "Where? Which?" they ask.

"Black hair, short, in a servant's uniform. Right there!" Callum continues to point, now moving his finger like an imaginary Kitaneh is on the run.

"Officer Morrisen to Chief Dunn: We've got a visual on the shooter. Send coverage to the rear stairwell, ASAP. Over," he says into his cuffcomm. The two men take off.

Two new officers approach to cover the post. Callum and I don't hesitate—we gallop up to the second floor. The hallway is empty, but the balcony is still covered in DI watching the ballroom. We keep low to the wall. At the last door on the left, I pause and turn the handle slowly, so the metal doesn't squeak.

"Ren?" I whisper as Callum touches the door closed behind us. "Are you here? It's me."

Off to the right, in the center of the room, the drapes open. Ren steps out, wiping her nose. She grips the glass of a small coffee table in front of her, like she can't stand without it. "Aven? You're not supposed to be here," she says, choking back tears.

She's crying. . . .

Not *just* crying. She looks like she wants to tear herself to

243

pieces. I rush over and wrap her up in my arms. She collapses into me—*I've never seen her like this before.* She presses her face into my shoulder, shaking. She stomps her foot and pulls away. She tries to tug her hair, but she doesn't have enough. She presses her hands against her ears like she's trying to shut something out. Something that's inside her.

She crosses her legs and sits on the floor. I can't see her anymore, hidden by the bulky wooden coffee table.

"What's wrong?" I ask, glancing at Callum. He's hanging back by the door, on guard duty.

"We're safe here," he says to me quietly. "For the time being, at least. No one saw us slip past."

"He's my father, Aven—*Voss.*"

What? I feel her hurt like it's my own—I'm stabbed from the inside. *How can* he *be her father?* "Are you sure?" I lower down beside her, and now we're both hidden behind the coffee table. "How do you know?" I ask.

But the look on her face . . . she just knows.

Ren glances past my shoulder, like she's about to tell me something. I turn around and see a cot covered by a blue blanket. Under it, I can make out the shape of a person, her black dress draped off the edge. "His wife," she says blankly. "My mother."

I rock Ren back and forth in my arms, wanting to say something to make it go away. That's not how pain works, though. "Renny . . . ," I start, not knowing how to say the thing I want to say. "You're my person. My favorite person. On this planet and every other planet . . . including ones that haven't been discovered yet. Even though I think you're nutty sometimes.

And even though we're as different as different gets, you're my sister. Am I your sister too?"

She looks up at me, eyes bloodshot from crying. "You know you are."

"But we're not blood, right?"

She shakes her head and coughs out a laugh, drying the corners of her eyes with her sleeve.

"Blood is just science. Family isn't science. If Governor Voss really is your father—it just means you share similar science. That's all." I kiss her wet cheek and continue hugging her.

"But, Aven . . . ," she says, and I can feel her words fighting a lump in her throat. "That's *exactly* what scares me."

Hearing us, Callum gives up on guard duty—he walks over and kneels in front us. The look Ren gives him could cause a second Wash Out, if that were possible. He's about to say something, when the door swings open. Two officers stride in.

Ren grabs me and Callum, hiding us behind the drapes. She opens up a window that leads to a small balcony. "Shh," she whispers into her index finger as we step out into the night. Pointing down to the ground floor, we see a patio that leads to the ballroom. It's a ten-foot drop—she wants us to jump. Ren closes the window behind Callum, and she begins to climb over the edge.

She hangs from the railing with her feet dangling free. Her hands let go, she drops, and she lands in a crouch on the red-tiled patio below.

Callum and I look at each other, both wearing the same

expression: *Ten feet isn't so bad . . . right?* We straddle the banister, lowering ourselves down until we're both dangling there. Inhaling, I let go—

My body falls through the air. Just like Ren, I land low. Ren shakes my shoulder with a grin, as we wait for Callum to fall next.

Beyond the double doors to our right, Dunn gives some sort of speech from the balcony pulpit. His mic'd voice drones through the glass. "We have all been betrayed," I hear him saying. "And I am deeply regretful of the orders I carried out in former Governor Voss's name. As chief of the Division Interial, I humbly step forward to offer leadership. I ask you to remember this: I am not Governor Voss—I was acting as a servant of the UMI. Now, as legally sanctioned acting governor, I serve *you*. It is my belief—"

A dart . . .

It sings past my head, sinking its fangs into the red tile. The net follows, attached to its tail. Its electric, twinkling blue lights blanket through the air, until I can't see anything else. A hundred shocking stars bite my skin. They confuse my nerves, making it impossible to move—until Ren throws me aside.

I'm paralyzed.

42

REN
8:45 P.M., FRIDAY

Coming to, my muscles feel like raw meat. Both eyelids twitch open.

"Ren?" Callum shakes me back into the world, but everywhere his hands touch, my skin stings in response. I'm dotted with red marks from the net, and my head throbs. Groaning, I lift myself—only to be yanked back by the metal leg of a table bolted to the floor.

We're cuffed.

Panicky, I glance around. Metal cabinets line the walls, overflowing with wires and monitors, or other DI devices. *She's not here—*

"You pushed her aside in time. I don't think she was seen," Callum says. He cranes his neck sideways, eyeing the partially open door. "Where do you think we are?"

Inside the attached room, a team of doctors has wheeled in a surgical table and a stretcher. Behind them—wall-to-wall glass screens, and the circular door to the causeway. Tools from the surgical table are picked up and replaced, clinking with each round.

"That *was* the security room," I say. "Now it's an operating room. We must be in some sort of storage unit."

Someone shuts the door the rest of the way. Vaguely, I wonder what's going on in there, but I can't quite muster up the energy to care.

The table leg's hard edge digs into my spine. Aven's words still echo in my head: *It means you share similar science.*

I wonder what other similarities Voss and I share.

Callum shifts from his awkward, hunched position under the table, deep in thought. "It makes perfect sense, really," he says after a few minutes, and rubs his jaw.

"What does?"

He can't be referring to what I think he is. *Nothing* makes sense.

"You . . . your blood, I mean," he answers. "After the DI left, I looked at it again under the microscope—I just couldn't understand why that dropper would have had such a destructive effect on the ecosystem."

"The dropper with my blood?"

"Yes, that one," Callum says. "I'd accidentally used it in the mini tank, right before everything died off."

I wait for him tell me what it all means. Instead, he pauses. "Backtrack just a moment," he says, waving his hands like he's erasing the air. "Assume that the governor and his wife were drinking daily doses of the water when you were conceived. What if the mushroom's genetic material, combined with the governor's and Emilce's, altered your own code in the womb? Under the 'scope, I saw that your blood contains a protein . . . the same protein that, in high concentrations, kills the algae."

I scratch my head, only to be jerked backward by the cuff. "So you think the water changed me?" I ask, swapping hands.

"Have you *ever* been sick?"

Never—but the possibility is too much for me to wrap my head around. "I scrape and bruise just like the next person, though."

"Your recovery time could be shorter," Callum suggests. "Really, it's impossible to say which portions of the mushroom's code you might've inherited. Some links could be weaker than others. Some might not have been passed down at all. Genetics are unpredictable that way."

"So, what you're saying is . . ." I pause, because the delivery has to be just right. "I'm part *mushroom*. Did I get that right?"

Callum sighs. I'm glad Aven's not trapped here with us . . . but if she were, she'd have laughed at that.

Comm static fills the other room—I lower myself onto the floor, cheek to the concrete, so I can listen under the door.

"Chief Dunn," a muffled voice says. "We removed the dart. . . . No, sir, there wasn't time to get him to the lab. . . . Security Room B. . . . The guard's outside, yes. . . . Sir, you should come here. Governor Voss's body has undergone . . .

rapid cellular turnover—he appears to be aging. We doubt he'll last the hour."

The doctor pauses.

I turn to face Callum, confused—"How . . . ?"

His free hand covers his mouth as he listens. "He was shot in the ballroom," he whispers.

"Chief, Governor is asking if you've found his . . . tonic?" By the way the doctor relays the message, he has no clue what the governor's really asking for.

A dizzying fog rolls in. *That's really Voss in there—about to die.* "This is a good thing," I say, but the moment is no longer simple. A day ago, it would have been. Voss was the Tètai's worst nightmare, I remind myself. The very reason they kept the spring hidden. He would have hunted it forever, killing anyone who stood in his way.

Through the closed door, a heart monitor beeps and we hear a deep, guttural whimper. I shiver. Back home, the meaner roof-rat kiddies sometimes played hacky-sack using sick, nearly dead birds. They'd lob the bodies back and forth. The sound Voss makes now ain't much different.

I almost want to pity him. *Almost.*

"I'll administer the Dilameth," someone says, and we hear more shuffling.

"That's not necessary, nurse. This dosage is perfectly sufficient."

Callum stiffens, his face ghostly pale. "They're withholding his pain meds on purpose," he tells me.

Under the door, there are moving feet and wheels. Doctors begin to exit through the causeway, pushing their cart of bloodied tools. The room is silent until we hear comm static.

"Chief, you've got someone watching screens in Security A. Can I just post up outside? Babysitting a dying politician wasn't exactly in the job description, y'know?"

A moment later, the door closes.

I bite my fist. *I wanted revenge, right? Well, here it is.* The governor's pathetic moans as he dies alone, right next door.

He won't last the hour. My father *won't last the hour.*

It's as if we're in a tunnel, and we're the only people alive.

I yank at my handcuff. Once, and then a dozen times more. Hard, then harder. "Do you know who I am?" I hiss at Voss, sure that he doesn't—Emilce sent me away. Kept me a secret. The governor may be as good as dead, but he's not there yet.

He will know.

Would it change him? Would he have some remorse? I want him to regret his entire life—every action that led him here, to this moment.

I try to squeeze my wrist through the aluminum, but my hand is too big. The base of my thumb purples as metal peels away skin.

I don't care—*I've never broken a bone.* Leaning back, I throw my weight away from the cuff. My hand crunches as I pull. Lava-blood pounds into my fingers. They're *red* red now, plump and stinging.

In my bones, I feel the thousand microfissures, marrow rips marrow, then mends. I howl. Gravity does the rest, breaking and unbreaking. Reeling backward, the cuff tears from my wrist, and I fall to the concrete.

I hurt, but nothing's mangled. Nothing's broken, just as

Callum guessed. I cradle my arm as I stand, watching the purple disappear. The door to the next room is locked, but through the window, I see him.

He's laid out on the stretcher, back comfortably lifted. Can't have him suffocating on a bloody lung, of course. He has the face of misshapen, molten steel.

I pound the window with my good hand. I slam it until the glass cracks, splintering into my palm. My blood smears, shards fracture and fall. "How could you do it to me!"

Through the broken window, the only answer I hear is a staggered, bubbling wheeze. He doesn't know who I am. He doesn't know what I'm talking about.

With the force of a dozen streaks of lightning hitting one lonely metal antenna, my entire life—every decision, every emotion—it becomes clear. *I've had Voss in me all along—*

The beast made of teeth. The infernal hook in my heart that wouldn't let go until I found a way to destroy the governor.

The moment I almost let Callum die.

Even my love for Aven, *tainted*. I'd never let her die if I could find a way to stop it . . . for her sake, but also for mine. I *am* selfish. I don't want to be around if she's not: She's my one link to goodness. Without her, what would I become?

I am my father's daughter.

"I was yours!" I scream, desperately forcing my voice through his drug haze. "Do you hear me? I am your daughter!"

The machine that tracks his heart rate beeps faster now.

I keep going. "That's right! You hear me, don't you! My own mother gave me up! The water you both drank? It's in me— it's in my blood! I'm different because of it. And I think she

252

was afraid . . . of *you*. I think she was terrified of what you'd do to me if you found out. Do you understand, monster?"

The words are hot, blackened volcanic vomit out of my mouth. In them are all the years I spent alone, fending for myself. Once in a while I'd wonder what it would be like, having parents who cared. Little did I know how lucky I was to grow up without them.

The hook is back, deeper this time. I no longer want revenge for what he did to Aven, or anyone else he ever wronged.

I want it for myself.

The beeping is faster now, so I know I'm getting through. He makes a sound. He has no voice, can speak only in whispers.

"You . . ."

That one word drags on, like he can't quite stop it. The vowel mixes with whatever air he's got in his one good lung. I'm in his breath.

"Me! Yes, me!"

He's watching now from under two weak eye slits. I don't see remorse. A flash of something, maybe. *Hope?* He lifts a finger, tries to raise the rest of his hand. It wavers in the air for just a moment before it falls.

"Help me," I hear him say. "You could help me. Your blood."

I'm sick again, hurling freshwater and now bile, because there's nothing left in my stomach to set free.

"You could be the way." Air hisses between his teeth. "You could save us all."

I scream one final time, spitting the last of my retching gut onto the floor. Footsteps echo outside the underground room. *If I wanted to see remorse, I didn't get it.* Even after everything he's put me through, Voss is who he is—he'd use me to the end if he could.

Through gritted teeth and clenched jaw, I tell him, "Die," and he does.

The beeping flatlines. Becomes one solid shrieking horizon that doesn't end. It extends forever in my head, and even when I press my hands up to my ears, desperate to drown it out, I can still hear. I'll never stop hearing the noise, I realize.

It's in my very bones.

43

AVEN
8:30 P.M., FRIDAY

The blue star blanket carries Ren and Callum in slow motion, up to the night sky. Everywhere the net touched, I hurt. Curled like a snake in the bushes, I watch— unable to move. Tears race over the bridge of my nose. I let them. I have no other choice.

In the ballroom, Chief Dunn gives his speech—I can hear him though the white double doors. Two black-gloved officers haul nets through the second-story window. One says, "Got 'em," into his comm, just as my rigid body begins to wake up. I spasm, muscles threatening to give me away—

A flashlight.

It sets my hiding space aglow. Bright green leaves bristle at my ear. I close my eyes. One by one, my nerves come alive—*now* of all times. Holding my breath, I pretend I'm still paralyzed. My heart bangs so loud, someone must hear it. The beam traces a path right over my head, hitting the building's brick facade behind me.

It outlines the mansion . . . and then stretches away to scan the bank. I exhale. Long minutes pass. *I have to get back inside. I won't let them take her.*

Flipping onto my stomach, I pull off one shoe—a distraction, while I make a dash for the double doors. Shaking the glue from my muscles, I wind up my arm. I bite my lip, I squint . . . I aim for a ground-floor window about thirty feet to my left. My stubby fingers grip the loafer oddly, and I hope I can still hit such a close target.

I hurl.

It flies into the glass—I bolt for the doors.

"There!" an officer patrolling the perimeter shouts. A dart cracks in the air as I touch the brass handle. Hissing, it misses me, connecting with the door frame instead.

I gasp and stumble into the packed ballroom. Dunn's faced away, talking into his comm. Hundreds of eyes turn. An officer posted at the door whips around. His eyes land on the dart still hissing in the wooden frame. *"Hey!"* he growls, and grabs my forearm. . . .

I'm dragged closer, as he reaches for the handcuffs dangling from his hip belt. I try to yank myself free, but I'm nowhere near strong enough—*I'm caught again.*

"That's her . . . that's *Aven*," one prisoner blurts, echoed by a dozen others. A woman shaped like a speedmobile steps between me and the officer. "What did you give us?" she asks in a wiry voice, breaking his grip. She isn't sure yet if I'm to be loved, or hated.

I stumble away, mouth open. *They deserve an answer—* but I can't give one right now. Choking back the lump in my throat, I drop to the floor and I duck between people's legs like a coward. I crawl into the crowd until it swallows me whole. Behind, the guard chases. He doesn't get very far. His black boots scuffle against the masses, prisoners falling to the side—the room's packed too tight.

He stops moving.

Ter, where are you?

I punch awkwardly into my comm, fingers hitting the wrong keys by accident. When he responds a moment later, I maneuver toward the kitchen, hiding behind my hair the whole way. I can't look them in the eye.

Ter wraps me in one of his famous bear hugs.

I stiffen, my eyes watering. The lump is still there—I'm too shaken to hug him back.

"What happened?"

I can't answer.

He gives me another quick hug and points to one corner of the ballroom, where Sipu and Derek are waiting for us. Then he leads the way, offering me a handful of tiny triangular sandwiches he must have snuck from the kitchen.

I turn them down. If I ate right now I'd only see it again later. He puts a few sandwiches in my hand anyway.

"I commed Benny—he's coming to get us. Where's Ren? Did you find Callum?" Ter asks, but the ballroom abrubtly quiets.

On the balcony, Chief Dunn has raised both his hands.

"Men, women, and children of the UMI: My first order of business as acting governor isn't going to be easy—what's necessary never is." He stops here. Half the people scowl, trusting nothing he says. The other half listen and wait before passing judgment. "*One* thing stands between us and a better way of life."

"*Freshwater . . . ,*" buzzes around the room, spreading like fire.

"Are you thinking about a Second Appeal?" a lone reporter shouts as she maneuvers her long mic in between the banisters.

Chief Dunn leans forward. He looks out at the crowd and nods.

"We don't know much about the cure you were given—*illegally*, I'd like to remind you all. Its regenerative side effect could last a few days, or a few weeks. We only know it's not permanent. *Now* is the time to strike Upstate—to demand Magistrate Harcourt reopen the main aqueduct."

One prisoner scoffs so loudly that others turn to look at him. "Why should we fight for you?" he yells.

Chief Dunn shakes his head. "Don't fight for me—*fight for yourselves*. Are you going to stand there and deny that you're *the* answer we've been waiting for? The drug you were given is nothing short of a miracle, and I want to use you. Our nation needs freshwater. I'm challenging you to *use yourselves*."

All the while he's been talking, I've forgotten to breathe. Dizzy, I glance around the room. The people are listening, considering.

"I'm not asking you to fight for free either. You'll receive compensation, just like any other officer. Payment for service. Free attendance to any West Isle school of your choosing. A clean DI record," he adds smoothly.

As the prisoners haggle, negotiating Dunn's terms—something else dawns on me. My stomach clenches, my vision blurs. The balcony shifts and retreats, until I realize it's me, swaying back and forth. "No," I whisper, sinking down to catch smooth, pale marble.

Ter touches my back. "Aven, what is it?"

I cradle my head in both hands, sure it's about to fall off. "My fault," I manage. "My idea . . . the water. If I'd listened to Ren, if I'd only waited . . ." I fold onto the floor, hiding my eyes.

I'm still being jolted stiff by the net's electric stars, shocked a hundred times in a hundred ways. Except, the shocks aren't on my skin—they're in the air.

I gave Chief Dunn the perfect army. Gift-wrapped with a bow, hand-delivered to his doorstep.

44

"**D**ane!"

Chief marches into the security room. He hears the monitor flatlining. He calls for the doctors, and a moment later, they appear. *"Time of death."* My father's body disappears in a flurry of white lab coats and gray hair.

The inventory door swings open.

"Chief," I answer, hoarse from screaming.

Hands square on his hips, Dunn finds me loose—and he don't even care. He pulls a glass vial of dark, silty liquid from his breast pocket and holds it up to my face. "The spring, Dane—where is it!"

Eyeing the contents, I can tell it's not the serum Callum made. It doesn't look like any of the vials I left for Derek either.

"Was this . . . Voss's?"

His name is a bullet in my mouth.

"Moment he was shot, he told me where to find it."

I say nothing, because I wouldn't have saved Voss either.

Chief shakes the vial like a snowglobe. As the silt sinks to the bottom, he whistles in sheer wonder. "Never actually thought anything of Voss's search for fresh. Not until you found the spring. There was office talk, sure, about him actually thinking he'd found the Fountain of Youth, but he never said anything to me. I thought it was all silly gossip."

Chief shrugs and returns the vial to his pocket. Paces the room, anxious. Callum, still cuffed to the table, keeps out of his way.

"No more games, Dane. I need the spring. I need it now."

I don't understand—*why now?* When I don't answer fast enough, he drags me into the security room. Points to one glass screen. "Look."

I choke. . . .

What was a ballroom an hour ago is being turned into a military base. Lines of prisoners receive blue fatigues, while servants hand out food and water. "A Second Appeal?" I whisper, touching the pixilated screen in disbelief.

"An *opportunity*, Dane. The plan's been in the works for years."

"And they just agreed?"

Chief Dunn brings his hand down against a table with a tinny smack. "Do you not see? The people need water!" he shouts, his eyes hard on mine.

He's not wrong, but . . . *this ain't the way.*

Digging my nails into my palms, I feel like a traitor. Chief is sending five hundred people like animals to the slaughter, just 'cause they've got the springwater in their systems. When it wears off, they're dead.

Is that on me?

"We leave in two hours—with or without your help. I've already reappropriated millions to secure a high-speed barge from a city on the Mainland; it's on its way as we speak. Every second I waste, the springwater loses its effectiveness. And just like last time, we're *vastly* outnumbered—we only stand a chance if we can *keep fighting*.

"Don't you want to bring freshwater to the UMI?"

I do—I do. . . . We deserve fresh as much as anyone, but . . .

What happens after *we win?* There's always gonna be another war to fight. If it ain't for water, it'll be for land. Or any other resource that catches our eye.

"Don't you want the UMI to be a great city again?"

An immortal city . . .

I clench my jaw, grinding my teeth so hard they just might turn to chalk. Voss is dead, but there's another waiting in the wings. What would a man like Dunn do with limitless power?

"Very well then," he says, stepping closer. "I tried talking to you, but you won't see reason." Dunn lifts his cuffcomm to his mouth. "Backup requested in Security A immediately," he says.

I step away, ready to make a run for the door when two officers burst in.

"Hold her."

They flank me, each grabbing an arm. I jerk away, trying to twist myself free, but then come the cuffs. With my wrists locked behind my back, I've got no power. I kick, but they force me down—I drop to my knees. Dunn braces himself against the wall. He lifts his leg. Looks at me. "Unless," he spits, throwing his boot into my ribs, "you care to lead a team of my men there. Now."

My body becomes a fist, clenched against the force. I grunt and spit. Callum launches from his spot, yanked back, forgetting the cuffs.

Dunn winds his leg again, this time striking it into my shoulder. His boot ricochets off my nose, bursting a vessel— fresh blood bubbles out my nostril.

"You can stop this," he says, using the sole of his shoe to lift my forehead. Metallic red smears up and down my face.

I gasp. *How can I stop this?* I rack my mind for an answer, but all I feel is hate for the spring that's destroyed as many lives as it's saved. It shouldn't be here, it was a mistake—a botanical error.

Because it was given to *people.*

Kitaneh once said the spring was a miracle and a curse— both. Now I understand. A miracle and a curse, because we are. Not even the Tètai were able to keep their hands clean; hiding the spring also ends in death.

With Callum holding my gaze, *I'm a botanical error too*, I realize.

I see in the twitch of his eyebrows, the slightest cock of his head—we're hitting on the same answer.

I could get rid of it. My blood could get rid of it forever.

Friendship may be the closest thing to telepathy we've got on this earth. Callum, ever so slightly, nods. In that tiny, atomic motion, he tells me he understands.

"Drop her."

The officers let go and I fall, dead weight on the concrete.

"In one minute I'm going to walk back in through that door. I expect to hear only one answer, understood?" Chief Dunn waves his guards out of the room, leaving me bloodied, like I've already been to battle. The war hasn't even begun. From across the room, Callum inches closer—as close as his handcuffs will let him.

"Ren," he says, hoarse with worry. "I know what you're thinking. . . . I thought it too. I can't stop you, I know. But I also can't let you. For a hundred reasons, but only one that matters, scientifically."

I wrench myself away, spitting out the tang of fresh blood. "What do you mean?"

"We don't know if you have enough blood in your body for this to even work," he says, pleading with his eyes.

"Isn't there some math magic you can do to find out?"

Chief Dunn walks back in, and Callum nods from under the table. Right now, I'm getting a firsthand look at the distance between the head and the heart. He understands why I need to do this, and he's hoping science can save me.

Funny, because science got me here.

Chief Dunn steps closer. "You ready to take a field trip, Dane?" He raises his leg a third time, waiting for my answer.

I am my mother's daughter. In the eleventh hour, I will make amends; I will right Governor Voss's wrongs.

I am also my father's daughter. A man who betrayed. His love, his people. His own humanity. *Humanity itself.*

Cool in the shadow of my own terrible greatness, I say, "Yes . . . I'll take you."

45

Like a fairy tale told backward, the ballroom transforms into Blues' barracks. Prisoners in fatigues line up to have their necks tattooed with Division Interial identification codes. Chief Dunn's abandoned his pulpit and left the captain in charge of organizing the ranks.

The ballroom is no longer safe.

Me, Ter, Sipu, and Derek head for the kitchen, searching for a better place to hide until Benny arrives. We weave through servers rushing to clean pots or put away cheeses and fruit, when Derek nudges us into an empty pantry not much smaller than our apartment back at the 'Racks.

I sit in silence under a row of imported tomato sauce tins.

"You really blame yourself?" Ter asks, and I just hug my knees closer.

I do.

He lays his hand on my back. "Aven, you don't control people's choices. This war is *not* your fault," he insists, but he doesn't understand—his dad is wealthy. When you're poor enough—*everyone* controls your choices. Dunn's taking advantage of the prisoners. Prisoners that *I* put in his lap.

"Hey, if the Second Appeal works, we'll be drinking fancy Falls fresh by next week!" Ter says, tapping my knee gently. "Ain't *so* bad."

Derek lowers down beside us. "Really? And what happens when Magistrate Harcourt sees an army of people who don't die? He'll open the aqueduct, sure. But do you think he'll forget what he saw?" Derek and Sipu exchange wary glances—they already know the answer: he won't.

"This isn't a permanent fix, Terrence," Sipu says. "Chief Dunn's just opening a different can of worms."

"We need to find Ren and Callum. When's Benny getting here? We need to do *something*." My voice sounds tougher than I feel. Stronger.

"Like what? Go there?" Ter says this like it's an impossible idea. I look at him, quite seriously, and he balks. "And then what?"

His cuffcomm goes off.

"It's Ren," Ter says, reading the message. "She wants us to jailbreak Callum. He's being transported from Security A this minute—so we gotta go, like, *now*." We stand to leave when a second message comes . . . this time for Derek.

He stares and stares before reading it aloud:

I'm taking Dunn. It's not what you think—I have a plan.

"To the spring?" Ter and I say in unison. I swallow, confused. *What is she doing?*

Derek edges toward the door, his copper brows pinched tight. "I'm going to find her. Comm me if you have trouble getting Callum."

As I move, about to follow, he lays a palm on my shoulder. "Ren won't want Chief Dunn to see you, Aven. He doesn't know my face. You guys go find Callum—*fast.*" Derek nods at Ter and Sipu before slipping into the kitchen.

"Jailbreak, then?" Ter says. "We gotta hurry if we're gonna find him."

We leave the pantry, swinging left out of the kitchen and into a crammed hall. New DI officers sit together, chugging full canteens. They don't pay attention when we bolt for the far stairwell, hopping between their thinly stuffed mats like cracks in the boardwalk.

Halfway down the stairs, Ter stops short. He's face-to-face with a handcuffed Callum . . . and the security officer standing right behind him. Slung over the guard's shoulder is a loaded shooter, ready for action—a dart pokes out of the barrel, unused.

The guard's eyes darken—*he recognizes us.* He lifts his shooter over Callum's shoulder, aiming it at Ter's nose. Bringing his cuffcomm to his mouth: "Backup needed on the rear stairwell—" he begins, but he doesn't get the chance to finish.

Ter lunges forward and grabs the barrel. He points it up—the guard pulls the trigger. A crack rips through air and smoke clouds the stairwell. As Callum wrestles himself free, the dart hurtles toward the ceiling. We cover our heads and sprint up the stairs. The electric blue net's paralyzing stars catapult far away, not touching one of us.

In the hallway, I have the lead—I jump from mat to mat, avoiding officers' legs. Our own commotion chases us, and Ter doesn't make it easier by grabbing a young soldier's shooter as we run. The boy shouts "Hey!" and both old and new DI officers catch on to our escape—but the hallway's too packed. No one can reach us fast enough.

"In here," I say, poking my head into the kitchen. I point past the cooks and servers to a window, and next to it, an exit.

While Ter types away at his comm, we race for the door.

I throw it open first, glancing around into the crisp, black night for a place to hide. Hedges illuminated by bright solar-powered bulbs outline the mansion, and two low trees frame the door.

"Look," I say, ducking under one. I wave for the others to follow and we crouch together, hidden by tough, fingerlike branches.

"Benny's here, you guys," Ter whispers, looking at his comm. "He's anchored off the west coast. He needs coordinates so he can get the Cloud ready to go."

"We can't go back to my place." Callum shakes his head as

Sipu tries to help him out of his handcuffs. "Chief Dunn's men completely destroyed my lab—and that's before he had evidence I was involved. Now that Dunn knows about Dr. Justin Cory, it'd be foolish to return."

"Well, we certainly can't return to mine," Sipu says, digging around in her hip belt.

Beside us, the moat ripples as a gale travels down the Hudson Strait from the north. From Upstate.

I swallow. *There's only one place for us to go.*

"We're taking it to the Falls."

Like a cartoon, three jaws drop. Six eyes come right out of their sockets. "I'm serious," I say, pointing to the ballroom. "In a few hours, Chief Dunn is sending an army Upstate. Not just any army—an army that can't be killed."

Turning to Callum, I tap his hand. "Remember the protest? That man said the Falls has surplus water stores. I know it's a long shot, but maybe if he saw our faces . . . if he realized that he's hurting actual people, he'd reopen the aqueduct. Just for a little while. Shouldn't we at least *see* if he's willing to negotiate?"

"Negotiate *how*, exactly?" Callum asks. "We've got nothing with which to bargain."

Indignant, I feel my cheeks flush hot red. How can people knowingly be so awful to one another? "Reason, maybe? Or compassion?" I snap through gritted teeth. "It is too much to expect that humans have some humanity?"

Sipu quiets me, her eyes glued to the window. Inside, a flock of heavyset officers are talking to the cook, asking questions. The cook nods and points to the exit.

"Hide."

Grabbing my hand, Ter pulls me behind the hedges, his newly stolen shooter banging against his hip. We lay lengthwise, crammed between sharp, leafy twigs and the mansion's foundation.

The kitchen door opens.

Five officers pass, boots trampling the moat's muddy bank.

I'm frozen, curled up against Ter. His heart beats against my spine. I'm so distracted by his closeness, my anger dissolves and I ignore the officers entirely. When Ter's sure they're gone, he pokes up his head.

"All right," he says, plucking a branch from my hair. "I'm gonna vote Upstate. Not because I think it'll work, but because, at the very least, Harcourt might feel like a scumbag after we leave. That'll be worth it."

I do *not* throw him a dirty look—that wasn't the answer I wanted, but it'll do.

Callum sits up from the bushes on the opposite side of the door. He brushes dirt off his nice black pants. "I'll come, but I don't know how much help I'll be. There's something I promised Ren I'd do."

"I'm staying," Sipu tells us. "I'll head back to the docking lot and get my mobile. That way, if the DI are tailing you, I'll hear it on the comm and I can offer you some coverage."

"Are you sure?" I ask. "You've already risked a lot."

She's quiet. Her blond hair falls in front of one eye, but she doesn't move it. "I agree with Ter—I'm not sure this will work, but I also agree with you, Aven. Humanity is a foreign word these days. I'd like to be optimistic again."

I meet her eyes and smile back, the closed-lip kind. She squeezes my hand once, then lets go.

"We've gotta roll." Ter scans the perimeter, using his cuffcomm like a compass. "Benny's intercepting their comms—he's drawn me a safe route to his mobile." Standing, he turns toward the island's west coast. "Follow me. Stay low."

It's happening, I think, racing after him. I can feel myself glowing again. I hug myself, but not from the cold—I'm warm all over.

I wonder if Ren was born with this feeling.

46

REN
9:32 P.M., FRIDAY

"Keep moving!" Chief yells from the ballroom balcony as I maneuver too slowly through the hallway of mattresses. The steel GPS tracking cuff he outfitted me with blinks red at my wrist. Dunn knows where I am and how slow I'm going. And if I stop moving, he knows when to bark at me.

I give him my best "Yessir" nod and quickly send off three comms: one to Derek, one to Ter—and the last to Callum, asking him not to tell Aven. I don't want her worrying about something that might not happen.

Looking up from my cuffcomm, I nearly collide with two girls in DI uniform, younger than Aven by no more than a year.

"What'll you do when you're rich?" I overhear.

The second girl grins and shrugs. "I'll wear my fancy clothes to my fancy school and eat anything I fancy," she answers between bites. "You?"

"Every time someone drinks water, I'll inform them that they should thank me for my contribution." The girls giggle, so damn ready for a future Dunn never should have promised in the first place.

My insides unravel.

Tomorrow, this kid's gonna see her blood spill on foreign soil. I'm not sure it matters that the wound won't last.

"Ren!"

Not Dunn this time—my black-and-blue heart jumps at the familiar voice. I spin around and find Derek right there. My rib cage clenches, squeezing my lungs of air. He looks at me, his hair the color of luck.

Once upon a time, I wanted luck from no one, not even Aven. *Good skill*, she said instead. Now, I'll take luck from anybody willing to hand it over. As I walk, I rub both pennies on my necklace. I wonder if they're dual-function charms: skill *and* luck would be great.

I turn away from Derek. "Dunn's watching. I can't stop," I say, and push toward the front entrance.

Making myself forget that I might not return from this.

"What is this plan, Ren?" He stops me, touches his hand to my shoulder. I survey the room to check if Dunn's watching—he's on the balcony, poring over at least a half dozen map holos with his second-in-command.

This could be our good-bye, I realize. *And we only just*

began. Without warning, I take Derek's arms and wrap them around my waist. Loving isn't something to be put off.

"I have to," I whisper into his mouth, then breathe a kiss onto his bottom lip. "I-I—can destroy it, Derek. With my blood . . . my parents, they—" The words cramp in my throat. "They knew about the spring. My mother drank it while she was pregnant, and now I have some poisonous protein in my blood. With enough of it, I can kill off the ecosystem. For good."

Derek's rust eyes search mine. "Who are your parents, Ren?"

I don't know how to tell him. I can barely say it myself. "I need you to trust me."

He stumbles over his words, runs a hand through his hair. "Ren, of course I trust you. I just—"

"There's no reason to stop me. Callum figured out a way to make more water . . . since you'll need it."

From the balcony, Dunn shouts, *"What did I say, Agent Dane!* Report to the front entrance *immediately*—my unit is waiting on you!" In the grand space his voice booms, and now I've got everyone's eyes on my back.

Derek's attention is elsewhere. "Dammit," he curses, looking over my shoulder. "Kitaneh."

I turn—a girl with onyx hair spilling behind her like a black flag rushes for the entrance. She casts us a cutthroat look before disappearing through the double doors.

Brack.

"Now she knows I'm leading a unit," I whisper, kicking my

275

heel against the marble floor. "Fantastic."

"I'll comm her—let her know this isn't what it looks like. May not do any good, though; she's been unreachable since I left."

"I have to go," I tell him again once Kitaneh's out of sight.

The entire walk to the front entrance, Derek's at my side, shuffling to keep up. When I don't slow down, it hits him: This is for real. I'm not turning back.

"Don't do it, Ren," he begs, resting a hand on my elbow. "If what you're saying is true—if your blood really could—you don't know how much . . ."

. . . blood I'd need to spill for it to work.

"Callum's doing the math."

"Even if you do have enough blood . . . ," Derek goes on. He's afraid for me, and it's made him agitated. "You could die too soon, before the ecosystem does. Your heart would stop pumping."

That is a great point.

"Then I'll have to stay alive until it's done."

As I stop at the front entrance, Derek's whole body tenses up under his lab coat.

"Once I get to your apartment, I won't know how to reach the cave. Kitaneh's gonna be ready—Lucas too, and with the DI along for the ride, I'll need your help holding them off. Will you help me?"

Derek looks away. He's steeling himself—against *me*. Against what I'm about to do, and what I'm asking of him. He gives a sharp nod. He doesn't want me to do this thing, but he knows there's no use arguing. "I'll see you on the other side, then."

He is referring to the other side of the Hudson Strait, that I know.

But I can't ignore the double meaning.

47

"Into the Cloud!" Benny shouts, as if it were our very own battleship—not the word for fluffy white sky bunnies. He steers up to the coast, engine sputtering. "Now what's this about going to the Falls?" he says as Ter jumps in, tossing his new shooter under the seat. Callum follows, wriggling over the rail and cursing the cuffs still locked around his wrists.

"Dunn's got an army," I say, and throw one leg into the boat.

"Yes, yes, that I heard over their comms." Benny holds out his arm for me but Ter nudges him out of the way. I let him give me a little lift.

"An *invincible* army," I clarify.

Benny shoots us a look. "Young folk should never tease their elders."

"No one's teasing." Agitated, Ter scratches his temple and gives Benny the abridged version of our night. "Aven wants to talk to Magistrate Harcourt. She thinks that, maybe, if we put a face on the UMI's situation, he might have a change of heart."

Benny rubs his wiry whiskers, considering. "Perhaps," he says. "It's certainly a different approach. Still, we should be prepared for disappointment; I don't trust Harcourt will be so easily swayed. Those in power usually aren't. It makes them look bad, even when it's human decency on the line."

Ter grips my arm and listens to the wind. Benny hears it too. Behind us, the rumbling of revved-up engines chase across the islet. They're headed for us.

"T-minus now!" Benny shouts, throwing the wheel right. His Cloud kicks a great frothy wave against the bank as we speed along the wooded islet. I fall into the plush white vinyl seat, thankful for its cloudiness.

A pair of beamers carves around the islet's tail, careening over black water. Another follows, racing to catch up with the first.

"A chase will just eat up gas," Benny says, cutting the lights. The Cloud slows to a crawl along Castle Islet's swampy west coast. Long branches dip their fingers into the water, and roots claw at us from underneath.

We veer around trees wider than the chief's own body. Benny parks between two giant trunks, both with cascading greenish leaves. We're in almost total darkness now, except for the moon and the yellow headlights.

Through the branches, both Omnis veer closer. They're

only a few hundred feet away. When the second one drops behind the first, Ter squints, shaking his head. "What's he doing?" he asks.

A scraping noise claws apart the quiet. The second Omni collides into the first, tearing off his rear propellers—they spin off, cutting up the water.

"That's Sipu . . . ," I whisper, clutching the rail. In the pit, I see her bleached hair, as bright as a lighthouse.

The DI Omni seesaws—Sipu pushes him into the coast. Her mobile, relatively undamaged, reverses. All's quiet until she bumps the DI mobile again . . . this time, she doesn't back away. She uses the mobile's bullet-shaped nose to steer him toward a massive tree's tangled roots. Then she slips underwater. She lifts the DI Omni from its undercarriage and deposits him even deeper into the thicket.

"She's jamming his comm," Ter says, and Benny nods in agreement.

The DI can't free himself, not without the use of its rear propellers—he's stuck there.

"Let's go," Ter says, fumbling through Benny's dash. Finding a spool of thick boating wire, he plops down in front of Callum and begins poking around in the handcuff's lock.

Benny brings us out of the watery forest and follows the coast north. On our right, a few hundred feet off, we pass Castle Isle's north pier—and a half dozen docked Omnis.

No one breathes.

The Hudson Strait opens up in front of us, two miles wide. The Ward's toothy, spired skyline shoots up from the other coast. A steady breeze plays over the river's black water and

Sipu trails our sluggish wake.

The half dozen DI Omnis recede into the distance, staying where they are.

Callum exhales as his metal handcuffs fall to the floor with a *chink*.

Thank you, he mouths to Ter, flexing his wrists.

After a few silent minutes, Benny reaches under his seat. He lays a large, old piece of paper on the wheel.

"Where we headed?" Ter asks, gathering around. I join too, but Callum stays where he is, fumbling with his comm.

Benny points to a spot north of us. "About thirty miles more."

"Thirty miles doesn't sound that bad. From top to bottom the Ward is about ten, right?" I say.

"DI," Callum warns, pointing back toward the north pier. A single yellow beam swings away from the Castle Isle coastline. It shoots forward into the middle of the strait . . . still a good mile away, though.

I grip the rail with both hands. "You think he sees us?"

"No idea," Ter answers.

"Let's give Sipu a chance to head him off," Callum says. "If we jump the gun, we'll end up with a dozen of them on our back." Benny agrees and holds course, not driving faster or slower.

Leaning against the Cloud's rail, Ter, Callum, and I watch as the Omni swings left. North—*toward us.*

"We stay as we are." Benny's voice is firm. "We'll give her two minutes. If after two minutes, nothing—"

He doesn't need to finish his sentence: immediately, we

hear the high-pitched sounds of metal scraping metal, like two mobiles grinding sides. The DI Omni nears, zigzagging down the strait, but never losing pace.

"Does anyone have Sipu's comm ID? Can we reach her?" Benny asks.

Callum, Ter, and I exchange glances—no one answers.

Then Sipu's Omni rises out of the water. She races forward, and for a few seconds, it's a battle of speed. The two are neck and neck. She spins her wheel, cutting into his, but he doesn't slow. He only veers farther and farther east, until he's able to make a complete turn, facing back in our direction.

The inside of my palms sting from clutching the rail so tight.

Ter takes my hand and holds it flat against his. "It's not even a competition."

I frown, feeling my palm grow sticky against his, but I see he's right—Sipu's Omni has taken off again.

She's gunned her engine until she and the DI are parallel, and then she rides it even harder. Her mobile flies over rocking waves, gaining speed, moving ever faster. It reminds me of a holo I once saw showing the moment a meteor broke the atmosphere, seconds before becoming a fiery mess.

She whooshes past the DI's mobile on the left and, spinning the wheel, she cuts him off at a T. Then she kills the engine.

"What's she doing?" I ask. At the same time, I cover my mouth with understanding.

A white-hot boom cracks the night wide open. Like a sun

exploding, the two mobiles fly together, then apart, in great pops of spewing metal—an orange cloud burns on the horizon, violent, sparking into the water.

I gasp, choking on air. I shake my head as the tears crawl against my eyes. "B-but—" I stammer. "Did they both . . . ?"

"That kind of crash, at that speed," Ter says, lowering his eyes. He lays his hand on the small of my back. The Cloud revs to life. I'm thrown hard into the rail, like I've been punched in the gut. My hair curtains out around my head, a white tunnel trailing the Cloud. Strands stick to my cheeks.

In the distance—one final, blazing gasp. It sets the black water aglow, and then the strait swallows it whole.

It's consumed everything.

Left nothing behind.

48

REN
9:51 P.M., FRIDAY

In the shallow moat, Dunn has assembled a unit of four Omnis docked side by side. Their black chrome exteriors are nearly invisible in the water. Meanwhile, a giant red-bottomed vessel churns downriver. Fluorescent floodlights illuminate a bare deck—*the barge*.

Fighting a tightness in my throat, I hop into the only Omni still empty—a single-seater, best for navigating small spaces. The convex moonroof shudders closed, giving me a plastic view of the night sky.

A panel of neon-green buttons on the dashboard control shi-shi things: internal temperature and the gender of the VoiceNav. I tap the screen, and it draws me an underwater map of the UMI.

The VoiceNav beeps twice, ready for me to tell it where to go.

"Lihn's Take-Out," I say into the mic.

That'll get me close enough, as the restaurant and Derek's place neighbor each other. It also won't give Dunn an exact location. On the Nav screen, a fat yellow line worms its way through the old city's rubbish, ending at my destination.

Estimated time is about thirty-five minutes to cross the strait.

The mobile submerges. Bubbles trace around the moon-roof and disappear. I don't have to step on nothin'—the Omni does all the work: a mobile with military capabilities adapted for even the laziest of folk. It spins out east, head-long into the strait. Like a needle of light, its beamers pierce the brack water. They shine on the sunken city—geometric structures covered in fuzzy green.

I take even breaths, force the calm down into my nervous system. I think about being inside a twister, where they say you don't get swept up. Through the rounded glass, building remnants give way to a riverbed of seaweed. Schools of fish shimmer past.

Flanked by two DI Omni and trailed by a third, I make my way across the strait. No scenic underwater buildings here, just days and days of open water. I adjust the speed to an easy cruise, and I wait.

"In approximately three hundred feet, you will have arrived at your destination," the Nav's cool voice informs before I get a visual confirmation. Moments later, boxy structures wrapped in green wool are my welcoming committee. Hairy plants wave us by in slow motion.

The mobile veers between two buildings, down what was once a road. Its internal proximity sensor kicks in—a sharp left, then right. It even avoids land mobiles, now no more than muddy, leftover lumps.

I feel useless, despite my lofty decision—destroying this planet's greatest curse and its greatest miracle.

In the rear and side mirrors, three Omnis still surround me.

A few blocks from the famous Lihn's Take-Out, I spot twin black chrome Omnis. Our parade of headlights has caught their attention, blood in the water. One for Kitaneh and one for Lucas.

Guess Derek's comm disappeared into the void.

The mobiles cross each other, then blow toward me.

Now's no time for autopilot. Reaching under the wheel, I disengage so I'm back in manual.

"Agent Dane!" I hear through the mobile's internal comm— it's from one of the other Omnis. "Explain to me why we are under attack—"

The speaker cuts out, replaced with white noise. I try to send a message to Dunn from my own cuffcomm, but the timewheel just spins around and around and the message never sends. Nav system's gone dark as well.

Only one answer: Kitaneh's jammed both the GPS and all outgoing radio signals . . . she don't want anyone finding out where we are. I might be able to receive messages, but I'd have to get one to know.

I do the only sane thing I can think of—gun the engine and make off like a tuna fish with a rocket on its back. Thankfully, in this baby, there's no lag time.

I slingshot right past one of the black bullets.

Through the window, I spot the Derek look-alike. His square jaw has more iron than his brother's.

Spinning the wheel to the right, I take off down a sliver of a road. An alley, hardly wider than this Omni. I'm right where I found the airlock. That time, I broke the code and swam to the spring from inside.

Doubt it'll work twice. Kitaneh would have changed the code, for sure. *I need Derek to find me a different way in.*

I check the rear, curious to see how she's handling three DI all by her lonesome. She dives under one Omni, scraping its undercarriage. It takes me a moment, but then I see what she's doing—she's trying to either jam their artillery barrel with the darts inside, or knock them loose.

Like a black cloud, Lucas's mobile floats into the cramped alley, blocking my view.

I angle my wheel upward to bring the Omni diagonal. Then, straight vertical. Finally, I'm rolling backward, nose over butt in a perfect 180.

I hope my heart doesn't fall out of my mouth like emptying the garbage. Dangling by the grace of my seat belt, the blood rushes to my eyeballs. I flex my quads, using the muscle as a buffer between the seat belt and my thigh fat.

I gun the engine, leaving Lucas behind.

Ahead, Kitaneh's playing cat and mouse, attacking and

dodging at the last possible moment. One DI tries to launch a dart into her mobile, but it sputters underneath him—her sabotage was a success. The two Omnis go nose-to-nose, at a stalemate.

A fifth DI joins the fray.

It targets another DI Omni. A dart ejects from its undercarriage, followed by a net. The dart strikes home, and the net wraps itself around the mobile. Its props slow, caught up in the tough cord.

It's Derek—I inhale, spotting his lucky hair glinting in the cockpit.

He targets the Omni still nose-to-nose with Kitaneh.

No dart this time—he just catapults himself through the water.

It's a suicide mission . . . Derek's ten feet from the other Omni. Eight feet, no intention of slowing. *What's he playing at?* My knuckles go bone-white on the steering wheel. I hold my breath, watching. Kitaneh, however, seems like she might have a clue. She waits there, eye-to-eye with the DI mobile, as Derek races closer.

Moments before the two collide, Derek dives from the airlock. I gasp, loosening my grip on the wheel. A beamer severed from the totaled Omni floats to the riverbed, lighting up Derek's hair. He's a copper fish swimming through river mud, appearing in my windshield. Past him, I can make out Kitaneh's headlights—she cuts around a corner, disappearing.

Tap, tap, tap—

Frenzied, I glance around the pit. Finding the button that opens the airlock, I slam it down much harder than necessary.

Derek swims in. The airlock closes behind him and water drains away. He falls into the small space behind my seat, a soggy, sodden mess.

"You pulled a me," I inform him, impressed, keeping an eye on the remaining two Omnis. Their yellow beamers zig and zag, aimless. They're blind as bats until the mud settles.

Derek shakes his head like a dog, brack water spitting around the pit. "To the cave?" he asks, hoping I've changed my mind.

I haven't.

I nod.

Derek's cuffcomm buzzes. "It's Sipu," he says, confused. "She just sent me coordinates."

"Coordinates?"

Shrugging, he shows me the message:

40°46'42.46"N, 74° 0'11.37"W

"No idea," he says, lowering his wrist.

Kneeling behind me, Derek lays his hand on my knee. "I can get us to the cave—*us*, Ren. I'm coming with you. You're not dying, not on my watch. If that means I have to keep you alive every step of the way, that's what I'm doing."

I take his hand in mine. Our fingers interlock, and we

squeeze palms. If he's expecting me to put up a fight, he's mistaken. "Okay," I say.

That's my only answer.

I don't want to do this alone.

49

AVEN
10:25 P.M., FRIDAY

Thirty miles turn to twenty, then fifteen.

A perfect circle of a moon hangs in the sky, lighting up forests on both sides of the strait. This far north, it's more of a river. Hundreds of trees hug the coast, more types than I ever knew existed. Dark, furry, cone-shaped ones. Fluttery mammoths that shiver all over with the wind. They swallow the ground. You'd never know there was ground.

A few miles downriver, strange lights dot the bank.

I join Benny at the helm and inspect his map. We learned geography at Nale's, but that was ages ago. Although Upstate is considered a single region, it's actually split into thirty: one for each reservoir. They have *that* many.

Only one aqueduct, however, can still supply the UMI with fresh . . . the one in Falls.

In the back of the Cloud, Callum frantically draws math on the air. "Benny, you wouldn't happen to have a pen and paper, would you?" he asks, pausing and cursing. "I can't remember this many numbers."

Benny rummages around in the glove compartment. "I don't know," he grumbles, skeptical.

"What are you doing?" Ter asks, sitting next to him.

Callum doesn't answer.

"Use the back." Benny hands over a stick of black chalk and a folded-up map. He returns to the wheel, frazzled gray hair sticking out in a hundred directions. His looks like one of those globe things we had in Nale's science room, with electric lightning inside.

"Nearly there, kiddos," he says.

Turning face-front again, I gasp.

Fluorescent towers rise into the sky, each level shaped like a flat wheel. Inside—*farms*. I've never seen one for real, just on holos in class. Upstate exports all sorts of fresh produce, since they have the water: another reason why they wanted to cut off their supply.

Squinting, I make out yellow and red and blue fruits growing against the glass. At the center, a mega-sprinkler goes *ch-ch-ch*, dousing them with water.

More towers line the coast, bright glass farms that spiral up into the sky. Between each, greenery takes over. If I didn't know a place like the Ward existed, nothing about this strange land would make me believe—back home is so different.

"Guys . . . how will we even find the magistrate?" I ask,

realizing I know nothing about Falls—I'll have no idea what to do when we get there.

No one answers.

I go backward in my mind through all of Nale's forgotten classes, trying to think of something that will help. Remembering the protest, I turn to the others. "What day of the month is it?"

"The thirtieth, maybe? Or the first . . ." Ter checks his comm. "Thirtieth. Why?"

"And what days of the month are the water auctions held?"

Callum doesn't look up from his work. "The first, the seventh, the fifteenth, and the thirtieth, I believe," he answers, still drawing his math squiggles. "At midnight, they release the dam into the winning aqueducts."

"The auction," Benny says, tapping his temple.

Callum curses. He throws his fist into the back of his soft, cushioned seat. "Dammit," he says again, staring into the air. The map, now covered in black, falls off his lap.

"What is it?" Ter asks, but Callum presses his lips together.

Defeated, he shakes his head. He won't tell us. "Dammit," he says again. This time it's just a whisper.

Squeezing into the plush seat next to him, I ask, "What did Ren ask you? If it has to do with her, it has to do with me too."

Callum folds up the map. "It's nothing," he says softly. "She made me promise."

"I'm making you unpromise. Tell me."

He laughs, barely, and stands. "She has her reasons, Aven. She doesn't want you to worry about her," he says, handing Benny the blackened paper.

"But *should* I be worried?"

"Maybe she doesn't know herself." He returns to his seat and avoids my eyes.

My heart cowers. I keep very still. He won't let me pry this thing out of him—no means no. And if I want to fight with that answer, I can't.

East of us, higher up, headlights flash by. Shadows run across the river. Engines *vroom* against concrete.

"They're mobiles, for land. Cars." Benny points to a road nestled in the hill. "With the price of gasoline, though, anyone still driving one is probably wealthier than we can imagine." He pauses, awed, watching the cars go by. A gargantuan, brightly lit sign hangs over the eastern road. On it, green painted trees and the words—

"Welcome to the Falls!" Ter bellows as we pass it by.

We're really here.

My insides shudder like someone's banging on the window. Wringing my hands, I press my fingernail-less fingers against my lips.

Can we really stop a war?

50

ike sharks dancing, three identical Omnis duck and
dodge in the murk. Kitaneh veers for mine, but one DI
guy blocks her off, their mobiles screeching underwater.
"How do we get into the cave?" I ask Derek.

From the way he's looking at me, I can tell he's not excited
about the answer. "Find your way back to the airlock," he
says, twisting around in his seat, unsure of the direction.

Thankfully, my trusty Nav don't need eyes. Following the
screen, I reverse and turn right into the narrow underwater
alley. There, a few feet above the muddy sand, is a circular
steel door—the airlock, built right into Derek's building.

"Okay," he begins, pointing. "You see how there's a few
feet of brick between the airlock and the riverbed? If you
could drill a hole into that gap under the airlock, you'll wind

up in the drainage tank. From there you're only about thirty feet from the cave."

"*Drill* a hole?" I balk—I didn't bring my drills. "And how do you propose we do that?"

Derek glances around the pit.

"*We* are the drill. Wonderful. You've got no back doors? Nothing?"

"Kitaneh changed all the locks, and our rainwater-collection drains are too narrow. This is our way in.

"But, Ren—" he warns. "The building is thick. You'll need to gather enough speed to break through the brick."

"It won't work." I shake my head, eyeing the narrow alley between Derek's building and the one next door. "Both this alley and this mobile are about ten feet. I can't get the momentum I'll need."

Derek looks out the windshield. A school of dark fish swims out the window of the opposite building. "What about a window? Ground floor, across from the airlock?"

I inhale, skeptical, but I lower the Omni closer to the riverbed. The opposite building has at least four ground-floor windows—one almost directly across from the airlock. It's the color of mold, green with overgrowth, thick and fuzzy. Ain't even a window no more, which is probably why I didn't think of using it first.

I bite my nail and nod, inspecting it. *This could work.*

Like parallel parking a grown man in a shoe box, I reverse through the water. Then forward. Then reverse. Again and again, until I step on it, driving right into the algae-coated glass. My cuffcomm buzzes, but this kind of maneuvering requires both hands.

The window groans against my Omni. I hear it cracking, breaking away from its frame. Uneven green triangles shower down, bouncing off my mobile's nose and continuing to sink.

The debris clears, and I steer us into what looks like it once was a child's room. Clouds of plankton hover over an algae-coated crib. Holding my breath, I doughnut us around till the nose faces the window.

This is it, I think. Last time I pulled a stunt like this, I had the good sense *not* to be inside the damn thing when it crashed. "We can't use autopilot, right?" I groan, knowing the answer.

"If you want to risk not hitting the proper speed, sure. Or it could malfunction. You'd end up drilling a hole two feet off-course, which would be completely useless."

Again, my comm buzzes, this time with a second message. It's from Callum. I swallow and read the message.

> 5 liters. You won't make it... Ren, we can find another way—don't do it.

The Omni starts to feel like a death trap. "Derek," I say, dizzy in my seat. "How much blood is in the human body?"

He knows why I'm asking, and reaches for my comm. "About five liters," he whispers, reading Callum's message for himself.

"I don't believe it," he says, squeezing my hand. He moves out of his seat and crouches next to me. "Don't do this," he asks. Pleads. He lays his forehead against my thigh. "You don't have to. . . ."

I don't have to, he's right.

Am I willing to die so that humanity can die also?

I'd be leaving Aven on purpose.

Every day of her life that I wouldn't be around for—I imagine them. . . .

Her first real kiss. The first time she gets behind the wheel of an Omni. Her first date. Sometimes, she talked about wanting to work the rooftop gardens if she ever got better. . . . I imagine her face the first day she plants a seedling, and I laugh out loud with her, here in this Omni, the first day it sprouts up green.

The imaginings don't stop. They come to me like memories, like moments that have already happened, they're so precise. She's in white now—I knew she'd get married before me, had no doubts there. I'd be the happiest person just to get to hold her train.

A baby . . .

Could she forgive me for this? Would she understand?

The Omni shrinks, or I grow in size, suddenly too large for this measly body I was born into. The air in my lungs dies, collapses; there's still so much for us to do together. How can this be the right decision when it means I have to leave her?

I'll never be ready to leave Aven.

And then, something else occurs to me. . . .

Every moment I want to spend with her, every milestone—you only hit them because life moves forward, because death is out there, waiting.

Without death, without risk, where is failure?

And if you always have another chance . . . how do you make the most of each moment?

The spring is a threat to humanity at its very core.

"Derek," I say, running my fingers through his hair. "I'm doing it. I'm doing it now." He looks up at me with eyes so bloodshot they're red, not rust.

Braced against my knee, he lifts himself and moves to the backseat. He searches for the safety belt and locks himself in. "All right," he says, because that's all he can manage.

Five seconds' worth of fear, I tell myself. The Omni hovers in the child's waterlogged bedroom, about fifteen feet from the window, giving us a total of twenty feet to hit the right speed. I can see the airlock, and underneath, those few feet of brick we've gotta hit to make it into the drainage tank.

I wish Benny were here—his voice in my ear, all confidence. He'd have calculated the exact distance and speed necessary. With his old maps, he'd have been able to figure out how thick the wall was. But he's not here. It's like racing with a blindfold.

I take a deep breath and close my eyes. No more than five seconds.

Five . . . *What if I miss the airlock?*

Four . . . *What if the crash kills me first?*

Three . . . *What if I can't escape the mobile?*

Two . . . *What if I drown?*

One . . . *What if—what if I actually do it?*

Zero . . . *Enough.*

51

AVEN
10:45 P.M., FRIDAY

"Looks like we're here," Benny says as the river forks. Brassy music and rowdy laughter floats over our heads, carried downriver. He leans on the engine and we boat uphill, steering right past a brack waterfall. Then the shallow waterway dies out, spilling over smooth, flat rocks.

A tall stone wall stops us from going any farther. Twinkling gold ropes of light dangle from end to end. It reminds me of the pearl-like necklace Mama used to wear.

Pitched atop the wall, red and white tents fatten with a gust of wind. We're thrown the scent of food like tossing table scraps to a pet. It's real food too, farm-grown, probably cultivated in the very same towers we just passed.

My mouth waters on cue—Ren and I went for so long with too little. I don't even care that I've turned stray again, begging for a place at a table, any table.

This is the dam, I realize—the stony barrier that cuts off their reservoir, plugging up our aqueducts so we're always thirsty. It's how they keep the water to themselves.

We're in its very shadow.

And everyone is dancing on it? Laughing? Eating and drinking? They must have forgotten us. It was decades ago that we fought them for water, and then the Blight hit—other nations wouldn't come near us with a ten-foot pole. They ignored us; we disappeared from memory. There's no other explanation.

Bolted to the massive gray stones, a sign reads: *Ye Old Dam Faire.*

Benny chuckles. "'Dam Faire.' Ha. Clever bunch." He brings the Cloud to a full stop and pulls a wheel of rope from its center hatch.

"Tie her tight, Aven. We still need to get home," he says, throwing me the line.

The others might be glad he didn't ask them, but I'm not. This is new—getting to be useful. For so long, Ren did so much for me.

I like it this way.

Hopping over the side, I find a metal handle drilled between the rocks, exactly for this purpose. The others join me as I easily tie off the knot with two near-complete hands.

Then we turn our eyes to the dam—it doesn't cut the river in a straight line. Instead, it curves backward, morphing into a rounded stone staircase. As I get closer, I realize the first few stairs are as tall as I am, and it's not actually a staircase at all.

A man-made waterfall must have flowed over this, once.

I begin climbing the bottom tier. The others tell me to wait, but the stairs shorten as they rise, and it only becomes easier. I let them yell—they'll catch up.

Soon the stairs end, and I'm face-to-face with a flat wall. To my right, I spot an *actual* staircase. It spirals all the way to the top. I crawl over the rail, one leg at a time, and climb, feeling every one of my muscles flex and burn.

I'm breathing harder, and my head feels light—but even as my body hurts, I love it. Before, my world used to be so small. A room, a bed, pain. My brain is still catching up, growing.

More quickly than I expect, I reach the top.

Everywhere it smells of cooked food. A dense crowd walks up and down the narrow stone pathway. Weaving through, I cross over to the other side of the dam, wanting a better view of the reservoir. There, I look out over the edge.

The freshwater goes on for miles.

As I take a step back from the wall, I notice something unusual—the top row of boulders isn't the same color as the rest. It's a darker shade of gray, like it hasn't been bleached by the sun yet. When the others join me, I point. "Look at the color."

Ter, Callum, and Benny—still breathing deeply from the climb—squint until they see what I mean.

"Do you think . . . ?" Benny asks, grazing the stonework with one finger.

"The dam was raised, wasn't it?" I say, already knowing the answer. "They *do* have extra water."

"Could be they've opted to sell less." Callum inspects the dark, heavy boulders against the lighter ones. "Agriculture might have proven more lucrative, and with drought season coming, it'd make sense to stock up."

"Perhaps," Benny says, his voice still ragged from the haul up. He bends down and looks closer at the stonework. "Perhaps not."

Leaning back against the dam, Callum crosses his arms. "You have a different hypothesis?"

"No," Benny says, shaking his head. "But this raise wasn't added in a day. Take a look." He points from one boulder to the next, until he taps the stones from the original dam. "Even more gradations in the color of the rock, see?"

We all bend down—he's right. The lower the boulders, the more bleached they get . . . by just a hair.

"An unaccounted surplus . . . ," Ter says, scratching the dark fuzz at the nape of his neck. Benny nods his head vigorously.

"From where, do you think?" I ask.

"Let's find out." Benny steps away from the wall, and we follow him into the throngs of the fair.

Under smoke-filled tents, striped red and white like Christmas candy canes, I bump into a woman—she's wearing a white apron, selling some type of food. It's long, yellow, and white, wrapped in open, stringy green leaves.

Regretfully, I show her my empty pockets and keep walking, even though my mouth is hurting from hunger. A moment later, Ter runs up to me, only to hurry us away from her stall. When we're out of her sight, he opens my palm. In it, he places the same yellow food.

Now, Ter's dad is wealthy, but last I checked we didn't exactly bring spending money in our DI uniforms. "How'd you—" I start, but stop when Ter casts me a sneaky smile.

I'm about to eat stolen goods.

I grin, not caring in the least. I'm hungry, and the woman selling the yellow food looked okay. Peering closer at the pale little buttons, I recognize them: corn. We used to get it at Nale's, but the buttons were all separated in a pile.

Someone passes me, also holding the corn, I watch as they eat, hoping for instructions. They bring the whole thing to their mouth and take a bite.

I do the same.

The tiny pieces pop open in my mouth, sweet and buttery. *This is food*, I realize. Not the protein bars or rehydrated soup that Ren and I are used to. *Real food.*

The feeling I had before returns. It's ugly. . . . I've only had it a few times. It's how I felt seeing Ren, healthy, sometimes.

The envy leaves me bitter. I try to shake away the scorched feeling, but I can't. These people—they have enough to share with us, and they choose not to.

"How is it?" Ter asks, smiling and drooling a little.

I want to smile back at him, but the anger in my stomach has infected all the other feelings too. Instead, I push him the corn.

He tries it, and his green eyes roll back into his head. He raises one clawed hand into the air. "Heaven," he moans, wiping butter from his chin.

Then, his face drops. He knows what I'm thinking—I'm judging their happiness. Wondering if they deserve it more than me, or Ren, or him, or anyone else I care about.

They don't deserve it more.

From the west end of the dam, an announcer beckons everyone to come close. His voice is staticky through the megaphone. Benny and Callum catch up, and together we follow the flocks.

This is it—Harcourt's here. He'll hear me speak my piece, and I'll make him understand. I have to.

Swallowing, I step deeper into the crowd.

"The auction is *open!*"

52

REN
10:45 P.M., FRIDAY

I force my fear into the backseat, focusing on the end goal. I've got the perfect view—a near straight shot to the airlock, and below, the drainage tank.

"Here goes," I say to Derek, nothing left holding me back.

I lay my sole into the pedal.

Inhaling, my head whips against the headrest. The Omni bucks forward. As it scrapes the window frame, the angle gets thrown; I readjust the wheel. We shoot through the water. Ahead, the bricks get closer and closer. My beamers shine on the airlock, the metal so bright it's like driving into the sun.

Any second now.

We're feet away. Three, then two, then—

Like a fist, metal flies into brick.

The Omni screams as the wall jigsaws apart. Somewhere between the bulding and the drainage tank, its nose crumples like balled-up paper. *Stupid alloy metals mixed in*, I realize too late. *Damn swanky mobiles.*

The headlights flicker twice, then go out. Brack water sprays in from a hole under the nose. Then, like a ball being hit by a bat, I'm swung again—this time sideways.

I slam into the opposite side of the pit, my head colliding with steel. Tiny bees swarm my vision, stinging the nerves behind my eyeballs.

"It's Lucas!" Derek yells over the screeching of metal on metal.

It happens again—

Over and over, my mobile gets clobbered, lodged between the building and the airlock's empty drainage tank. More water needles itself into the pit, stabbing me in the shoulder blade. Somewhere, a crack widens—the needle becomes a jetstream, and the mobile fills. *We've got to get out.*

"I'm opening the moonroof now!" I yell to Derek, pushing the button—the plastic lifts. I squeeze out of the Omni, only to bump my head against the airlock above and land in water up to my knees. I turn to check on Derek.

He's . . . leaving?

He's trying to wiggle back into the alley, his body fighting brack water as it shoots through the hole in the building. *Why?*

My heart takes over. It beats like a propeller picking up speed, faster and faster, until I'm afraid it will explode. It's not that I don't want to do this alone . . . *I* can't *do this alone.*

The tank's almost fully flooded—water wraps around my ribs. A long, high-pitched beep fills the airlock above. Again, my head bumps the grate. Treading in the brack, I turn . . .

. . . to find Kitaneh standing over me, locking the steel door to the basement. This is why she disappeared—she wanted to cut me off from the inside. The blade at her belt glistens under the fluorescent bulb.

"You led them *here*?" She kneels down, grabs me by my necklace, and yanks. Both lucky pennies—Aven's and Callum's—stab against my windpipe.

I gasp, but air can't make it in.

"You're weak—just like I told Derek. I knew it—the moment someone you love was threatened, you folded."

Not true . . . I think, digging my nails under the chain. Blood rushes to my head and black squeezes at my periphery.

Holding her apple-shaped face inches from mine, Kitaneh lifts me from the water. "I should have killed you when I had the chance," she says, scowling. Dark and ready, she tips her chin.

I don't see Kitaneh reaching for her knife . . . or the blade's tip gouging my stomach.

I don't even see my blood as it spits against her chest—a jolt of bright red.

I feel only the hot blade slicing into me with liquid ease. It lodges deep inside as water slaps my back. I gag; both pennies continue to cut off air.

My heart powers on like something electronic. It beats at a pace I can't keep up with, like there's one long razor blade being dragged around inside my chest. Dizziness makes my stomach twist, and the knife inside sets sunflares off in my veins—blinding bursts of crimson and canary.

Then, the necklace loosens. . . .

My leaden body drops into the brack, released without warning. I'm wrapped in liquid warmth, shivering. In the water my blood parachutes out of me—I watch it like I've watched my breath hang in the air on a cold day. A reminder of life. When the red stops, I'll stop too . . . but I'm not ready yet.

I'm not where I need to be.

I won't die here.

53

AVEN
11:15 P.M., FRIDAY

"**M**agistrate Harcourt, please read off the opening bids."

On cue, everyone cheers.

A man, wide like a balloon, takes the megaphone from the announcer. His white shirt puckers, too tight at his waist, and hair pokes through the gaps between his buttons. He eats enough.

Behind him stand two men and one woman—each in green, wearing dark ties and beige wide-brimmed hats. A small gold shield on their breast pockets reads: *City of Falls, Ranger.* They're holding rifles, real rifles, across their chests, guarding a corridor. At its end, the sign on a plain, brown door reads: *Distributary.*

Where they must control the ducts . . .

Magistrate Harcourt reads off numbers too fast; I can't

understand him. When he pauses, people make megaphone-hands and hoot—that's how high the bids are. Their hollers echo over the reservoir.

The magistrate names places I've never heard of and some that I have. He pauses. "This week's winner is the township of Engle!" The round man laughs, bowing to the crowd.

Everyone claps, smiling at the closing bid.

Engle . . . I try to remember maps from school—Engle's on the Mainland, only a few miles north of the UMI.

"Engle hasn't participated in our auction for quite a few months. We're glad to see they're back on their feet. Enjoy the fair, everyone!" Magistrate Harcourt says, winking. People disperse, some shaking his hand and thanking him.

Benny lays both palms on my shoulders.

Now.

"Magistrate Harcourt!" I say firmly.

Hands clasped behind his back, the magistrate strides over wearing a wide grin. "Yes? How can I help you?"

He takes a moment to examine us. Ren used to tell me that the racers' girlfriends would look at her this way. He steps back. "You're not from around here."

I glance at the others. Callum's still in his fancy suit, but Ter and I are in DI uniform, and Benny's wearing jeans so old they're brown.

Compared to everyone else here, we look like paupers.

Compared to everyone else here, we *are* paupers.

Seeing the UMI insignia on our uniform's arm patch, the magistrate takes many more steps back. "Get away," he says, shuddering. "Leave. I won't have you infecting my citizens with your virus. Guards!"

Callum approaches him—"I'm Dr. Justin Cory," he says, holding out his hand. In his nice black coat and pants, the magistrate pauses. When it's clear Harcourt has no intention of shaking hands, Callum pulls an ID card from inside his jacket instead. "On my honor as a medical practitioner, I can personally attest to these people's health. No one here is sick, I promise."

Magistrate Harcourt examines the card. "Why are you here?" I close my eyes, arms crossed behind me. The others think what I'm about to ask is crazy, and maybe it is. But that alone—is even *crazier*. This is everyone's planet and everyone's water, and people should take care of one another.

I swallow my doubts. I have to.

"We're here to ask . . . ," I start. My voice breaks. I try again. "We're here to ask if you could open the aqueduct to the UMI. Please."

"Excuse me?" The magistrate cocks his head, smiling.

I say it again.

He does a double take and points to the megaphone stand. "I'm sorry, did you not just witness the auction?" he asks politely. He thinks *I'm* confused—

He's the one who's oblivious.

That bitterness rises from my stomach up into my throat. Swallowing the anger, I walk to the north side of the dam and look out over the reservoir—inky water for miles.

"You have so much fresh, more than you need. So much more, that you built the dam higher to make room for it all."

313

I stop to breathe, so nervous, my leg muscles are shaking. When I look up at the magistrate, he's red-faced, guiltily avoiding my eyes. "Just thirty miles south, people are spending all their money buying black market, preparing for the drought. Why *wouldn't* you want to help?"

Magistrate Harcourt scoffs, then claps his hands in laughter. His stomach shivers, straining the buttons even further. He scratches his head. "Child," he says, and already I know I'm not going to like what follows. "That is not how the world works; no one likes to be asked for handouts. It's been decades since the disaster. Take some responsibility."

"But *that's* not how the world works either!" I cry, wagging my finger at him. *He's blind.* "Sometimes the hole's too deep and you can't dig yourself out. The longer it goes on, the harder it gets, until the only way is for someone to help you out."

Magistrate Harcourt stops laughing and shakes his head. "Have you heard the saying, 'survival of the fittest'? None of this is my problem. A lion doesn't send back the goat, because he's the lucky one born with teeth. You have your rainwater—you're standing here; the collection systems must be working. These are *our* natural resources."

Magistrate Harcourt's fat brown eyes glare down at me, as hard and unyielding as this dam.

"Put simply," he continues, "this water is ours. If you want it, you will have to pay for it at auction, just like everyone else. The UMI is not my responsibility. I am sorry."

He doesn't look sorry. "So that's your answer?" My voice croaks, pitifully. I don't know what else to say. I could tell him about Dunn's army—throw it in his face that they'll arrive on his doorstep in a few hours—but I'd never sell us out like that.

"That's all?"

He sighs, exasperated. The conversation is over. "Since you are already here," he says with a false smile as he spreads his arms wide, "you may as well enjoy the fair."

Swiftly, he drops his hands and his fake kindness. "But I expect you to be gone by morning."

With those last words he shuffles off, not one glance back.

From some tent, a balloon bursts in the air. A girl squeals in laughter. The ding of some lively bell, the cheering chorus. Sounds blur together.

The happy fair goes on.

54

I leave Kitaneh's knife in.

Once it's out, I'll bleed freely. Too soon for that.

My penny necklace weighs tons—it wants to sink me—and my eyes burn. Not from the salty brack, but from tears. I'm crying, swallowing water, and I need air. I clutch the hilt in my belly and using only one arm I swim up, reaching, fumbling for the grate.

I grab its edge—

Derek?

He's grappling with Kitaneh—he must've followed her into the apartment. He tries to restrain her from behind, but she jerks sideways. Too fast, he winds his arms tight around her body. She can't free herself. And now, she's got no knife to fight with.

316

Derek presses his mouth to her ear, struggling to keep her still. "Ren can do it. She can destroy the spring." Kitaneh bucks, almost breaking free. Derek doesn't allow it.

"Impossible," she spits back, but her voice is soft—like maybe she hopes she's wrong.

"Voss was my father. Emilce, my mother," I say in a voice so weak it's hardly my own.

Derek's face drops.

Even with a knife in my gut, I find myself thinking crazy things . . . things that won't matter a half hour from now: I hope he might come to love me someday, knowing whose blood runs through my veins.

I'm barely able to hold on to the grate, but Kitaneh needs to hear the rest. "I didn't know until today . . . there's something with my blood—a protein—the right amount will kill the ecosystem." I take deep breaths as my vision narrows and my toes go numb.

Kitaneh stops fighting. She slumps over Derek's arms, and I think if he weren't holding on to her, she might collapse.

"She'd be willing to die for this?" Her voice is hoarse as Derek lets her go.

I nod, salty tears gathered at the corners of my mouth.

Kitaneh's eyes redden and her tanned face pales. When she meets Derek's gaze, it's like watching someone discover birth and death in the same moment.

"So many centuries we've kept the spring hidden," she whispers, staring into nothing. "Forever, it seems. Protecting humanity from their very own nature. Secretly . . ." She chokes on a feeble laugh. "Secretly, I'd hoped there was a different reason. That perhaps, we weren't just hiding it—we were preserving it. For a better kind of human."

Derek is quiet. He nods his head gently, like he too might've harbored that secret hope. Outside, a dull thud shakes the building's foundation—it must be Lucas and the remaining DI.

When my wrist buzzes, I barely feel it over the pain in my gut. Static fills the airlock. "Respond, dammit!" Chief Dunn's voice crackles through the comm's weak audio. "I've sent another unit to the last known GPS coordinates. They'll be there shortly. And Dane, if I find out you knowingly led my men into some kind of trap . . ."

I don't hear the rest. Dunn's threats don't matter no more.

Kitaneh reaches for the wheel, about to open the basement-side airlock. "Lucas can't hold them off alone. I'll let him know what you're doing. We'll keep them away for as long as we can." Her hand lingers there.

She spins the wheel. "Do it."

Pressing another button, the grate under Derek's feet retracts.

He jumps into the water and the airlock continues to flood. Taking one long inhale, he wraps his arm across my chest and leads me to the cave. I trail behind, too weak to swim on my own.

The sides narrow around us. I'm banged against slick rock. Without light, we're unable to see how tight the space has become and I tuck in my limbs to avoid getting bumped again.

The first air-hunger pang hits. This time, with a knife

fixed in my gut, it's harder to force back the ache. I malfunction, dizzied, swallowing back vomit. My throat contracts as my jaw clenches, but I defy the need to open my mouth. I kick, but almost immediately, my kneecaps ache. I just don't have the energy.

Derek's pulling me along faster than I could swim on my own, and soon, the cave widens, curving upward. I barely stick my tongue out, and it comes back with a sweet taste. Then, like an ice cube dropped into hot water, my skin melts into a new heat. I'm wrapped up in it, warmed straight through to my core.

For a split second, I'm too hot, anxiety-ridden—*this might not work.* My thoughts spirals toward every worst-case scenario.

I've led Dunn straight here.

It will never, ever end.

Air . . .

Derek and I gasp into the pitch-black cove smaller than Benny's cloud—a watery pool spotted with neon-green-capped mushroom stars. Fresh spills into my mouth. Out of habit, I spit as he cradles me against his chest.

"You're sure about this?" Derek asks, trembling under his wet cotton T-shirt.

"Too late not to be, ain't it?"

Water drips like rain onto my nose and between my lips. I blink, confused, because my face is above the surface.

I'm swallowing his tears.

"Go."

A jab under my ribs sends shock waves throughout my

entire body. My teeth chatter. He's twisting the blade. I can feel the blood as it's wrung from me. I imagine red clouds like nuclear warfare covering every glowing organism in the cave. It surges over the algae and the spores, and every mushroom. My mind is a bonfire, searing against the underwater universe.

I cough blood and fire and smoke.

The basic drive to survive overrides my mission, as if my mind has pulled on the emergency brakes. My rib cage is a straitjacket. I buck against Derek's arms, springwater splashing onto my stomach.

Like a storm passing, the searing disappears. My flank stops throbbing, my breathing steadies.

The damn water. It's healing me. How can I bleed out if it's closing up my wound?

It's too strong.

"Twist again," I tell Derek. "Lift me from the water and hold on tighter." If I can't fight the instinct to survive, he has to fight it for me.

Again, he rotates the hilt. It's a metal helix drilling my stomach, while my own helixes escape.

Did you know that the heart only gets one billion beats in a lifetime?

I told that to Aven once. Now I'm proving myself wrong.

Like flipping a switch, my eyesight turns off. Before, I was seeing by the light of a hundred million green plants. Now it's just an empty night.

From a distant planet, somewhere light years away, Aven calls my name. *Ren!* It's as though the rocky cave wall is speaking to me. Derek hears nothing. I alone hear the whispering walls. They quiet, though.

The blade drills deeper.

My body burns up in the sky. All my thoughts are trapped under glass. I'm outside the glass. I see my sister, a bird, living on a branch out of my reach. She's happy. She looks away.

I open my eyes, or maybe they were open all along and only now they're working again.

The spring's green twinkles.

I cannot take this going and coming.

"Higher," I croak. Derek raises me up. I'm lifted like a living constellation and hung on to the sky, where even dead things go to be immortal. Blood makes highways over my body, dripping into the pool.

Derek shakes. His whole body convulses over mine, sending ripples of blood-soaked spring water into green algae. It drinks the poison.

"I'm here, Ren. . . ."

He tells me I walked into his betting office like a bomb going off. That I made him cower and I made him laugh. He thought I was the toughest metal, but he was wrong. I was a mirror. He says words like *unfair* and *why her*, as my memory begins to melt.

Why am I in his arms if I can't hold them? Why does he have lips if I'm a ghost? Can a thought also be a kiss? I pretend it doesn't taste like a blank wall.

His name . . . what is his name?

"You're not alone," someone sobs, but I don't hear anything—just a passing cloud giving up the rain.

I am dying.

In my ears, the howl of death dogs. I bare my teeth in reply: *Take me.* From the back of my throat, a gurgling pours out. My heart is a breaking clock.

I'm dissecting myself like the frog in Nale's classroom—examining what's inside.

In me are all the things Voss and I have in common: Our blood, yes, but in that, a desperate clinging to the ones we love. Our relentlessness—the way we don't understand the word *no*. And . . . the legacy we leave behind.

I'm dying for Death.

Even as I undo the damage Voss caused, I will betray humanity too. Except, I'll do it uniquely, in my own way . . . as a daughter should—by denying them my faith. I don't harbor Kitaneh's secret hope.

Was this the right thing?

The question will live longer than I will.

Along the cave wall, green stars flicker in the water. Red laps up against slick algae, bathing their stems.

I'm being emptied into the universe.

One by one, the stars go out.

55

AVEN
11:30 P.M., FRIDAY

*W*e failed.

Like ants, we climb down the black spiral staircase. The Cloud bobs in the distance, tethered to the rocks, waiting. We're all so quiet there might've been a death. In a way, that's not wrong. Only it wasn't a person, it was an idea. Tiny and perfect, not yet met with the future. It was hope.

We failed.

I hate those words. Ren wouldn't think them. She doesn't allow it. Since the first time I saw her sneaking off to the races, she's been that way. Maybe that's why she always succeeds.

I won't fail, then. I won't accept defeat.

"We're not leaving," I say, halfway down the dam. "I want

to know where the extra water comes from. Did you see the magistrate's face when I mentioned it? I thought he felt guilty about not sharing, but that couldn't be less true, clearly. So, if he's not guilty about that, what *is* he guilty of?"

"You think he's hiding something?" Ter asks as both he and Callum skip stairs to catch up.

"It's the only answer that makes sense."

"The entrance to the distributary was heavily guarded," Callum says, glancing back at the dam. "I'm not sure how easy it'll be to investigate."

We need another way in. . . .

A gust of wind takes my hair, and I stifle a sigh. I imagine what it will look like at midnight—someone pushing the button: The aqueduct opens. Hundreds of gallons of reservoir fresh surge into the winner's city.

I look around, but all I see are stone and stairs, and the river forking ahead of us. The cusp of a brack waterfall flows white.

A waterfall . . .

At Nale's, we used to get holo time, when she'd replay old cartoons and movies. Characters were always hiding doors behind waterfalls. Even Robin Hood did it, and he was a fox.

Scrambling to the bottom of the stairs, I leap over rocks to cross the river. Once on the opposite bank, I race downhill, looking for a side view.

A *crunch-crunch, crunch-crunch* stops me in my tracks. I duck behind a boulder and freeze as a beam of light carves up and down the woods.

Patrolling the nearby grounds is a ranger—he's making

his way uphill, boots trampling the underbrush. Scanning downhill for more of them, another light catches my eye. About a hundred feet off, a woman sits inside an outpost flush with the treeline. Behind it, deeper in the woods, I spot a fenced area—it's dimly lit, but I can't tell if it's being patrolled.

Then I realize this side of the river is dotted with outposts . . . all hidden just deep enough in the woods that they're invisible from the river.

Only one directly faces the waterfall, though.

I'm onto something . . . and I'm trapped.

"Aven! Where'd you go?" Ter calls from a rock in the middle of the river.

The patrolling ranger shines his light on him. "State your business!" Inside the outpost, another ranger stands and peers through the glass to get a better look.

My chance.

Staying low, I scuffle downhill, dragging dirt and twigs under my feet. I don't slow until I'm directly in line with the outpost. To my left, a ravine drops at least fifty feet into the river below. To my right, the ranger. She casts unsure glances in Ter's direction.

As I inspect the waterfall, gusts of brack spray my face— I'm looking for an arc wide enough to fit a pathway.

All I see is the ravine. No path.

A yellow beam cuts across the grass just inches from my feet. I turn—*I'm too close to the waterfall*—but the ravine's right behind me; there's no place to go. The light swings closer. Without thinking, I avoid it. . . .

I step backward into the ravine.

My heart races, drugging me with adrenaline. I cry out, but it's swallowed by the rushing water. I wait for gravity to catch me and throw me down, but—

I'm not falling.

I've landed on . . . *glass*? A thick, clear ledge extends wide enough to walk along. My burning muscles shake with relief, calmed by the waterfall's cool drizzle. Choking on laughter, I crawl along the path, too shaky to stand. When it narrows, I have no choice; I pretend I'm walking a roof gutter or doing a balancing act for the circus. Soon it's barely wide enough for one foot, but I find a handle drilled into the gray rock face. Brack spray clings to my eyelashes and wets my lips, salty. Spotting a gray camouflaged door, I begin to feel heady, like I can do anything. *I was right.*

I touch the handle.

Then I read the sign.

Emergency Exit. Alarm Will Sound.

There's a keypad to the door's right—it locks electronically. I can't get in without the code. My stomach curdles. *Of course it's locked.* Turning back, I follow the ledge, but I don't cross onto the bank—I've already made it this far.

Instead, I type a message:

> Found the emergency exit, but it's got an electrical key-code lock. Any ideas?

As I wait for Ter's answer, the ranger stationed by the tree draws semicircles with her flashlight. The beam passes over the river and the waterfall, through the woods, then swings back over the waterfall again. I flatten myself, cheek to the glass, letting it pass me by, and wait for what seems like hours. They have to come up with a plan, I know . . . but the glass is cold, and the water is cold. I begin to shiver, so I curl into a ball. Finally, my wrist buzzes.

Callum's going to distract the rangers while Benny figures out a way to cut the power. He thinks he knows where they keep the circuit breaker. And I'm finding you.

As I type my reply, a second comm follows:

Where exactly are you?

I explain as best I can and press send, wondering about Callum's distraction. Creeping closer to the bank, my teeth chattering, I get a better look.

I don't have to wonder long. Downriver I hear the crack and sizzle of a dart fired into the air. Just one at first, but Callum must be on the move. Every few hundred feet, he fires another, then another.

In the sky, electric nets burst like blue fireworks as dozens of flashlights come out of the woodwork. About half are ordered to follow the noise while the rest stand their ground, scanning the forest—I watch the lights converge on one spot, then race off in a different direction. My stomach twists. . . . *Don't catch him.*

Behind the outpost, a gray-haired shadow zigzags through

the trees. *Benny!* I nearly fall off the glass ledge as I catch him headed for the fenced area—where he thinks they keep the circuit breaker.

The woman in the outpost holds her wrist to her mouth. Rangers line up and down the bank, creating a wall. *But where's Ter?*

Seconds later, he comes tumbling down the dirt and diving under the waterfall—but I'm in his way. He slams me, the soles of his shoes smacking into my shoulders. My legs slide over the ledge. Water soaks my DI uniform, freezing me from the thighs down. "Ter!" I yell, grasping for his ankle as my heart plummets.

Ter sits up—grabs me with both hands. "Throw your leg over," he tells me, grunting, and I do. With one hand holding mine, and the other holding my knee, he pulls me the rest of the way.

Shivering, heaving—I collapse into him.

"Holy hell," Ter whispers into my ear as he strokes my damp hair. "Holy, holy hell."

My body warms quicker than it would if he were anyone else.

Then, a quiet hum I hadn't even noticed . . . stops. Along the bank, every outpost goes dark. Ter's cuffcomm buzzes, and we read the message together.

You have ten seconds until the generators kick in.

"Yeah, yeah, Benny!" Ter pumps his fist by his side, helping me up as he stands. "You ready?"

I'm soaked to the bone, I'm shivering, and I can't feel my feet.

"Totally," I say, and take the lead. We walk along the ledge, spines hugging the rock face, until it gets too narrow. Then I grip the metal handle in the wall. "Eight seconds," Ter says.

Hands stacked on the knob, Ter laces his fingers over mine. I feel him against my new skin in a different way, in places that are decidedly not my hand. The back of my neck. My belly button.

He looks at me, and it's like being wrapped in a blanket of grass.

We twist the handle.

56

The emergency exit door swings open without a sound.
Ter flips on his comm light and we step into a completely dark corridor carved straight through river rock.
We fly through it, about two hundred feet, when we reach another door—

DISTRIBUTARY CONTROL CENTER

The keypad on the right is dark. We crouch and hear confused yelling from the other side. He opens the door an inch, and we glance into another pitch-black hallway. Someone else's cuffcomm casts white light on a small room with dozens of blank screens.

"Dammit!" a woman says, slamming her hands against a darkened switchboard. "Why the hell aren't the generators on?"

"They're coming, any minute now. You know there's a

330

delay. Jack, why don't you find out what's wrong before Lil here throws herself over the dam?"

They must be the aqueduct switchboard operators.

Each of their cuffcomms buzz.

Tapping Ter's shoulder, I point to a tiny room across the hall. As quietly as possible, we tiptoe across, ducking under a counter and exhaling. His heart beats so fast I actually feel it bumping against my skin.

"Shit, you guys. Something's going on. Something big," the other man says, reading his message. "Jack, go check the hall. We may have a break-in on our hands."

Moments after Jack disappears into the corridor, blue overhead lights buzz on and a muted glow fills our tiny room. Ter and I tuck ourselves in the darkest corner. Across from us are maps—backlit black glass atlases outlining the entire Falls region. At least ten aqueduct lines snake out in neon green from this very dam, including the one that leads to the UMI. Most branch southeast, which makes sense; the Wash Out hit coasts the worst, affecting both groundwater and reservoirs.

"Thirty to midnight," the man behind the switchboard says as the door to the corridor swings open and Jack reappears. "Let's get started."

I grab Ter's arm and we slide even further under the counter. Jack takes his seat watching rows of screens.

Signs line the topmost row: *Engle, Bergen, Orange, Pelham, UMI,* and other places I don't recognize. The Engle duct is being aired right now—*BROADCAST* is illuminated in red, over its row.

331

Every other screen watches a different section of its city's aqueduct. But under *Engle* only half the screens are on.

I scan the other cameras.

Inside each city's duct, leftover water pools at the bottom. And at the end of each row, I see in red lights: *WEIGHT: 0 gallons.*

This is how they do it, I realize. *This is where the surplus comes from—leftover water.* The weight reads zero gallons in the duct, but right there, I'm seeing it's not true. There's not a lot of water in there now, but after decades and decades, it would add up . . . wouldn't it?

I poke Ter in the shoulder and mouth to him what I've just discovered. He points to my cuffcomm, trying to tell my something.

"Video it," he whispers, and he taps his wrist.

A recording. Wiggling off my comm, I adjust the settings. Then I aim it at the switchboard, making sure it's in view of every screen. I zoom in on the Engle row.

"Hello, Engle," the woman says, tapping her headset's mic. "We're commencing delivery of your fifty million gallo—"

Before she can finish, the distributary goes dark.

I grab Ter's hand—*this isn't good.*

Red strobing lights tucked into every corner click on, sparking my heartbeat to life. An alarm sounds.

"This is not a drill. Remain where you are. Commencing lockdown of all aqueducts and distributary entrances and exits in ten, nine, eight . . . ," a woman's computerized voice announces, continuing to count down.

"Holy shit, you guys. The Hudson security cam—"

I peer into the hallway, trying to catch a glimpe of the screen, but it's behind a corner. Simultaneously, both Ter's and my comm buzz. It's Callum.

They're here.

"Did you hear that?" the woman asks, and all three of the distributary's technicians stand.

The computerize voice continues her countdown: *Six. Five. Four.*

"We gotta leave—we're about to be trapped," Ter says. Lifting me by the arm, he pulls me across the hall.

"Someone's inside!" one technician yells, just before seeing us.

Ter flings open the door and we sprint back through the rock-carved corridor, racing for the emergency exit. I'm breathing heavily, unused to so much running. As red lights chase us, the countdown continues.

Three. Ter slams into the door, reaching for the handle. *Two.* He presses down. *One.* It opens. We swing out the door and cross under the waterfall. As we jump onto the riverbank—

Rangers. By the thousands. . . .

Uniformed men and women take formation up and down the river, camouflaged against the woods. They march in units of ten or twenty, creating barricades with their bodies. Their rifles face the water.

In the distance, Dunn's barge powers upriver. It can't be carrying any more than a thousand—the five hundred prisoners, and the rest of the DI. Officers in blue fatigues hold position, shooters in hand.

We're outnumbered tenfold at least.

"Hands up!" a woman shouts—the unit of rangers stationed at the outpost turn their guns on us, while a troop of five form a closer semicircle.

They aim for our chests, dead center.

57

AVEN
12:03 A.M., SATURDAY

Ter and I raise our hands. Vomit rises from the fear curdling in my stomach.

"What are we gonna do?" I whisper, shaking.

The closest ranger jabs me in the ribs with the barrel of his gun—I drop my arms, bones throbbing. He does it again. "Hands up!"

Another ranger lifts his cuffcomm. "Magistrate Harcourt, we have the intruders. Bringing them to you now, as directed."

The man prods Ter and me uphill, toward the dam's stony wall. He brings us to a second winding staircase this side of the river.

At the top, two hundred rangers point their guns over the stone embankment. Magistrate Harcourt stands in the middle of the pathway, speaking feverishly with a group of men and women. The rangers usher Ter and me under an abandoned candy-cane-striped tent, where we're met with Benny and Callum, whose his cheek and jaw have started to turn purple. We cast each other looks, no idea how we're going to get out of this mess.

A few hundred feet downriver, where it's too shallow for such a large vessel, Chief Dunn's barge slows to a stop.

"Open the duct, Harcourt!" he commands, the ship's intercom at his mouth. His voice booms through the internal speakers. In unison, the thousand officers slam their barrels against the ship's floor. Then they slam again. It starts slow, but grows in speed. Soon, the rhythmic metal-on-metal echoes the pounding of a thousand hearts about to explode.

Magistrate Harcourt isn't shaken—he glares down at the chief, unknowing, barely offended by the threat. Holding his own megaphone, he hollers, "Quiet!" but the hammering only grows louder—until altogether, in unison, it stops.

The magistrate takes five seconds of calculated silence before speaking. "Chief Dunn! You recklessly put your people at risk! I don't want a massacre on my hands, so I have to ask: What are you playing at?"

"You think I'll show my cards that easily?" Dunn laughs, a tinny sound through the megaphone.

"I, Chief Craig Dunn, acting governor of the United Metro Islets, come to you with a single, peaceful request: Open. Our. Aqueduct. The city of Falls gets only one chance at peaceful negotiation."

Magistrate Harcourt turns to a woman on his left with

auburn hair and deep crow's-feet. The two confer. Nodding, he shifts to the bald man listening at his other side. His face is expressionless. Their eyes meet; he agrees.

"This can't come to blows," Callum whispers. "No news would spread faster across the globe."

The magistrate calls over the nearest ranger and whispers something in her ear. A moment later, a troop surrounds Ter, Callum, Benny, and me.

What's going on?

The magistrate doesn't take his eyes off the chief. "Because I'm not a heartless man, I'm returning your paltry excuse for an espionage unit . . . albeit with a message."

Unable to see us, Chief Dunn turns to his captain, confused.

"Girl." Harcourt waves me over. "You're to tell your superior the following: The city of Falls does not, under any circumstance, comply with Chief Dunn's 'peaceful' demand. You may play whatever cards you wish." He whispers something to another ranger, and adds, "We are not afraid of war."

Like a balloon popping, my lungs empty. I take breath after breath, but a tightness squeezes against my brain, and I can't catch air. *Me? I have to pass Dunn this message?*

Ter touches my back, only to have his hand swatted away by a gun.

Harcourt looks back over the embankment and reproachfully clicks his tongue. "Really, Dunn," he says with mock pity, sending us down the stairwell, rangers at our backs. "Three children and an old man?"

By the time Dunn opens his mouth to deny it, we're

halfway down. He recognizes us, covers the megaphone to argue with his captain. They wait in silence.

All the way down the riverbank and through the tall grass, our circle of rangers follow. When I snag my foot on a rock and stumble, I'm shoved onward by a gun's thick barrel. Ter tries to take my hand, but another ranger divides us with her rifle.

Nearer now, we see how massive the barge really is—it's as wide as this river, with heavy-duty light fixtures built directly into its red metal siding.

On the hull, a painted tiger bares its teeth.

Chief stands at the ship's bow, unmoving. Only the twitch of his mustache declares him human, not statue. He's as taut as an arrow held back too long, hands crossed behind his back.

The docking ramp lowers.

Ter risks a touch—his fingers reach for mine. I grab on to them, panting. My palms begin to sweat, and I wipe them against my fatigues.

The rangers prod me forward, but not the others. I walk the plank in reverse, more afraid of Dunn than all the rangers combined. The barge carrying a thousand makes no noise as I step onto the vessel.

Chief Dunn stops me—I'm patted down by the five closest officers. I cover my body, shaking in anger. Water pricks at my eyes, so I bite the inside of my cheek to stop it.

I stare at the floor until they're done.

The orange-and-white tiger—she bares her teeth at me from the ship's bottom. Wide block letters circle her: *THE*

ENGLE BENGAL, COMMERCIAL SHIPPING AND FREIGHT.

When an officer announces that I'm clean, I grit my teeth. My cuffcomm is a snare, biting my wrist until I free the recording inside. *Chief Dunn needs to know Harcourt's stealing water.*

It could stop this war from going any further.

I'm a battlefield of nerves, skin ice-cold. The rangers behind Ter, Callum, and Benny haven't lowered their guns.

"The city of Falls does n-not—" I stammer. My tongue buckles under the weight of Harcourt's message. "—under any circumstance, comply with Chief Dunn's 'peaceful' demand. You may play whatever cards you wish." Pausing, I add, "Those were his exact words."

A gun is fired.

I spin around.

The first act of war—Benny is doubled over the water's edge, gray smoke wisping from the ranger's gun. His white shirt turns the color of hate as he bleeds into the river, while Ter rushes to his side.

In unison, all the other rangers lift their weapons.

The shot was a message from Harcourt: He will not negotiate. Leave, or enjoy the blood he's not afraid to shed.

"Ready!" Chief Dunn shouts, loading his shooter. He drops to one knee and rests the barrel over the stern. Behind him, our thousand soldiers load their shooters as well.

Dunn raises his hand.

"Aim!"

My ribs burn, straining against my heart, and the world rolls away like a pair of dice—in seconds, it will land on a number. The number amounts to the history of the world, about to change forever. An avalanche opens up beneath my feet, and I can see straight through the fire inside.

Hot tears collapse onto the ship, but I am not weak. I am no child. *I'm human.* I cry and I shake, because I am afraid of things bigger than Chief Dunn or a bullet in my chest.

"Wait!"

My voice whirlpools in the air, drawing every last officer's attention. It's hundreds in one, far louder than I thought was possible—I'm not just speaking for myself. It's a voice that would stop even Ren. "Harcourt has been stealing water from everyone—that's where all his extra comes from," I announce, and quickly remove my cuffcomm. "I have proof. He was about to steal from Engle before you got here."

I hold the comm for Chief to take.

His hand lingers in the air. The word *fire* sits on the tip of his tongue.

"Even more reason to lodge a dart between his eyes," Dunn finally says, head cocked, peering into the shooter's viewfinder. Eyes never leaving his target, Dunn lowers his hand and gestures for the captain to take my comm.

"Hold fire!"

The captain projects the video onto the ship floor, and Dunn calls for two teams of officers. He sends one below deck. Moments later, they return with a yellow plastic gurney, and the second team marches down the ramp. As gently as possible, they lift Benny from the riverbank. Ter and Callum follow as they lay him, slack and barely breathing, onto the cot.

From there, Callum takes over, calling out supplies left and right.

Chief begins watching the holo projection, eyes dark. I rush past him, falling at Benny's side. His blue-veined hand is ice in mine. I breathe into it, watching the rise and fall of his chest like it's an antenna trying to catch a signal. His face is marble-white. Choking back a sob, I lay my head against his leg.

This would break Ren. . . .

"Up, up," Benny breathes, tugging his hand free and waving me off his leg. "I'm not dead yet, kiddo." I laugh at him and cry at the same time. Slowly, he opens his pale gray eyes. As he blinks, water runs down his temples; he's crying too. He looks like he saw a ghost. An officer hands me his canteen, and I bring it to Benny's mouth.

"Today's your lucky day," Callum says, cauterizing the wound.

Benny winces, his face scrunching up. He stifles a yowl. Even his whiskers look wilty. "Do tell."

"The bullet went straight through your shoulder. It did not hit *one* artery." Callum begins wrapping Benny's shoulder in gauze. "A very clean wound."

"So, Harcourt," Chief says, having seen enough of the video. "Should I get Engle on the shortwave transmitter?"

Small and far from atop the dam, the magistrate doesn't answer. His wide bulk turns left, then right, arguing with his advisers. The bald man and the auburn-haired woman disagree—their hands wave in the air as they shoot each other ruffled looks.

"Do it," Chief commands, and the captain reaches for a black box left of the helm. He lifts the intercom and begins twisting a dial, flipping through channels.

"Dunn!"

Magistrate Harcourt's voice rings out, echoing downriver. "How much do you want?"

Now, Dunn lifts his eye from the viewfinder. "A lifetime supply," he answers easily.

Harcourt shakes his head, waving his hand over the dam. "You're joking." His thin laugh echoes through the megaphone. "Try again."

Dunn repeats himself. "A lifetime supply."

"That'll cost me more than it would to admit fault, save face, and return the surplus! Never."

"This is not negotiable. I'm getting Engle—and any other city you've cheated—on the intercom."

No one notices the invisible signal Harcourt sent to his military. But like a clock striking midnight, each and every ranger drops to one knee.

Thousands of muzzles point at the barge simultaneously. Thousands of fingers, triggers, and bullets wait for the magistrate to give the final signal. I imagine the rounds being fired into the first five hundred of our small army—the bullets hitting organs. Organs repairing themselves. Officers standing and taking it again, round after round, until the water's all used up and the regeneration slows . . .

Stops.

In the tense air, Dunn's cuffcomm crackles with static. "Sir—"

Dunn's hand is back on the shooter, eyes focused on his target—now hidden behind a row of his rangers. Dunn doesn't move a muscle. His ears just listen.

"Sir—" the voice repeats, pitched with excitement. "We have found *freshwater.* I repeat. We have found *freshwater.*"

Dunn's gaze loosens. "Repeat that," he says, loud enough for his comm's mic to pick it up.

"Freshwater, sir. We've found it. That ex-agent of yours— the Dane girl? She brought us right there. Died smack in the middle too. Her boyfriend had to fish her out and everything—a damn disgusting scene. But it's a freshwater spring, all right, deep enough to pipe off."

Everything stops here.

I rush for the intercom. I'm water, screaming over rocks. Dunn's arm throws me to the floor—he holds up his other arm in a time-out, high enough for the magistrate to see. There's more negotiating, then jumping and screaming, hugging and shouting—electric nets fired into the sky.

I don't hear it. I cry into the orange-and-white tiger's heart, pummeling her with both my fists. I want her to fight back— she has to fight back. Because she's a tiger . . . and that's what tigers do.

Ren doesn't just die. *It's not possible.*

58

REN

I am emptied from one universe into another universe.

It has no stars. No galaxies growing in wombs, no cells dividing. No double-crossing double helixes. It has no planets. No gravity. It has the color black, but black's not a color, just an absence.

It doesn't even have me. Not really, not yet.

It has nothing—it's a void.

Deep in the absence, a spectrum ignites. At the speed of disappearing light, the curved universe flexes around the nothing of me, like a muscle. I fall and I fall through a dark matter tunnel, a barren wasteland.

The absence has dropped me.

I'm thrown into light but not air. In my third universe, I can't breathe. . . .

I'm born mostly dead.

"The umbilical cord—" a woman in a white coat says, then she curses. "It's wrapped around her neck." She counts how many times it's tried to strangle me. The number is five. "I need you to push, Emilce. We have to get her out, *now*."

"Stay strong, sister," says a woman with a loose topknot.

But my shoulders are too wide . . . *now* isn't possible.

Here for half a moment, I'm emptied yet again—and for the first time—funneled back into absence. The black, curving void holds me. Because I am nothing, I have eyes everywhere: I watch as my mother pushes, but it's too late.

I'm already here, in the absence.

Twenty minutes later, the doctor pulls a still, blue body out from my mother. Her face, freckled and dark and round, changes shape. Horror fills the gasping O her mouth makes. The woman with the topknot, Miss Nale, rushes to Emilce's side. She squeezes her hand, kissing it a hundred times.

"I'll give you a moment while I inform your husband," and I watch my mother cradle the body as the doctor leaves the room. My mother cries against the skin I was born into.

Her tears are my first rainfall.

Like a ragged animal cursing the moon, she screams. Her scream carries through universes. It pokes holes in the void, it wakes the strange blood in my body. It calls it to action. *Come back*, it begs. *Come back.*

I see now, this universe—it has a bone to pick.

Laying out the whirlpool of time, it finds a chaos that hasn't been ordered: A spring. A test. The first man who killed too many to make it his own. The second man. And the girl he made, who could undo it.

Humanity will fail the test, but they will fail with flying colors.

Seeing all of time's forward-backward tumbling, the Earthbound universe intervenes, and the absence obliges.

It unhooks me. Throws me into the spectrum.

I scream.

My mother's face is a sun rising in the west. She cleans my body. She kisses my wet, round cheek—the one with freckles, soon.

"What in God's name . . ." Miss Nale staggers backward and clutches the headboard for support. "How can this be real?" she whispers.

My mother's hand cradles my head and then, like tripping on a rock, her smile slips away. I feel her heartbeat chase itself into the distance, each one faster than the next. She holds me close, pats my back, but her anxiety is in my blood too.

"Shut the door!" Emilce yells when the doctor returns.

The woman steps back. Hands cupped over her mouth, she whispers, "She couldn't breathe for twenty minutes. . . ." Her eyes dart between us. "I'll get your husband—"

Emilce's eyes don't leave mine. "No—you will do no such thing," she says softly. She doesn't want me to worry. "Neither of you will ever say a word about this to my husband. Or to anyone else, for that matter."

Beaming down at my round face, Emilce coos.

The doctor lays her stethoscope against my back, breathes, "But—but this is a miracle."

"Exactly," Emilce says. "My husband . . . he will ruin this child. She wouldn't be his daughter . . . she would be his greatest advantage. He'd find out what makes the miracle tick. He'd say it was for the 'greater good,' but she'd still end up empty. He'd empty her. And I don't care about the greater good. I care only about the precious face staring back into mine."

"I'm not sure I understand," the doctor says, puzzled, as she looks at Emilce.

Miss Nale touches her sister's shoulder, and her worried eyes meet mine.

"My husband is not the man I once married. He's grown obsessed—" My mother looks away shiftily, not wanting to say too much. "He will want to find out just how big of a miracle she truly is. And if I'm right—if he's changed as much as I fear he has—she could spend the first year of her life in a lab." Emilce closes her eyes and exhales. One last time, she kisses my forehead and then passes me to the doctor. She dries her nose with a handkerchief.

"Will you take her back to the Ward with you?" Emilce asks Miss Nale.

The doctor, jaw agape, reaches for Emilce's shoulder. "Mrs. Voss, you're tired," she says with sympathy. "You don't know what you're asking of your stepsister. Why don't we leave you and your child alone, and we'll see how you feel in an hour?"

"Doctor, I have all my wits about me. I had a clean delivery, no drugs. My mind is not addled. Sister, tell me, will you do this thing I ask? Will you take her?"

Miss Nale kisses Emilce's head and retrieves the blue quilt from a chair in the corner. She wraps me up in it, then cradles me in her arms, and that is her answer.

"Doctor." Emilce's voice is pure iron. "If I learn that you've told anyone about this, you will see your future as a medical professional ruined. Am I understood?"

The doctor points at my mother, opens her mouth. She quickly closes it. "It seems I have no choice," she says bitterly. "I only hope you're making the right decision."

"Time will be the decider in that. Not you, and not I."

"Don't you want to give her a name?" the doctor asks accusingly.

Emilce thinks. "My husband is a great Latin scholar. I think the name 'Renata' fits her well, 'reborn' as she was."

"Renata," Miss Nale whispers, tucking me away.

"Renata," my mother echoes, watching as I'm taken.

The scene evaporates behind us as the universe tumbles ahead. I'm fast-forwarded through moments like seedlings, reliving every juncture that grows me into *me*—who I am, or was, when I left the universe in Derek's arms.

I'm six, looking out at the West Isle, and for the first time, I understand they have more.

The first girl I almost become friends with shakes my hand. She's taken to a sickhouse the next day.

The first mother and father glance around Nale's classroom, looking for a child—I ignore them, and they ignore me.

Kids taunt me, call me mean, and so I get mean.

Aven . . .

When I see her, time and space stop. This Earthbound

universe closes its eyes. Bending to one knee, it places infinity in my hands. Asks if I want to take it. If I say yes, Aven and I could spin off together, create new universes. She wouldn't get the Blight and I'd be born with uncomplicated blood. We'd be adopted. Together—sisters.

It would let me out of here, if I wanted.

A choice.

Because the universe has rules, and even it is not free to break them. It saw a chaos; it intervened. But actions have equal, yet opposite, reactions, and now . . . now it must turn a blind eye. Tumbling backward and forward through infinity, I'm being given the opportunity to live for myself—not die for *it.*

I could say yes.

I could.

But I won't.

Back in the cave, I decided to be the thing that ends it. You don't just return from a choice like that, even when a universe offers you paradise. I'm changed . . . freed. I already broke my paradise apart and gave its nucleus away. Now there are thousands of new paradises germinating without me. No single one—not even my own—could grow so large.

I close the fist of the universe.

59

Ter carries me from the barge. He lays me down in the front seat of the Cloud, and then he takes the wheel. I don't speak. I don't move. I don't know what words are anymore. They can't bring her back.

Callum directs a team of officers to transport Benny's gurney off the barge—Benny's choice. Something about trusting his own equipment and not wanting to see his Cloud abandoned in enemy territory. I think the truth is he'd just rather be here with us.

As Callum ties the gurney down, his cuffcomm buzzes.

"Who is it?" I ask, making a ball of myself in the seat corner.

Callum reads the message. "It's Derek," he says, hesitating.

"He wants us to meet him at the Bone Vault."

I swallow a hundred times, but more tears escape. They find their way down the sides of my nose and the banks of my cheeks, into my mouth and behind my ears. I shiver thinking about where we're headed.

The Bone Vault.

A place to pray for the dead, decorated entirely in bones. The last place in the world I ever wanted to go—I imagine it's like being inside the stomach of some monster. *Ren knows this.*

"But—I don't understand . . . ," I say, watching my tears make tiny pools on the floor between the seat and the Cloud's hull. "How did she do it?"

Callum explains—her blood, the protein. The way she never got sick once in her life, never even broke a bone. Understanding crashes over me. Every cell in my body reacts, shaking, frenzied. *She gave her blood to destroy the spring.*

"You said her plan was risky, Callum, you didn't say it was suicide!" I cry, digging my palms into his knees, wanting to hurt him. "You didn't tell me, how could you not tell me?"

"Is there any chance she survived?" Benny asks slowly, his voice thin.

Callum rubs the bridge of his nose. "My calculations . . . I found that she'd need every ounce in her body to raise the protein concentration high enough. Otherwise, it wouldn't kill off the entire ecosystem. I told her this.

"And now that we're meeting Derek at the Bone Vault—I

351

think it's safe to assume . . ." His voice trails off.

Ter guns the Cloud; its engine bawls into the dark. "We could have done something. We could have stopped her!" I cry over the noise.

Can she really be gone?

I don't know if I can believe that yet. Ren was never the one who'd die first—I've never even thought about it.

I cover my mouth as something else occurs to me. "The water," I whisper. "We don't even have it anymore."

Ter's jaw drops—we're thinking the same thing. He slumps forward over the wheel. "Was it . . . ?" he begins, and I nod.

Sipu's Omni.

"What?" Callum asks. "What happened to it?"

Ter answers so I don't have to speak the words. They're the final nail in the coffin.

"Aven had both bags at Sybil's Cove, when we met Sipu. The first bag went to prisoners, but the second one . . ."

"The crash," Callum breathes, sliding on the floor of the Cloud. "That bag had everything—the spores, the algae, the rocks. Without the spores, the water's gone for good."

Over our heads, a hawk shrieks like he understands.

Ter reaches for me. I stop him. There's no such thing as comfort right now. There's only me and every memory I have left. I can't forget any of them, not one. I have to remember, otherwise she really is gone.

I start at the beginning, with the day we met—from that first moment, she was my favorite. She was standing there at the edge of Nale's roof, a loner, and she didn't even look up when Miss Nale introduced me. Everyone else said, "Nice to meet you, Aventine," in a tone Miss Nale would approve of. But Renny just stayed where she was, staring off. Nale didn't make her do anything—Ren was a lifer at the orphanage, there since before she could make memories. Other kids said she was mean, but I knew different. It was because she was afraid. People came and went, or people came and died. I wanted to make her less afraid. I wanted to be her One. I knew I could do it too.

I knew she'd like me.

As soon as she agreed to be friends that night before the races, it's like we made a secret pact to never die on each other. I was the first to almost break it, getting sick with the Blight. Never in a million years did I think . . . did I think—

Folding into myself, face slick with salt water, I clutch at my penny necklace. She's wearing hers now, I bet. I gave it to her because it was lucky, but she said she didn't want luck. So I told her "Good skill" instead, and she liked that.

I liked it too, because Ren never needed luck.

Maybe, this time, she did.

I force my head up, hair unsticking from my cheeks. *I can't believe it, I won't.* Leaning my head against the rail, I pretend to sleep so that the others leave me alone. Really, I'm feeling the wind against my eyelids, hoping it freezes the tears underneath.

I wonder if it's cold where she is too.

60

REN

The closed fist of the universe isn't done with me.

It takes off, wheeling through every moment of the rest of my short life.

Benny—he called me "kiddo" during my first race and I wanted to smack him. . . . The night I was nabbed, Aven hiding behind a corner, watching. Later, when it wasn't so sad anymore, she said it was like watching me be carried off by the worst stork ever. . . . The day I enlisted with the Blues as a mole—I was already hated, and the pay was decent. . . . Returning to the Ward. I hunted Aven for weeks, found her nearly dead in a sickhouse. It was the most terrible feeling I'd ever known. . . . Becoming a dragster, officially. . . . Meeting my very own bookie, a guy named Derek. . . . Crushing impossibly on said bookie . . . Race after race after race . . . Callum . . . The spring . . . Delivering the serum . . . The raid . . . Aven, kidnapped . . . Our escape . . . *Bellum pestilentia* . . . My mother, my father . . .

My choice.

I'm seconds away from my second death—

The cave . . . Derek speaking to me in words I don't understand now—only dying me could understand those words. Him holding me to his chest, while water soaked up every ounce of my blood.

I empty away, a destroyer.

For a third time, the absence folds itself around me. I'm back in the universe that is between others, cast in nothing. I'm in its very eye, watching all that is Earthbound go on without me.

Which is, I guess, why I did what I did.

Earth's history unfolds like a spherical holo right before my eyes. It happens in the closest thing I have to real time, because here in the nothing, time is also nothing. It's watery. It travels in whichever direction I push.

The view is panoramic. Every thought, every wish, I hear them spoken in my mind, part of some core I can't begin to understand.

Curious, I roll the ball of Time back toward my body— toward Derek.

I watch as he swims fast from the dying cave. From the fresh memories of me dying and of me dead. My limp body floats behind him like a comet's tail, knees banging against the walls. I'm not there to feel it.

Now, seeing Derek like this, thinking his thoughts—I

understand. He needed me more than I ever needed him. I *wanted* him—a different thing. Distantly, I call myself cruel. I begged for us to begin, and we did. Then, I ended us.

My everywhere eyes pull back—Aven's voice cracks dimensions. I travel the Ping-Pong globe of Earth thirty miles north, where armies converge—and there she is, the axis balancing two heavily weighted scales.

I deny that there is no center of the universe: my chosen sister is living proof.

Vision shifts again—

The DI unit breaks into the airlock. A man in a wet suit swims to the last location saved in my GPS tracker and finds shriveled, dead caps hovering on the water's surface. He did not find what he was looking for—

He finds something else.

Fresh.

In the stairwell, Derek carries me up three flights of stairs. Then he carries me to the dock where, with his eyes closed, he pulls the knife from my body. He doesn't want the others to see it. I'm slack in his arms as he lays me in one of the Tètai's Omnis. Underwater, he finds two black, battered, sunken mobiles—one belonging to Lucas and one to Kitaneh. In both pits, gray-haired skeletal frames. Time caught up.

Then . . . the Bone Vault.

My body arrives like a rainstorm no one sees coming. One minute the sky is fine. The next, everything's changed. Under a vertebrae chandelier, Derek lowers my body down onto the stone. If I could feel, it would be cold.

There, he waits.

I watch as the Cloud pulls up to the dock, solemn. Aven hangs back in the boat with Benny, telling the others to go without her.

There is a part of me that rejects the in-between universe—that still thinks of life as mine—and hates myself for making Aven come here. It's the part that still calls myself "I," even when I don't exist.

She wonders if she wants to see me at all.

Ter's first through the canopy of clavicles. *Oh, Ter.* Still a teddy bear, even rocking those Blue fatigues. For some reason, I never thought of him as a brother. Maybe it's because I had Aven. I just didn't consider adding more to the list. Not until now, hearing him call me "sister," do I realize how blind I'd been. Afraid.

Callum follows. His eyes are shiny from tears he's not allowing himself. When he looks at my body, I hear every word he never said—his wishing that he'd tried to kiss me, just once, to see if I'd kiss back. In the void, I realize I would have, but then I'd wish I hadn't.

My blood was too angry for his. Too volatile. I needed a mistake-maker. Someone who'd understand what selfish felt like. He stands over my body, with all his wishing, very still. He knows why he never tried.

Benny's back in the Cloud, too weak to make it into the Bone Vault. He lays on the gurney and in his mind, calls me his child—an answer to a question I'd never been brave enough to think. In a dark corner of my heart, it existed only as a hope . . . that I could choose my father, same as I chose my sister.

Aven is last to cross the threshold. She's trying not to imagine stepping inside a beast that eats other beasts, then swallows their bones whole. She stands in the shadow of a candlelit gaping jaw. It flickers against the wall. Ter tries to take her hand, but she's limp, unable to hold him back.

She thinks I've betrayed her by leaving. She doesn't want to feel that way; it doesn't seem right. But she feels it nonetheless. In a whirlwind of white hair, she rushes for my body. Falls to the stone. The cry she makes must come from someplace else—it can't be from her. It's too wild, too monstrous and hurting. She's only fourteen. She shouldn't know how to make that sound.

Holding my hand to her cheek, I hear her yell, "She's cold—" It shakes me even here in the nothing. "She needs a blanket!"

If my mother's tears were my first rainfall, Aven's are my last.

"How could you leave me?" she cries into my palm, kissing it over and over. Folding my slack arm around her shoulders, she lays on the stone beside me. Her voice is a whisper I hear through the universe's ears, and not my own. "Come back? Please?"

I don't have a beating heart to break.

Patient, the absence watches as I reach for the closed fist of this universe. Moments ago—days . . . years—I was given a choice. Wrestling with the fist, I howl, "I want my choice back! I'm cashing in now; you have no say!"

I wait for its answer, but the language of the universe is silence.

"Do you hear?" I shout again, and then I wonder . . . *Maybe it doesn't.* Maybe it isn't even listening.

Maybe its eyes are still closed—

Its equal, yet opposite, reaction hasn't been met.

Without a heart to break, I break the void instead. I claw toward the spectrum, scraping off the tunnel's black like it's a bad paint job. The absence doesn't fight me, but my body does. Without the universe's help—its eyes still closed to me—I have to do its work.

I have to put myself together, alone.

I crawl inside my body and find no blood. None but what's left in the chamber of my unmoving heart. Still in this between place, this megacosmic corridor, I use its eyes, which are everywhere.

I look only for one thing: a single molecule.

I find it where the blade is no longer lodged. One droplet of springwater in my stomach's viscera, waiting. I call it up through my veins, sailing it into muscle. *Right vena cava, right atrium, right ventricle. Artery.* I bathe the watery molecule in a pool of blue blood. *Lungs, veins. Left atrium, ventricle.*

Aorta.

Like a mother singing to a child, I sing to my own heart.

Rules unbreak.

The equal, yet opposite, reaction reacts. Black gives way to color, and the gravity of bodies and hearts and hands greets

359

me. Absence and its tunneling vortex of nothing whorls away. It leaves me and my body for another time.

The Earthbound universe opens its eyes.

It does, and so do I.

EPILOGUE

AVEN
24 HOURS LATER

Blue and gold fireworks burst, splashing over the Milky Way and a clear, moonless night. In the Cloud, they arc over the strait from both coastlines—the Ward and the West Isle. Sparks fall over our heads like a wedding veil made of stars. No tricks, no tests. Just thousands of people and their wild rooftop rumpus.

Tomorrow, we'll begin repairing the pipes in preparation for a five-year supply of Falls' fresh. And next year, we'll be piping off the Minetta Brook, so it'll be ready before the contract with Harcourt runs out. Chief Dunn sent my recording to his own comm, in case the magistrate ever has second thoughts about the deal.

I poke Ren with my entire finger—almost. The fingernails never grew back, but I don't mind. Their absence reminds me how much I nearly lost. "You want to watch?" I ask, but she's dead asleep, curled in my lap.

I've been poking her every so often to make sure she's not *dead* dead. Each time, she swats me away, and each time, immediately after, she grabs my finger. She falls back asleep just like that, without letting go. I've had to alternate poking hands.

A spray of brack fans over the Cloud, wetting everyone— Callum and Derek cover their heads. Not Ter at the helm, and certainly not me or Ren. We don't even feel it. It could be snowing and I don't think we'd care.

"You have arrived at your destination: 40°46'42.46"N, 74° 0'11.37"W" the Voice Nav announces. It's a mouthful, even for a robot. Green froth churns against the Cloud's hull as Ter slows the engine.

"We're here," Callum says, but he doesn't look ready. "Derek, did Sipu comm you anything else?"

Derek shakes his head.

"We're here," I echo, tickling Ren's ear. "Wake up, sleepy-head."

Ren mumbles something not even I can translate. When she opens her eyes, the first thing she does is close them again. "We're here?" she says, nestling closer.

"Here we are," I answer, and I smush her nose. Ter cuts the engine. In the rough water, the Cloud bobs up and down.

Ren sits up like a bullet, remembering what we've come to do. Across the Cloud, she exchanges a nervous look with Derek. He's in his all-black wet suit, rubber flippers on his feet. New silver streaks already shine in his copper hair.

Kneeling, he pulls a vial from his backpack and drinks a sip. After this, he has only one more vial left.

"We'll find the second bag," Ren says. "She must've tossed it before the crash. Sipu wouldn't have commed you otherwise."

Derek nods, fixing his mask. He throws an oxygen tank over his back, and like a penguin in his awkward flippers, steps over the rail. Callum gives a hopeful pat on the shoulder as Derek drops into the strait.

Water splashes around him in an O—the underwater light strapped to his tank looks like a sinking sun as he swims through bright turquoise. We watch until we can't see him anymore, when Terrence turns to Ren.

He reaches into his pocket. "For you," he says, handing her a crumpled envelope. "Miss Nale caught me at Benny's as I was picking up the Cloud."

The paper is old, stained brown with time. It reads: *Renata* in handwritten cursive letters. She tenses up, holding the letter and staring at it. I touch her elbow.

Shaking herself, she glances south down the strait.

The mourning barge is still burning.

Ren was awake to see Governor Dunn push it from the DI dock. She watched until her mother and father were no more than a hot blaze smoking up the stars.

"Tell me if it's worth it," she says, pulling soft, clothlike paper from the envelope and handing it to me.

It wilts in my hands like a dead plant. Holding it stiff, I read. By the time I reach the signature, *Ever your loving mother, Emilce Voss*, I'm crying.

"Good or bad?"

I nod, sniffing, and I wipe my nose.

"Jeez," Ren says, rolling her eyes as she swipes the letter. "If you're blubbering and it's from *my* dead mom, I'm gonna be a train wreck. Who here has steel tear ducts they'd care to loan?"

Callum holds out his hand. She gives him a weak smile before passing the letter. "Thank you."

"'For you, Ren,'" he reads, softly looking at her once before continuing. "'This story begins long before I was born.

"'Hundreds of years ago, my husband's ancestor wrote of a spring with miraculous properties. Hundreds of years later, my husband found that same spring. He left with enough water to prolong his life for decades, thinking he'd be able to return.

"'But the Wash Out destroyed any trace of this spring.

"'Many years later, I met this man, Harlan Voss. Young and in love, he shared his water with me. Knowing the spring flowed from an underground river, he believed he would find it again.

"'Then came the assassination attempts. He was on the right track. The spring still existed, somewhere—but it was being protected. Harlan dreamed of eradicating death—he thought it was a disease. He wanted to "revolutionize life."

"'I became pregnant.

"'My child, a baby girl, was born dead. The umbilical cord had wrapped around her neck, denying her air for twenty minutes.

"'But her death was not permanent. . . .

"'Screaming into life, she was returned to me. The water

had changed her—that was the only explanation.

"'I couldn't keep my girl. . . . I didn't trust my husband. Harlan Voss had become Governor Voss, a man who sought greatness for the UMI, power and immortality for himself, and me. But his supply of water was dwindling, and he was growing desperate. I didn't like the things I heard him say— horrifying plans to force the Tètai's hand and provide him with the spring's location.

"'I was afraid he'd keep my girl hidden away in a lab, unlocking the mystery of her rebirth. So I asked my step-sister, Ann—you know her as Miss Nale—to care for you. In your name lies the secret of your birth:

"'Renata.

"'"Reborn."

"'How cruel that I knew you'd be safer without us.

"'As your mother, perhaps it's selfish that this comes to you so late, but you must hear me: I have been in love with you from the moment you were a hope to the moment you were a truth. From the day you died to the day you came back, and every day thereafter.

"'Ann tells me of your friend Aventine—how she keeps you grounded, and you raise her up. She worries because the girl has begun to look sick, and you've grown so protective.

"Renata, know this: death is not the end. You will meet your soul mates, and they will be with you even when the day comes that they are gone. That is how soul mates work.

"'Do not fear Aven's death.

"'Do not fear your own either.

"'Life is both a give and a take. The sweet and the bitter.

Without either, the other cannot exist. I have learned that living forever is not as important as living well. So let life be the wondrous thing it is, with all its fullness and frailty, and yes, its horrors. Without those things, it is not life.

"'I am sorry for everything that I know to be sorry for, and I am also sorry for the many things I don't.

"'I love you.

"'Ever your loving mother, Emilce Voss.'"

When Callum stops reading, Ren's eyes glisten but her face is tough. She takes the letter back and carefully, she stuffs it into its envelope.

"Good or bad?" I ask.

"Good enough."

Again she looks south. Now the horizon is dark. The barge has sunk.

A circle of light rises from underwater. Derek's head breaks the surface, brack rippling against the boat. He hoots, holding up a large, clear, waterproof sack.

He climbs the ladder back into the boat and lowers our buried treasure. It rolls a few times before coming to a complete stop. We circle around, frozen.

"She really did it," Ter says softly. For a moment, we're all quiet.

Sipu is gone, under the water, and we're not. We can't even say thank you. They're homeless words.

Callum kneels. He undoes the clasp at the top of the bag and it folds open. Peering inside, he laughs. "It's all here," he says, awed, pulling out the smaller, individually wrapped sacks. "Rocks, algae, fungus, water."

"Now you can make more?" I ask.

"I can."

"So . . . what are you guys gonna do with it?" Ter lowers down, taking a look at the piecemeal ecosystem before Callum stuffs it back into the bag.

"We," Ren corrects. She's thinking something. "What if . . . we gave it away?"

Of course the others gawk at her. They don't know what she means.

I do. Our eyes meet, brains firing off in exactly the same places, arriving at exactly the same conclusions.

"Callum, you'd have to get rid of the immortality phyto-things," I say. "But you could make more medicine—lots of medicine . . . for viruses and for tumors. Or for people who lost limbs."

Ren nods. She bites back a smile. "We'll travel . . . not just to the UMI. We'll go to the Mainland, Upstate. And we won't ask for money."

Derek laughs as he sits down, his wet suit pooling around him. "A new sort of Tètai . . . ," he muses.

"We'll come in the night," Ren says theatrically, pretending to hold a sword.

I jump forward and I point to the sky. "Wearing masks!"

With a heavy gust of wind, Ren lowers her fake sword. "Naturally," she says, glancing up. She loses herself, absorbed by the night.

"Whatcha looking at?" I ask, leaning against her shoulder. She shrugs. "Just the black."

Another gust sweeps the purple clouds from the sky,

freeing Orion and a dozen more immortal warriors. They can stalk the night now. They're watching us. Maybe Athena's even there.

Stepping away from the rail, Ren curls her arms around me. We press foreheads. The old president on my copper penny meets the old president on hers—head to head, luck to luck, skill to skill.

"Can we really do this?" I whisper into her ear. "Can we keep it safe?"

Something growls in the sky. Millions of light years away, stellar dust shivers. Immortal beasts bare their teeth, protecting immortal things.

"The universe did *not* see this coming," Ren says, grinning, but I'm not sure what she means.

The night wind shouldn't taste like promise if it did.

ACKNOWLEDGMENTS

There's a saying, "It takes a village to raise a child." Well, similarly, it took nearly the entire island of Manhattan (and some very special New Jerseyites) to help bring *The Ward* and *The Isle* into the world. Thank you, Lauren Frankel, my brilliant cousin, who set the ball in motion. She showed me her copy of *The Hunger Games*, and YA had me hooked.

To Claudia Gabel: Life changed in the most wonderful ways because of you. I'm forever grateful that I got to be in your MediaBistro class, and that you wanted to take a chance on me (and Ren!). You're made of nothing but pure, Grade A fairy dust.

Thank you, Ben Rosenthal, for your editorial eye, and for your patience as I caught up. *The Isle* would be a cartoon without you.

Thank you to my agent, Ginger Clark. You continue to be my cloak of invisibility and my Excalibur all in one.

Carol Fitzgerald and Tom Donadio and everyone else at the Book Report Network, you taught me about the book world. This process would have been far scarier were it not for TBRN. Thank you! Rebecca and Jeremy Wallace-Segall, thank you for sharing Writopia with me—I am immeasurably better for it, in ways I'm continuing to understand. Linn

Prentis, for showing me the SF/sci-fi ropes. I learned so much during our time working together! Thank you, Jaimee Garbacik, Elyse Tanzillo, and Frank Weimann, for taking a chance on a poetry grad. Jaimee, for your creative editorial support early on. And Elyse . . . Oh, Elyse. What would these books be you? You are my human deus ex machina, a miraculous fix from above swooping in at the last minute.

Thank you Ryan Elwood, Seastar, for living in the water with me. I love you, Adam Courtney, for my stellar website photos and for your esoteric knowledge on the habits of villains. You know far too much to be one of the good guys. Kurt Ritta, for your cabin in the woods; Amy Dupcek, for our "writing" dates—I REGRET NOTHING; Aurora Wells . . . for you; Lindsay Turner, for being my rainbow; Jenny Williamson, for being a brain I adore storming around with.

Justin Barad, you are my very own Dr. Justin Corey/Callum Pace. You deserve a medal and a real PhD for all the hours you spent on the phone with me, researching. Frederic Pryor, Senior Research Scholar of Economics at Swarthmore College, for discussing the economics of a water stress situation with me; Germán Mora, Department Chair of Environmental Studies at Goucher College, for a crash course in climate change; and Pat Rivera, of the Museum of Indian Culture in Allentown, Pennsylvania, for providing me with information about how the Lenni Lenape people lived in this area during the time of Dutch settlement.

Any errors in this book are my own.

To the inspiring English and creative writing instructors in my life: Micol Ostow, Beth Spires, Michelle Tokarczyk,

Arnold Sanders, Jeff Myers, Johnny Turtle, Lee Foust, T.J. Anderson, Rick Tretheway, Thorpe Moeckel, and Jeanne Larsen. Thank you.

An epic thank you to everyone at Katherine Tegen Books— my publisher, Katherine Tegen, my first editor Claudia Gabel, and Ben Rosenthal. Also Laurel Symonds, Melissa Miller, and Alexandra Arnold, and the entire art team for their work on the cover. And thank you to everyone at Curtis Brown—my agent Ginger Clark and also Holly Frederick and Kerry D'Agostino—for helping get *The Ward* out there.

Lastly, my fam—my sister, my cousins, my aunts and uncles. Your support knows no bounds. Grandma, I'm too lucky to have you in my life. Thank you for knowing me better than I knew myself, and for the gentle nudge in the right direction. Mom and Dad, I'm so very, very blessed to have you both on my team. Your faith in me is the only reason I took my own writing seriously.

Thank you.